# The Miller's Daughter

# Elizabeth Gill

# The Miller's Daughter

Quercus

First published in Great Britain in 2021 by

Quercus Editions Ltd
Carmelite House
50 Victoria Embankment
London EC4Y 0DZ

An Hachette UK company

A CIP catalogue record for this book is available
from the British Library

HB ISBN 978 1 78747 345 4

10 9 8 7 6 5 4 3 2 1

Printed

Papers used by Qu

A.

sible sources.

*For the members of the Coven — Jezza, Priscilla and Sweet Pea.*
*Thank you for making me laugh so much on Thursdays,*
*it carries me through the week. Love you. Laffy*

# One

*The Foundling School for Girls, summer 1861*

Sister Madeline was sitting in her office, worrying. There was nothing new in that, she was always worrying about something. She wasn't sure whether it was a fault or something to be recommended, but she tried to act on her worries constructively.

Since she had come here to the wilds up on the moors of north-west Durham from the city of Newcastle upon Tyne some six years ago to establish this foundling school a great deal had happened, and each time she solved a problem it seemed to her that another five sprung up in its place, as though the enemy had stolen in during the night and planted tares among her wheat.

She had had two nuns to help her, but Sister Hilary had married Mr Nattrass and now seemed very happy at the small farm about a mile away from the foundling school. The other nun, Abigail, was now Maddy's right-hand woman. They were both in the their middle thirties, perhaps the best age for a woman to be, Maddy thought. They were energetic, full of ideas, capable of spending long days in both physical and mental activity, and they had respect as well as liking for one another, and yet Maddy sometimes reflected that they came from such different backgrounds that she was always surprised they got on so well.

Abigail had been an orphaned child taken by the nuns from the Newcastle streets, tiny, starving, she had still been alive because of her wits. She had been a thief, stole to live, and there was an early time in the convent when she took the gold candlesticks from the altar and tried to sell them. She had never grown much, the result of her early childhood with little food and no care, but she had soon become a valuable member of the convent, which was all the more reason that Maddy felt gratitude when the Mother Superior sent Abigail with her to this wild place to start a refuge for homeless children.

Maddy had come from a respectable middle-class back-ground, but impoverished by her selfish though brilliant father, she had been penniless when he died and had gone to the nuns in despair.

Maddy could have married when she was young and some-times if she was having a bad day she remembered how Jay Gilbraith had wanted to marry her when she was twenty and he a young businessman of thirty. Her father had refused because Jay had also been a child of the streets. He had had no background, no family, and had fought his way up, making his own money. Her father was too proud of his daughter and their name to let her marry a nobody.

Now Jay had created this village, a place where he gathered up people who needed a new start, a decent place to live. Maddy had no romantic thoughts of him any more, those she did have were caught up in her early life and were besieged by the misery of her father's behaviour, so she did not dwell on these things.

In some ways she thanked God that they had not been allowed to marry. It was strange how when you looked back you thought that there was an unseen hand guiding your life, and though it was not what you wanted at the time, you could achieve so much more by giving your life to a much more worthy idea than having children and just going on. She was proud of what they had achieved with God's help, and grateful that somehow she had ended up in this wild and beautiful place.

Now she needed a replacement for Hilary, she needed another shoulder to the wheel, if you like, she thought.

That morning she had a letter from the Mother Superior in Newcastle and it was an instruction, Maddy did not doubt it. She was sending a nun to help, and she trusted that Sister Madeline and Sister Abigail would make her welcome and help her to settle in. Mother did not say that the new nun was to be a replacement for Hilary, and Maddy thought it was as well unsaid. Hilary was a huge loss since she had married Mr Nattrass and although they lived nearby it could never be the same and Maddy was not sufficiently selfish to wish it so.

The new nun was Sister Lydia. She had many talents – Mother was a believer in there being 'no lights under bushels but men light a candle', Maddy thought – talent was her oft-used word and, unlike many religious orders, the Daughters of Charity were allowed to use their talents as best they chose to enable other people to be well and prosper, and they could leave the order if they wanted. Maddy thought this was sensible though not godly, it depended on how you looked at such things.

Maddy also discerned in the letter that Mother knew Maddy was not keen on having other nuns there, she was too worried they might cause disruption, but since to Mother this was firstly a religious venture Maddy knew that she would have to put up with Sister Lydia, no matter what kind of person she was.

Abigail felt the same. They had sufficient help in the community so as not to need any more religious figures, but then perhaps they were both wrong, so privately they stopped laughing about the idea as they had when they thought it was not a serious possibility.

The nun arrived on the kind of day that only made its appearance perhaps twice a month, if that. It was a perfect day up on the tops, a clear sky, the odd white cloud disappearing as it broke across the horizon. Everything looked as though it flourished without effort.

Maddy had gone to greet the new arrival. Abigail was left to mind everything else, but then Abigail was not wont to say nothing when she thought there was anything to be said, so it was safer to leave her at the school and go and see the new help alone. Maddy expected nothing and hoped for nothing and knew there was no way in which she could win, she must accept what she was given and be thankful.

At first, as Sister Lydia was helped down from the pony and cart, her face was nicely blank, so Maddy made hers the same. She called herself stupid and pessimistic. Mother had sent a woman she thought would be of great help, indeed her letter had said so.

The new nun looked all around her, ignoring Maddy, not deliberately, Maddy thought, but just that she had never been anywhere like this and was bemused and possibly scared too. So she came closer and made the first move. She welcomed her, introduced herself, and the other nun was polite enough to look and smile and nod.

Maddy was surprised at how young this woman was – she could not have been more than twenty, or maybe she looked younger because she had exquisitely fair skin, like peaches and cream as the old saying went. She was slender and large-eyed and had about her a look that Maddy could only think of as vacant. She dismissed the idea. Mother would never send her somebody incompetent.

As Abigail said later, 'She looks like she belongs in one of them tea houses in Newcastle, lifting her little finger with her teacup and nibbling the edge off Victoria sponge cakes.'

She was very slight, 'As though the wind off the Tyne would carry her away,' Abigail said.

She was also one of the most beautiful girls either of them had ever seen. 'She's got eyes just like Dobber,' Abigail said, Dobber being one of Mr Nattrass's sheepdogs.

Her eyes were indeed dark brown, and her lashes when she cast them low hid a great many things in her face. She had delicate hands that looked as if they had seen no work, and there was to her face a gentle blush amidst the whiteness of her skin.

'Lydia.'

Abigail said she had never known of a nun called such a name and had no idea where it came from. Maddy had the feeling there had been a Saint Lydia at some point.

Sister Lydia looked shocked when she saw the children, and Maddy understood why. There was a great deal of noise in the dining room. A lot of people might have hushed them, but these children had come from difficult circumstances so as long as they did not quarrel or fight at the table she did not care. She had never thought about the noise before, but she felt sure it sounded tremendous.

She and Abigail always sat among the children, nowhere near one another, it worked better that way, they had control. She sat Sister Lydia down by her side so that the young nun would not be overwhelmed. The children ignored her and, although they made a great deal of noise, they were also conscious that they were being well fed so it was all good-humoured.

Many of them knew what it was like to starve, the rest were grateful for their education, and since the bigger boys were the only ones who might have disrupted things and had been sent to learn at various farms in the district – something Maddy became more and more grateful for as time went by – they ate well. She insisted on them using knives and forks and having table manners. Abigail had a habit of rapping people across the knuckles for not eating properly at the table – no elbows, fork in left hand, held with prongs downward, knife in right hand, held the correct way up so that it cut properly, and not to put too much into your mouth at once in case you might choke. Table manners were a matter of common sense, Abigail said.

'These are knives and forks, not shovels, and we are responsible for the manners that you take out into the world, and on such things you will be judged, so take heed.' Abigail could be so correct, Maddy thought, in awe considering she had never seen the inside of a house at seven years old.

The children soon learned, and also after the first meal or two that they need not fear, or eat as if they would never get another meal. Everybody here ate three meals a day and drank goat's milk in the mornings – Abigail now had three nanny goats and a young man to look after and milk them. Jim Slater's lad, Robert, who was helping his father to fit windowpanes and doors in the new houses, took on the duty with relish. With the milk there were often newly baked biscuits. Maddy was aware they were not so well baked as they had been when Hilary ran the kitchen. She tried to push away such thoughts. She told herself that Sister Lydia would turn out to be a surprise and that perhaps she was a wizard in what she still thought of as Hilary's kitchen.

After a day or two the children would settle down and sleep well. Mr Gray, the local doctor, looked after the village so that every child who was hurt or ailing was soon helped, and Maddy prided herself that no child was ever neglected after coming to her.

Sister Lydia did not eat much that first day. She seemed aghast and when she was assigned kitchen duties she blenched visibly. 'That woman has never peeled a carrot in her life,' Abigail said the following day, coming into Maddy's office and closing the door, which she did when she wanted to say something disagreeable.

'We must give her time,' Maddy said.

Abigail looked hard at her and then went back to the kitchen to see how the meals were going for the rest of the day.

Things had been difficult in the kitchen since Hilary had married. The women who helped were competent, but nothing more, and Abigail's cooking was so plain that Maddy would have suggested differently had she dared. Abigail too did not like the work, though she would never have said so. She preferred being with families and helping in houses and looking after the welfare of various young women in the village. Maddy knew well that if Lydia had been able to take over the kitchen it would have worked well, but Lydia showed no aptitude. Maddy thought the nun's neat white hands and upper-middle-class accent and good looks meant that Abigail was right, Lydia had never been in a kitchen before, so she could hardly be expected to cope now without a lot of help. In the end Maddy found a woman from the village to run the kitchen, which solved a lot of problems. She was widowed without children and had helped her husband run an inn in Stanhope. Having nowhere to go she had ended up here and Maddy saw as soon as the woman arrived that she would take over care of the kitchen. Abigail was so relieved that Maddy could see it in her face. Maddy just wished she could have discovered anything that Lydia was remotely good at. Typically Mother had given her no clue, it was so like her to let Maddy work out such things for herself.

In the end she asked Sister Lydia if she had any teaching

skills, but that too was a bad idea. She couldn't keep the children quiet. She couldn't engross them in any subject at all, and it was so obvious she was hopeless that Maddy despaired. She could not sew or knit, she could not sing a note. Maddy half wished that Hilary had never married, but it was far too late for all that.

# Two

Cowshill, Weardale, 1861

It was July, the first week of the month, and Mary Barnfather's favourite time of year. The back gardens were full of greens – carrot fronds waving in the wind, leeks peeping up from their trenches criss-crossed, creamy cauliflowers fat and round like bouquets, spinach and lettuce and onions. The potatoes were at their best, all you had to do was rub their skins so that they flaked off under your thumbs and they were ready to be cooked. Most memorable of all was mint, and here she remembered being a small child sent out to pick the mint so that her mother could use it to go with the lamb on special Sundays. Vinegar, sugar, and the mint bruised for its smell coated the lamb and new potatoes, with lots of butter and salt, was the perfect accompaniment.

The nights were barely dark and the days were long and sunny for the most part, but then thunder and lightning would prevail alongside huge downpours so that nothing wilted, everything grew.

She had spent the majority of her days playing with her siblings in the burn, which flowed through the village where her father ran the flour mill. They would spend hours trying to dam the stream, moving large stones to stop the water. Abe, the eldest at fourteen, was good at that, she mostly gave him directions. The six-year-old, Flo, was happy just to plodge in the water, and two-year-old, Rosie stayed in the house, her mother being convinced that they would let the poor child drown because they weren't capable of looking after her.

Her mother was always urging Mary to help, she was ten now and could do most things, but her mother didn't say much about it, although she got fed up because Abe was not capable of looking after Rosie by himself.

Abe was different than other people and spent a lot of time gazing into nowhere. Mary went to school, Abe didn't, and nobody tried to push him after he went the first few times, didn't know where he was, and ran for home. Six-year-old Flo didn't go either because she didn't like it, and Mary felt a bit bad about the whole thing because her mother insisted on her going. She liked it.

'It might get you out of this godforsaken hole if you could learn something useful,' her mother said.

Her mother complained a lot, everything was somebody else's fault, but since nobody took any notice and nothing changed she would shut up in the end. She'd often say that she wished she had never got married and had children.

There weren't many unmarried women here and either they were dressmakers or went as help to the small farms, and they were generally not considered of any importance. Great shame was heaped on those who could not attract a man.

Mrs Carlton, who lived four doors along, was respected because her man had died in the quarry and the management had paid out money because they deemed it was not his fault, but still she had to take in washing because she had three children and nobody to lock the doors.

Mary's father was always at the mill, which was just across

from the house and over the stream. He would come in three times a day for his meals but often he was so busy that Mary would have to take his meals to him, and something for the lad who worked with him, Kenny, so there were always a lot of meals to be made. Mary was amazed her mother had time for anything else, though she felt a little guilty because she could have been of help but didn't like being inside.

Of late she had taken meals over and only Kenny had been at the mill, and there was no point in talking to Kenny because as far as she knew he never spoke. How the two men communicated was beyond her. She didn't even know where Kenny lived. She had the feeling that he slept on the premises, and the few times lately when her dad had not been there Kenny had happily eaten both meals. Mary didn't tell her mother that her father was not there, if he had other business it was nothing to do with her.

Her father was a quiet man, he had few words to give to the world, as though he was somehow storing them for future use, as if he might be giving out diamonds on his breath. So mostly he just went about his business, got on with his day. Her mother was noisy, perhaps that was why he was quiet. She went on talking and grumbling, regardless of whether there was anybody around to hear her.

Mary would come in sometimes, thinking that they had a visitor, most unusual, but her mother was just going about her tasks, cooking and washing up and scrubbing floors and making their clothes.

She was a seamstress and very good at it, so Mary wondered why she had married when she had such a skill and resolved that there had been no need of it. Most women were good at such things, their mothers taught them to be. It made her sad to think that her mother had had nothing to look forward to other than this.

It was summer and the days were warm and long, so the nights were too, the windows always open to what breeze they could catch, and up there on the felltops there was almost always a breeze. When the night was blue and as dark as it would get, the moon was big and round in the sky, giving light behind the clouds and making Mary feel so alive that often she would stay by the window while the others slept.

School was finished, she was so relieved because, although she enjoyed school, her freedom was the most important thing of all. She loved her home. Harebells so blue, and clover purple and white, long stemmed big white daisies in the grass by the roadside, and purple vetch. The stream was low because there had not been much rain lately, but from time to time it would come down in torrents as though aware it was not doing its job properly.

Her father was a proud man and although they were not rich he paid his way, he never let a bill go unattended and everybody in the area knew that he was honest and hardworking. Also, if people were stuck he would help them with money or time, and her mother protested that he was trying to keep the whole dale and that one of these fine days they would have nothing to eat and nowhere to go.

Mary was pleased that he was her dad. She thought he was wonderful. He was tall and slender and smart, with bright red hair like carrots and cool green eyes. He had a milky skin such as most men didn't. He had a smiling mouth and although he didn't say much Mary knew that he loved them. He would talk to them softly, he never beat them when they did what her mother thought was wrong, so her mother could never say, 'wait until your dad gets home', partly because he was nearby and partly because he didn't lift a hand to anybody.

His only failing was that she was his favourite. She knew that he didn't mean to set her apart from the others and also she knew that if Abe had been like other lads she would probably have come with the rest of the children after him, but since he wasn't, her father took to her and she enjoyed it. She knew how unfair it was, but saw that he couldn't help it. Her mother seemed not to see it, and Mary hoped she never would. In any case, she said nothing.

Her father took Mary walking with him sometimes on Sunday afternoons. He didn't ask anybody else to go, she couldn't remember when they had not done such things. In a way she felt like she was the nearest thing her father had to a son, despite Abe.

He taught her how to tickle fish and how to push back their heads so that they died and how to slit their bellies and take out their insides with your forefinger. He took her shooting for rabbits and pigeons and let her shoot while he knelt down and she rested the gun on his shoulder.

He taught her how to skin rabbits and pluck pigeons. She wished she could go to work in the mill with him, but when she suggested it he laughed and looked pleased and said that when she was older she could go in, when she was stronger she could help, and she was amazed and grateful because girls didn't do things like that.

Her mother taught her to cook and bake and sew and knit. Mary was not good at sewing and knitting, she thought it boring. All she wanted was to play outside with the others, dream of when she would be old enough and strong enough to look after the mill, to help her father when he aged and couldn't do it any more, but she accepted the things her mother taught her because it would have been wrong to refuse. And her mother wouldn't have stood for it.

As the days went forward she was taking three meals a day to the mill. Her father was sometimes there at night, but often he was missing through the day and she could not help worrying that there would be problems. Whatever was he doing that he did not come to work?

By now she was lying awake half the night, long after her mother softly snored and the children around her slept. Abe always slept well. She was convinced that if the house were burning down she would have had to waken him to make sure they left safely.

It was August when she heard her father get up in the middle of the night and creep about as though not wanting to disturb anyone. Perhaps he needed to get to the mill early and make up for the time he had lost, but he had gone downstairs and did not come back, and yet neither did he leave the house.

Eventually she trod barefoot down the stairs, her feet making no noise and her nightgown long and white, with embroidered butterflies such as she had requested when her mother made this garment for her. She had been so proud of the butterflies. They were brown and orange and had yellow spots on their wings, which was exactly what she had asked for.

It was shadowed but not dark and somehow she had the feeling that summer was over. She paused at the bottom of the stairs because she could see his figure, and then he saw her.

'Daddy. Are you going out?' she said.

'Yes, I – yes, I am.' He stopped there and looked up at her, his green eyes so bright, and then he said slowly, 'Would you like to come with me?'

She stared at him.

'No,' he said immediately. 'How foolish was I? You cannot come with me. You must stay here and look after everybody.'

'I can dress in a minute,' she offered.

He seemed to think about it, and then shook his head.

'No,' he said, 'it wouldn't do. I can't have you along.'

'Are you going far?'

'A fair way, yes.' He sounded reluctant, as though she could change his mind if only she could think of the right thing to say or do, but nothing came to her, and her insides panicked that she could not hold him.

'Will you be back in the morning?'

He was no longer looking at her. He didn't even look at the door. She thought he was going to put down the bags that he held in his hands but he didn't. He clutched at them ever harder, his face set, and then he unlatched the door and all he said was, 'Look after the others,' and then he opened the door and closed it after him.

Mary never forgot the little click as the latch came down. There was something so final about it that she did not run after him as she had thought she might. She stood there, thinking about what it would be like if she put on her clothes and the lovely shawl that her mother had made for her, but thinking about that shawl she knew she could not go. It was such a pretty dark heather, the colour she had requested because heather was her favourite colour, her favourite flower.

She hesitated, not sure about which way her mind would choose to go, but she did nothing. She could have put on her clothes and followed him, so why didn't she? She didn't know. Just that somehow she divined it was of no use. It would do no good. There had been something about his stance and the turn of his head and the look in his eyes that stopped her.

After he had gone all she could smell was flour and the dying kitchen fire and the remains of the meal her mother had made so faithfully. The meals had been better than ever of late, and she thought that perhaps her mother had seen that her father was distracted and tried to put things right in one of the few ways she knew.

Mary tried not to think that he had gone for more than a day. Could she have mistaken his words, his intent, but then he had never said such things before, had never gone like that in such a way.

He wasn't there the following morning and when she took out the breakfast to the mill he wasn't there either. She started waiting for him, looking for sight of him, listening for the sound of his heavy-treaded boots, but he wasn't there the day after, nor the one after that, and she lay awake in the darkness, lost as to what to think.

Her mother seemed unaware that her husband was not at the mill and did not come home at night. Since she was not alarmed, Mary tried not to be, but as two days turned into three and three into four and she was still taking three meals a day over to the mill and watching Kenny gleefully demolish the lot she became more and more worried. She did ask Kenny where her father had gone, did he know when he would be back, but Kenny kept shrugging his shoulders, eating and drinking and saying nothing.

How could her mother not know that her father was not there at all? Mary didn't know whether to say something, but it didn't seem right that she should.

But then she could not go on like this, not saying that her father was not there, and she could not tell her mother the truth of it. It weighed heavily on her. Sooner or later, especially when there was no work being done at the mill, as surely Kenny could not do it all, her mother would notice.

She wished she had somebody to talk to. She started to fear the worst, so that when she finally got back to the house she couldn't eat. When the squire, Mr Long, discovered her father was not there any longer, they would lose the mill and the house.

Her mother complained about her not eating, but she couldn't get a morsel down after five days of her father's absence.

'You're not ailing, are you?' her mother said, putting a hand to her clammy forehead. 'You're hot and sticky. Do you feel ill?'

'No. No, I'm fine.'

Mary could see her mother was surprised that day because rather than going outside with the others on such a fine day she helped without being asked.

'Now I know you're ill,' her mother joked.

The morning was endless and yet noon came and her mother packed food off to the mill.

Mary tried questioning him again, but Kenny went on eating, looked blankly at her and all around, as if her father would suddenly appear. He really was quite daft, she thought.

So she didn't linger to collect the plates. She went back into the house and told her mother that she had left the plates with Kenny because her dad wasn't there.

Her mother thought nothing of that, why would she? It was again an endless time until tea, but when she took the meal over she knew that she would be faced with the same thing again and so it was. It was awful, the time trickled past like an almost dried-up stream.

This time her mother frowned but said nothing. Everything changed that night. Her mother waited up and Mary could not sleep and finally when her mother went to bed she knew that nothing would ever be the same again. Everything in their lives was altered and nothing could or would go back.

Her mother did not sleep. She kept walking about and then going downstairs, and finally Mary knew that her mother had lit a candle and gone to the mill. She would probably find Kenny sleeping there. Did her mother suspect that he slept there?

She was not long in coming back. By then Mary had crept down the stairs and was waiting by the door. It really was dark and, as her mother came in with the candle still alight, she spied Mary and said, 'Goodness, child, what are you doing still up?'

'Is something wrong?' Mary tried to be innocent about it but she felt guilty.

'Your father isn't there. I think that perhaps he has had an accident.'

Mary couldn't think of a thing to say, and then her mother paused inside the door.

'Why, his coat isn't here.'

Mary tried to look surprised and remembered her father had his coat on when he left, even though the night was warm, and that should have told her he was not coming back. And then a thought occurred to her. Maybe he would come back. She couldn't understand why he had gone. Or where?

Her mother was examining the place behind the door where his coat lived as though her hands would make him appear, and then Mary thought, the truth began to dawn.

'Where could he have gone?'

It finally occurred to Mary that her mother had been hoping and praying as she had been, that she too had been worried for some time but had not liked to admit it in front of her children, could not live with the idea that her husband had left them.

Mary hovered on the stairs.

'Go back to bed, child. There's no point in you being here.'

Mary went, but her mother did not come back up the stairs and Mary couldn't sleep. She felt guilty. She felt as though she ought to go down and tell her mother that she had seen him leave. She felt as if she should have awoken her mother then, but it was too late for all this and nothing could be gained. Her guilt about it might be replaced by more guilt.

Her mother would feel that it had been all her fault. She finally fell asleep just as morning arrived and then her mother was shouting up the stairs for her to get up. When she did so, instead of giving her breakfast, her mother sent her to the mill to enquire whether her father was there. It was a useless errand, Mary knew, but she dutifully went and of course he was not there. Kenny looked disappointed when he saw that there was only one breakfast.

After that nothing more was said, but her mother began sending one lot of meals to the mill. Kenny was asked to the house. He had never been in the house before and hovered in the kitchen, smelling of flour and well, of himself. Mary thought he must never have washed in his life though where he could do so except in the stream she couldn't think. Her mother asked him questions, but Mary need not have worried. Kenny didn't know what day of the week it was, never mind when was the last time his boss had been there.

And Mary's mother did not realize that Kenny had been eating double his food for almost two weeks. He certainly didn't look fatter, but then he spent all his days heaving sacks of grain and flour about, so why would he? His face was blank as her mother questioned him. He didn't know when Mr Barnfather had last been there, leaving Mary's mother with the impression that her husband had been gone but a short time.

After that Kenny went outside and continued to have his

meals sent over, and her mother continued to wait for her husband to come back. Mary felt awful. She waited too and she prayed night and morning, but after another few days Mr Long himself turned up at the mill. Mary's heart did horrible things, down past her boots. She felt sick.

'I understand that Mr Barnfather is not at home,' he said, and Mary's mother wrung her hands to find the squire unexpectedly in her kitchen since he had come in the back way. She offered him the front room, but for some reason he declined it.

'I don't know where he is, sir, indeed I don't,' she said, and then the poor woman retreated into the pinafore which she lifted to her eyes.

'I will make enquiries,' Mr Long said, and then he went away and left her mother bemoaning the state of her house, her kitchen, and herself.

Her mother was fractious. She burned the meals, she shouted at the children and yet when they went outside to get away she shouted at them for leaving her, and so it went on. Her mother didn't sleep that night or the next, and then Mary didn't sleep either, increasing her prayers, doubling and then tripling them while her hands shook with dishonesty.

It was five days before Mr Long came back and her mother was flustered again to have such an important personage at her house twice in a week.

He asked if she would step outside since the day was rainy and the children were inside. The others thought nothing of it, but Mary stood by the window as the squire explained that something had happened. Furtively she opened the window and instantly wished she hadn't because the squire was saying to her mother, 'There is another woman. They went off together on Thursday night.'

Her mother stared at him.

'My husband went away with another woman?'

'I'm afraid so. Francine Butler, the daughter of the blacksmith at Lanehead. Her parents are angry and upset and she will never be able to go home. You must have heard that she disappeared several months ago. He has a little cottage there, and now they are going away together.'

'But – but he would never have done such a thing. We have always lived here, his father had the mill before him, you know he did.'

'Do you have anywhere to go?'

Mary gasped so loudly she thought they must have heard her.

'Go? Why, no, sir. I have no family left and my husband's family are all long since dead. You know that, they're in the churchyard and he was an only one. Abe cannot help him much, he is – not very bright.'

Her mother stopped there and Mary remembered the many times her father had tried to get Abe to understand things. Yes, they had a son, but he was incapable of being any use and Mary knew that they had longed for another son, and perhaps that was why he had spent so much time at the mill and away from the house and why there never seemed to be any conversation between her parents.

'He will come back,' she said now, trying to reassure both of them, Mary thought.

'He cannot come back, not after this, not after such disgrace. They are gone.' The squire coughed, like somebody who was finding this audience particularly difficult. 'They have a child, a little boy.'

Her mother cried out and then sobbed, and her apron, which had been particularly useful of late, Mary thought, went up to her eyes and stayed there as she tried to restrain her emotions and couldn't.

'I will try to get you a house in the village and perhaps you could find something useful to do there,' was all the squire said, and then he left.

Her mother stayed outside for a long time so that even the other children noticed and the younger two cried as children did when they were confused and had no idea what was going on. Nobody made dinner and when Mary went to find her mother she couldn't see her anywhere.

She gave the others sandwiches and put the fire on because she thought that her mother would need tea when she came back in, but she didn't come back. In the end, Mary took the children outside, mostly because she didn't trust Abe not to let the younger ones fall on the fire.

And then she looked around. They didn't notice her. She went next door to Mrs Wheatley's who had evidently heard what had happened and was guarded, not quite opening her door. She tried to be hearty and reassuring, but Mary was undeceived.

She went to all the neighbours, but none of them seemed to have any idea of what she might do and she knew that they were so poor they could barely afford to feed and house their own children, never mind anybody else's, so she came back, worrying that Rosie might have fallen into the stream. The only thing she was glad for was that Rosie was nowhere near the stream, they were playing just outside the house, though Abe had gone to sleep in the light sun that now pierced the thick green of the summer trees.

There was by this time little to eat, so Mary went to the hen-house and collected eggs, made bread, and was able to give the children some tea. After that, her mother still not having returned, she looked in the place her father kept his money, the little dresser that lived in their front room.

When she opened the middle drawer it was empty. She searched the other drawers, the cupboards, and everywhere in the house, afraid now. She did not want to think that not only had he gone off but he had left them without a penny. Thinking that Kenny was at the mill, though how he would have helped she had no idea, she set off, but the place was empty. Kenny, like a rat deserting a sinking ship she thought bitterly, had gone.

# Three

The first time that Lydia saw herself in a mirror after she left Newcastle she stared. There were no mirrors at the Newcastle convent so she had not caught a glimpse of herself in years, but at the orphanage there were small mirrors. Lydia was not quite sure why. Was it just that it was a place for children, but then why did children need mirrors? She could not help staring back at the beautiful creature her reflection was and then being so ashamed that she blushed and turned away. She didn't look again, but she could not forget how very lovely her face was, framed that way so that her eyes looked big and stark.

After that she noticed men in the village gazing at her as she went past on her way down to various houses or up to the foundling school, and then she understood why there were no mirrors at the convent, she should not notice them watching her. Nobody said anything and there was never anything threatening about it, it was just as though they were admiring a sunset or a view down the valley, and they didn't stare, so after a while she stopped thinking about it.

She knew that it was hard for Sister Madeline, trying to find a place for each nun where her best efforts would help the school most, but so far Lydia was afraid she was not making progress.

She had never been in a kitchen and that was the first place she was sent. She cut her fingers three times trying to peel carrots, and Sister Abigail complained, not just that her blood ran into the carrots but that there was scarcely any carrot left when she was done.

'You're meant to pare it, like this.' But Abigail did it so quickly that it didn't make any difference to how Lydia understood it. There was no way in which she was ever going to manage carrot peeling, and when she also reduced a potato to nothing but a pile of skin Abigail despaired and asked Maddy to move her, she knew. She did washing up for a while, but the plates and cups were always sliding from her hands on to the stone floor so that she was forever surrounded by shards of crockery, and then she would tear her hands more as she stooped to pick them up.

Abigail tried to show her how to hoe the weeds that were always springing up in the garden, but Lydia knew not a weed from a seed, that was what Abigail said with amazing patience, and so she was sent into the schoolroom.

Lydia had not known until that moment that children terrified her. Maddy spent days telling her about teaching and helping her to make the children regard her, but Lydia's voice forsook her and was lost in terror. The moment she was left alone she wanted to run out. It didn't matter how many attempts she made, she couldn't do it.

She hadn't been miserable since the day she left home, but she was now, and the more inadequate she thought she was the less she could do anything. She had loved life at the convent and wished herself back there very hard.


Lydia had been a meek child and never had any idea what she wanted to do. She was an only child and when her parents suggested she might marry the son of their greatest friends, although she had half expected it she realized that it was the last thing she had ever wanted. That was when she stopped being meek, and nobody was more surprised than she.

'But he's perfect for you,' her mother said.

Lydia couldn't believe it. She thought she had never met a man who was less likely to interest her, but she didn't want to say that. She never felt attracted to anyone. She thought that as an only child she might have enjoyed the company of other people, but the truth was that she liked being alone.

She did not want a man telling her what to do and she didn't want lots of children. She knew, though her mother had not said so, as far as she could remember, that her mother wanted a dozen grandchildren, having been unable to have more children herself, but Lydia was not about to fulfil her mother's second-hand dreams.

The young man was called David Welcome. She had known him all her life and never liked him. She spent a lot of time with him, since her parents and his parents were practically inseparable.

David had tried to teach her to ride until she begged him to stop. She hated being that far off the ground and when the horse moved she closed her eyes. David was the kind of boy who never read a book, was rarely inside, he spent most of his time hunting as he grew older, and since his father was Master of the Hunt he was always down at the stables helping with the hounds and seeing to the horses. He only seemed to like her because his parents encouraged it and if nothing else he was a most obedient child. Also the two families were as one, and she knew very well that they all wanted her to marry him.

She didn't even like how he looked. He was considered very

handsome, tall and lean and dark eyed and very merry with everybody, including herself. He would have danced all night with any girl who would dance, and because he was popular and well known and rich and landed gentry, her mother would never have understood why Lydia was not interested in him.

He was a big joker. He seemed to think telling jokes was conversation. He liked to make people laugh. He liked to party and dance and drink champagne, and every girl in the area around Newcastle liked him very much and several of them looked adoringly at him, but he didn't notice.

In the end he said bluntly to her, 'So when are we going to get married?'

They were standing in front of the huge, ugly and recently built mansion that had been in his family for hundreds of years, at least a house on that spot had been, they kept pulling down the houses and building new ones as though the future was necessarily better. And everything inside the house was renewed. His mother had no taste, Lydia thought. The library was cold and empty, the main rooms were full of chairs that matched but couldn't be sat upon for any length of time without discomfort, the hall was full of dead animals' heads, it was disgusting, Lydia thought. The table always groaned with food that would have fed a great many families, but nobody noticed there was a surfeit, so she only hoped it went to the servants at the end of the day. But they didn't think about it. The idea of having to live there with them was so awful that she couldn't even contemplate it.

There were few books in the house. The whole house was full of stuffed animals in glass boxes. Foxes with glinting eyes seemed to gape at her above the candlelight in the evenings. The talk bored her, it was all about killing things, and she was meant to wear beautiful dresses so she was always cold on these occasions because they were white silk or satin, and she had to wear pearls in her ears and around her neck and on her wrists as though she were an object herself.

It was a bright sunny morning, she had to say that. There had been a party the night before and David had drunk so much champagne that he had had to be carried to bed. The young men had thrown food at one another across the table and chased the maids through the hall, and everybody (except the maids presumably) thought it jolly good fun.

She thought he was joking at first. He looked pale and probably had a bad stomach upset. She would have recommended kaolin and morphine had she been asked. The local apothecary had recommended it when her mother had been ill some time recently, though her mother had not drunk too much champagne.

David was obviously what her mother called 'mis-stitched by her silence'.

'You're not saying anything, Lydia, I have the devil of a headache and Pa told me that if I didn't ask you soon he would do the work himself.' He seemed to think that funny and smirked.

'I don't want to marry you,' she said.

She would have walked away, but he would only have followed her. If ever there had been a spoiled child he was it. He had been denied nothing in his life, so she merely stood there while he frowned and looked at her as though being told the champagne had run out.

'What?' he said.

'I don't want to marry you.'

'But – but Lydia, that's ridiculous, damn it I'm the most eligible man in the whole area and it's all been settled. Your pa and my pa have done the paperwork, and we are to be married in the summer, you know it.' He was laughing openly now, showing his perfectly even white teeth. Ghastly, she thought. He was so absurdly physically well, a life which had had everything so far.

'I know nothing of the kind. Nobody has said anything to me.'

'Well, it was taken for granted. Of course you will marry me. What else would you do?'

'I'm thinking of becoming a nun.'

They both came from wealthy Catholic families and were devout, and in other generations both priests and nuns had been suitable roles for the extra children, especially girls who could find no partners, so it had been useful, but she was an only child. At first she said it just for something to say, to shock him, and he was certainly shocked.

He laughed again. He laughed long and loudly, but Lydia didn't laugh, so that in the end he stopped and stared at her, not believing what she said.

'Am I meant to tell my pa that not only will you not marry me but you are giving yourself to God? He would thrash me for being drunk before breakfast.'

'Your father would never do anything of the kind,' she said, his father being the most idle man on the planet.

'I think you mean it. That's silly, Lydia, you know it is, any girl in the whole of the north-east would marry me.'

'It may seem ridiculous to you, but it doesn't seem that way to me at all.'

He stared even more and he laughed until she wished she could knock the laughter from his face. She wanted to tell him that she wouldn't marry him if he had been the last young man on earth, but she didn't, she was too well brought up for that, but she must let them all know that she would rather die than marry him.

There was hell on, that was what he told her, that there would be hell to pay and so there was. Her father was dumbfounded, her mother wept, and his mother wept, and his father had to leave the house, he was so upset. Strange how it became a reality.

Suddenly, becoming a nun seemed easier than all the other ways of living. Well, not easier, but more likely somehow, more feasible and certainly a lot safer than marrying somebody as crass as he was. She couldn't think of another way to handle it, another chance to get away, and get away she felt she must.

She was bored with the people in her life who cared for nothing but themselves and their wealth. Nobody read a book or watched a bird singing or did anything that was not so essentially selfish that it made her flinch. How had she been born like this? Pleasure was all they wanted or went towards.

Her father was upset and she could see it in his face.

'Why, Lydia why?'

'He bores me.'

He stared just as much as the boy had done.

'And that is why you don't want to marry him? You are being unreasonable.'

'I thought the Catholic church needed nuns.'

'Not like you. Not so exquisitely beautiful as you, or as well born. We have given you everything. Is this how you repay us?'

'You would rather sacrifice me to a man I don't care for?'

'Marriage is not a sacrifice, it's what women do, their role in life is to marry and give a man sons. How dare you?'

She met his eyes, possibly for the first time she had defied him, but she would not have this, she would not marry a man who was so stupid that she could not endure his company, much less his touch. He would never get so close as even to touch her hand, she swore to herself.

'I dare because I will not do it. I will not marry him, I don't care what any of you thinks or does and if you try to make me marry him I will run away.'

There was one young man she really liked. They played tennis. Not that she liked tennis. She had no real idea how tennis worked. You hit a ball back and forth across a net and then somehow, depending on where the ball landed, somebody won more points than the other person, and as far as she could see the whole thing was asinine.

She did like Clive Laidlaw. He liked playing tennis. She had known him when she was small, and playing tennis with him was easier than all the things she was supposed to be doing, like practising the piano, sewing, which she loathed, being fitted for new ball gowns or afternoon dresses, hats and so on. She was obliged to have tea with her mother at various houses where the conversation was all about marriage, who had married and who had failed to marry and why. And then it was all about children; to make young women feel that they had failed when they did not produce grandchildren to comfort the grandparents and carry on the line. The whole thing was so appalling, Lydia thought, like beasts on the farm.

At least at home she had books and there was a library. Unlike the Welcome household the library in her house had a fire unless it was very warm, and the servants, knowing that she loved that room and was the only person who ever went in it, made sure there was a fire from early morning until she went to bed. She had no idea who had chosen the books, perhaps her father in one of his moods when he liked a room to be what it was meant to be, and it was a treasure trove.

Perhaps he had employed somebody to see to what went into the library. If so then whoever had done it was wonderful. It was one thing she was grateful to him for. He seemed not to mind that she spent most of her life there, and she thought that occasionally he would buy and leave around the room various books he thought she might like, though nobody ever said anything. Her mother would have been horrified, but sometimes she would go into his study and put her lips to his cheek in thanks. It was her father she would miss most of all when she left, and she was loathe to cross him because he was a good, kind man, but she could not give in.

The library was her favourite room ever and sometimes she dreamed of staying there, not marrying, not moving on. She had no brother and in time would inherit the property, so if she didn't marry it would be hers and possibly that was the reason so many men courted her. If she didn't marry she would be able to sit over the fire for ever and never go beyond the gardens, which she liked, and the summerhouse where she sat when the weather was clement.

Her parents were always out at dinner parties and concerts and the theatre in Newcastle. Her mother wore gorgeous gowns, green with sequins and matching peacock coloured shoes with high heels. She wore fox fur around her neck and diamonds in her hair, and at her neck and on her wrists and in her ears. Lydia liked to see her parents dressed up to go out. She always uttered a sigh of relief when they were gone and then she would sit over the library fire with a good book, a comfortable chair, and eat apples and cheese instead of what Cook called 'a proper dinner'.

She knew also that the servants loved it when her parents went out. They sat over the kitchen fire and drank beer or gin and water and ate and did whatever they wanted to do. Lydia was very popular with them, because she was never any bother, Cook said.

She was fairly happy like that until she was sixteen, when she left school – she didn't want to leave, but her parents thought it indecent she should spend time in a classroom at her age. She missed it. Her enquiring mind was keen on working out how the human body functioned, but she dared not say so or even enquire. Her knowledge was discovered in the library because her teachers would not have wanted her to find out how people were made or gave birth or from what causes they died.

And she loved history, the Greeks, the Romans, anyone and everyone. She wished she could travel the world and see how the countries were in Europe and in remote places like Africa and in particular the Sahara, which sounded bleak and exciting.

Her mother got her decked out in gorgeous frocks and told her how lovely she was day after day.

They wanted to get her a maid of her own, but Lydia was horrified and refused. Imagine having to consider somebody else to that extent, for some poor girl having to sit up for her when her mother insisted on taking her to dances and pay somebody to dress her and do her hair and wait on her. The whole idea was distasteful.

She tried to be realistic. Her mother said it would be giving some poor girl a job, but she just couldn't do it. It was against everything she had ever thought she was about. She realized then that she was being prepared for marriage and imagined herself as a Christmas goose, plucked, gutted and put in a tin for the fire. She would be consumed by it all, but she must not give in, she did not understand what else she could do, but she must find something.

Having refused Welcome she did not therefore expect Clive to ask her to marry him.

Clive was nice, comfortable to be with. That was part of the problem. And strangely, as they sat down, taking it easy after a first set of tennis, he said in tepid tones, 'Did you want to get married, Lydia?'

She was aghast. Her mother would complain that she was sitting on the grass in her white clothes, which in a way was the compensation for having to play two long sets at least, except that again some wretched woman in the wash house would curse silently for her negligence.

'Of course not.'

He sighed.

'I did say so to my parents, but they seemed to think that since you had turned Welcome down there might be a shot in it for me.'

'You knew?'

'Everybody knows,' Clive said. 'And that you joked about becoming a nun, so they made me promise I would ask you.'

'But you don't have to marry me, you could have anybody. Your parents have oodles of money and background.' His mother was an earl's daughter and his father came from some-body very important in the Scottish Highlands with thousands of acres and castles and lots of other important things, she dared say.

He banged the tennis racket off his knee in a manner that Lydia thought would definitely break the strings, so enthusiastic was he in this work.

'They like you.'

'And do you like me?'

'I suppose.' He was looking down at his knees and his face was suffused with blushes, but Lydia knew it for modesty and that he would have liked to say a great deal more on the subject but didn't know how to. She had never thought that Clive loved her and she could not help being pleased.

'You suppose?'

He hesitated and then he looked straight at her and his eyes were clear and honest.

'I like you better than any other girl I have met. I don't particularly want to marry, but you don't seem that eager to take on Welcome and I know you like books so we could read a lot.' That made her smile. As reasons went for getting married she didn't think it was up there with the most useful ones, but it was certainly worth considering.

'I'm so tired of having to dance with girls I'm not interested in because they know I can afford to give them diamonds,' he said.

That did make her laugh.

'Oh, Clive,' she said.

'And I've got lots of money, you could have anything you wanted.'

'I don't think there is anything I want.'

'Look, Lydia, if you get stuck and they are trying to make you marry somebody else, tell me. We could always run away.'

'Where to?'

'I don't know. I could be a missionary and go to China.'

'Does the church allow that?'

'Positively dotes on it, I should think,' he said.

# Four

Jimmy Slater was the youngest of five, he was ten and three quarters and wished that he was eleven. He might be able to leave school then, he hoped so since he hated it. His father, Jim, was Mr Gilbraith's right-hand man, that's what everybody said, but he had started out, and still was to some extent, a carpenter. The eldest in the family, Robert, had long since left school and helped his dad in the carpentry business. He was in his early twenties.

'Making windows,' as he grumbled to Jimmy when they went to bed, 'I'm going to be making windows for the rest of my life.'

The three children in between were all girls. Jimmy couldn't stand two of them, Hester and Kitty, they were always telling him what to do. The other, Hannah, was lovely.

He had to go to school, his mother wouldn't stand for any nonsense, that was what she called it and so sometimes he went, but he would rather have been in the workshop with his father and Robert; and since Robert got up very early and went to the foundling school to milk the goats, Jimmy went with him.

He liked the goats, the way that they nuzzled his hands. Robert taught him to milk them and he liked their dark oblong eyes and the warmth of their bodies and the nutty smell of their black and white coats. They were beautiful creatures in their own way. Jimmy didn't really understand nuns, the women he knew were

all married and had children, and if Sister Abigail talked to him –
and she talked to everybody as far as he could tell – he didn't
know what to say and found his face going all hot until he had
to look away.

'They need to work and it's good for Jimmy to learn that once
he has said he will do a thing he has to do it,' Jimmy's father said
to his mother.

This was because Jimmy had decided he didn't want to be up
at the goat hut in the early mornings after the first few times
he'd gone, but his father wasn't having that. It did make a battle
at home with his mother wanting him at school and his father
wanting him to do what he said he would do all the time.

After that he did go and milk the goats twice a day. His father
didn't shout like his mother, but somehow he got you to do what
he said you must. Anyroad, Jimmy liked being with their Robert.
Robert was not like the girls, telling him what to do. Robert was
his only ally in the house and Jimmy really wanted to leave school
and go to the workshop.

He loved the smell of wood shavings and to see how the
doors and windows were constructed. His father also made special furniture which people admired, everybody wanted the small
tables and stools, but his father had little time to make them. The
trouble was that his father was now putting other men into the
workshop because he had so many more things to do and Robert
complained that it was not the same without him.

Their mother also complained because their father stopped
having proper hours as their mother called it, and was often busy
on Saturdays and Sundays and in the evenings.

Their mother also knew that Mr Gilbraith paid Jim Slater a
great deal of money and had offered him a bigger house. There
was a huge row when their mother found out.

'I had to hear it from other people,' she said, 'you didn't even talk to me about it. I would have liked to have been asked.'

'There was nothing to talk about. We don't need a bigger house, Kitty and Hester are going to be married, Hannah is nineteen—'

It was not the best thing to say, Jimmy knew, it galled his mother that two of her daughters were going to be married to men she cared nothing for and that her prettiest daughter showed no interest in men at all or in anything else, their mother said.

'It would be nice to have more space.'

'More space?' his father said, and he thought his mother should have held her tongue, she had gone too far. 'How much more space do you want, woman? We have three bedrooms, three rooms downstairs, a big yard, and it's all to heat and light and clean and keep right and we have five children and so far nobody else has looked after them or seen about anything.'

'We could have help.'

She had gone too far again, Jimmy surmised, and he was right.

'Help?' His father had turned red in the face and his blue eyes glinted with the temper he controlled.

'Mr Gilbraith has a lot of help,' his mother said.

'Mr Gilbraith has a whole village to see to. So far I've only got you and we have three daughters. We are not having help until you are having to do the lot on your own and so far you have plenty of help as far as I can see.'

Jimmy would have agreed to this, his three sisters being the most diligent girls he had ever seen. They washed and cleaned and scrubbed, they cooked and baked and sewed and mended, they embroidered and knitted. He had never seen one of them without something to do and for goodness' sake, as his mother had said, Hannah had begun reading Latin, she went to the chapel to see Sister Maddy.

'A long way may it get her,' said her mother who was against almost anything the nuns did though she wouldn't say so directly. 'The lads round here don't want a lass who knows dead languages.' But she couldn't complain much since Hannah could do just about anything in the house. 'Those nuns.'

She didn't complain any further but they didn't move and wouldn't, and anyway his mother had two daughters to set up for marriage and at the moment it was all about bottom drawers, something which apparently you put stuff into for when you got wed. It mystified Jimmy and every time one of their lads came to see them he had to give up his seat for them.

One was a right clot called Harold Smith – short and fat and not very clever, a labourer in house building – and the other was a pitman, Alf Smith, though the two were not related. He thought his mother disliked both her prospective sons-in-law but she could not say so. There were so many young women wanting husbands that she had to be grateful for what she got. Jimmy knew that since he listened through the wall to his parents talking about it late at night.

His father sighed and Jimmy could hear that he would be quite glad to get the two lasses off his hands and didn't really mind who they married so long as they were respectable lads. His mother said that she knew they deserved better but she doubted it was going to happen in such a small place as this in the middle of nowhere.

Also there was Polly Swift. Polly Swift lived in the next street down from the fell and Jimmy couldn't stand her. She was fat for a start, well not fat, but her top stuck out at the front and he tried not to stare but it wobbled and then her middle went a long way in and then she came out again with a startling bloom before her backside looked like a large pan. All the lads were after her, his mother said, because she was so bonny, she had hair you could nearly warm your hands on and bright green eyes and she was very keen on Robert. Whenever she and her mam came round Robert managed to be out, even when his mam told him he had to be at home.

He was like a cat Jimmy had once known who fled from the house as soon as there was any kind of noise. His mam got cross with him, but since his dad didn't say anything Robert took no notice.

Jimmy, being the youngest, you would think was not noticed by his mother with so much going on, but the trouble was that his mam's gaze was everywhere. He hated school and didn't like being at home. Now that he had learned to read, write and add up, he didn't see the point of school. The nuns had given up trying to get him to go, but he would turn up every couple of days demanding a new book and because the other lads didn't want the books, Jimmy ended up with them all to himself.

If the weather was good he would spend the day outside. If it wasn't, he would go to school but escape to a back room where there was a fire. The nuns let him get on with it most of the time because he was so far ahead of everybody else. They had tried to teach him more, but Jimmy got bored. He didn't think they knew much more about the things they tried to tell him than he did because a lot of the books they had dealt with nature and other places, far off lands and animals he had never met.

He longed to go to Africa and look for lions and had to be content with the cats who lived in the village. He watched them carefully and would have drawn them had he had paper and pencils and when he mentioned it to Sister Maddy she gave him these as he had known she would.

If he could find somewhere to sit by a fire at the foundling school the various cats would come with him and let him sketch them. In particular was Tiddles who belonged to Miss Proud and the others whose names he did not know, but they were happy to be where he was since he was a bit like a cat himself and always found the most comfortable places to be in the warmth.

His mam wasn't happy when she worked out that he was learning nothing more that she could see. His dad wasn't as bad as his mam, but since his mam complained to his dad his dad tried to get him to take part in things. Jimmy hated taking part. That meant dealing with other folk and that was hell. He didn't like to say it was hell, he would have been clipped around the ear for that by his mam, but it was true. He couldn't stand how stupid other folk were, he much preferred animals.

Home was full of other people and in particular Kitty and Hester who went on and on about getting married. Did their lads not have homes so they could go to theirs? Apparently not, or was it just that Jimmy's mam liked the two girls to spend as much time as possible at home before they were married and was given to crying in corners?

It wasn't as if they were going far. They had both been given houses, next to one another near the mill at the bottom of the village when they said to Mr Gilbraith that they were getting wed. Jimmy would be glad to see the back of them only he wasn't quite sure what home would be like then. Was silence any better than noise? He didn't know yet and wasn't sure he wanted to find out.

Their mother even considered the bottom of the bank too far. There was a lot of fuss about stuff like dresses and cakes and who was coming to the weddings and Jimmy liked to make himself as scarce as he could for fear that he would have to listen to much more of it.

'You aren't going to marry Polly Swift, are you?' he enquired of his brother one late night when Robert had just got in.

'Never in a million years,' Robert said.

This was a thing between them. They usually started off at never in a hundred, then never in a thousand, then never in a million, then never beyond the world into the stars before they both slept. Jimmy put quick prayers in to God that Robert wouldn't leave and marry her. He wasn't sure he wanted to be here by himself, with his parents having nobody else to fuss over.

# Five

Her mother would come back. Mary kept telling herself this the first day and the second. On the third day her mother came home and Mary was so pleased, she had been watching for hours. Her mother stumbled down the road towards the mill and that was when Mary ran towards her because it was clear that something was wrong and she was hurt.

She helped her mother inside and to bed. The doctor cost money and she had none. She tried telling the others that everything would be all right, but it was not. Her mother kept trying to get out of bed and then she was sick all over the bed and all over the floor and she said something about her head and her ears. When she insisted on getting up she swayed and then was throwing up again until she could not keep down even the sips of water which Mary felt sure she should be trying to give her because she was very hot.

Mary didn't like to leave the others to go for the doctor but in the end her mother got so hot that her forehead was burning and so Mary put out the only fire they had so nobody could fall into it, she told Abe to stay inside with the two small children, and then she ran as fast as she could to where the doctor lived at the bottom of the village. She banged hard on the door and the doctor's wife answered it.

'Why, Mary,' she said, 'whatever is the matter?'

'My father has gone away and my mother is ill.'

Mrs Cummings got her to describe the symptoms, and she didn't know when the doctor would be back but that he would come to her as soon as he could.

Mary wondered how she would pay him. There was nothing of worth left in the house. That day was surely the longest ever and the children cried. They had had nothing much to eat. Mary gave them everything she could find and eventually they went to bed.

Mary put cold cloths on her mother's forehead and tried also keeping her body as cool as she could, but her mother tossed and turned and eventually Mary was so worn down that she fell asleep on the floor.

By morning her mother was moving her head from side to side and saying very strange things and she was so hot that even through the cloths Mary could feel the burning.

All that day she waited for the doctor to come and by then there was very little in the house to eat and the hens had laid but two eggs and the two little girls cried and cried. Abe wasn't so bad, he just sat there and didn't say anything, as though he knew something had gone wrong but he wasn't sure what.

That night Mary didn't sleep at all and her mother grew worse. She said the kind of things which Mary didn't understand and she talked to people whom she thought were in the house. She kept looking at Mary while the sweat poured down her face and her neck and her whole body. Mary watched and tried to help, but by the time that the sun had come up her mother had ceased to breathe. She was like a tiny burned out fire, there was nothing left of her.

Mary didn't tell the others, there didn't seem to be much point. Halfway through the morning the doctor appeared.

'There was a problem at the mine,' he said. He meant one of the lead mines, the place was full of them. Mary didn't care about problems at the mines, all she knew was that she had lost both parents in a matter of days and nobody had seemed to care.

'There's not much point in you coming inside,' she said, 'my mother is dead and I have no money to pay you,' and she turned around and went in and slammed the door.

He banged on the door and said her name but she ignored him, she was so angry. There again Abe didn't notice. Mary didn't know what to do, but that evening Mrs Cummings, the doctor's wife, arrived.

'I'm so sorry,' she said. 'You know that he would have been here had he been able. Can I help?'

'I doubt it,' Mary said stiffly. 'Can you take us in?'

Mrs Cummings stuttered.

'No, of course you can't,' Mary said. 'You have nine children, don't you?'

'We will try to help you.'

Mary stared at her and that was when she saw that this woman was worn out with being the doctor's wife and possibly that was what women were like when they had borne nine children. She was permanently tired. Always running behind. Her own mother had been like that, only not as bad as this. Perhaps all women were, they had too much to cope with and some of them died, especially when their husbands had walked out and left them penniless with four children. The doctor's wife looked as if she was not long for this world either. Was this what women had to look forward to? A cold black grave after a short lifetime of giving birth?

'I have no money and nothing to eat and cannot afford to bury my mother. I have a brother who is daft and two small children. What do you think I should do?'

Mrs Cummings hesitated and then she produced some vegetables from her bag and she put them down on the table and she said, 'These may help,' and then she went away.

Oh yes, Mary thought, all I needed was a few carrots and some potatoes, but she put them on the fire in a pan and the children ate them gratefully. Other people were better. Once people knew that her mother was dead the local undertaker came and waved away the idea that Mary might in future be able to pay and he took away her mother's body. He organized a funeral. People did not come, only Mary, Abe and the children were there. The church was in the very centre of the village, but still nobody cared enough.

There was no service, her mother was buried and they watched her being lowered into the grave in a thin wooden coffin and that was all. Mary hurried them away from the place as soon as she could and swore never to go to church again. Abe followed. She thought that he understood but he didn't say much until they got home and then he went upstairs, sobbing.

She didn't know why people weren't there, she thought they imagined that her mother had had something catching and therefore kept out of the way. She understood, sort of, but she felt as bad as she had ever felt. Worse still, after the funeral the squire came to the house and looked apologetic but was nothing of the sort. Mary didn't rescue him. She looked through him.

'I'm sure you have somewhere to go.'

'We have nowhere to go,' she said.

He smiled. Mary would always remember that smile, she thought, it was pitiless. They didn't matter, they were just children, and as far as he was concerned they could starve by the side of the road. She swore she would get him back for it one day.

'I have found new tenants for the mill.'

There was no mention of a house in the village, it had been nothing but a sop, Mary thought. Now that they had no parent they didn't matter, they were nothing but an encumbrance.

Mary did not say anything but she felt anger as she had never felt it before. She wished she had a kitchen knife to stick into him. She was horrified and yet rather pleased at this. She didn't say that she would stay here until she had to go, but that afternoon she took Flo and went around the neighbours' doors and then she took all the foodstuffs they had in good faith and from guilt given her, and after that she and the others holed up in the house with the doors closed and bolted.

Luckily it began to rain and when it rained here in late July and early August it didn't know when to stop. The children begged to be outside but when Mary showed them what it was like through the windows they changed their minds. It was hard to keep them busy, and Abe had no ideas.

After five days of continual rain she heard a huge banging on the door at the back, away from the river. She ignored it. They all huddled together, afraid now, and then there was a bigger noise and after several goes at the door men broke it down and streamed in. They probably knew her, but they did not care, they did not look at her.

'I gave you every chance, now you must go,' the squire said.

They were left outside and then the house was boarded up so that they could not go back and then the squire moved away and so did the men.

At that point the grocer's wife, Mrs Wanless, came to her and said, 'Bring your little family to us, Mary,' and so it was that they were taken in. They were given a meal and the little ones were put to bed in nothing but blankets and pillows on the floor.

These people had big families and spent their time trying to feed them, so Mary was truly grateful.

'My Fred is going into Stanhope tomorrow so he can give you a lift and somebody there told him that up on the tops there is a school for orphans,' Mrs Wanless said.

Mary had not until that point realized that they were orphans, but she said sensibly, 'And how much further is it on from there?'

'About six miles, I think, mostly uphill. It might take you all day with this lot because the little ones cannot walk far, but I will give you food and water.'

Mary was astonished at her kindness and would have hugged the woman had anything like that been usual, but since it was not she merely nodded and thanked her.

She slept that night under her neighbour's roof and swore that if ever she could afford it she would repay them for their incredible kindness among all this grief. In the morning Mr Wanless got them on to his cart and took them to Stanhope.

It was a very long way, it seemed to Mary that it took ages, but the time went too fast for her and she was worried about what would happen when there was nobody to help. He dropped them off and left a couple of blankets with them and she did not like to mention that they had nowhere to sleep, she just thanked him for all he had done and let him go. The sight of the pony and cart going away from her was one of the hardest things she had had yet to put up with. But at least it wasn't raining.

There was no point in going anywhere that day but when the rain began in the early evening it was relentless, they were soaked and both little girls cried. She managed to shelter them in a shop doorway and even then they were not left alone. Somebody said late that night when she was almost asleep, 'You cannot stay here.'

She had no idea who it was, just a tall figure in the darkness.

'We are leaving in the morning.'

'You must leave now.'

Mary didn't argue, she just pulled the two children to her, Abe had not woken up and after a while whoever it was went and left them. She was so relieved.

The next day was slow going with the two small girls, they made it into Wolsingham and there they stopped before they began the climb up out of the dale. Had Mary been alone it would have been nothing but with two small children, one of whom was tiny, and a disgruntled brother who disliked exercise, it took her a long time to get to the tops and even then she could see nothing except what looked in the distance like a town.

It was at least a mile or a mile and a half and they had to go down the hill again, up the other side and then they were still faced with a climb. Only the idea that nobody would take them in at this point drove her forward.

It was very late in the day when they arrived and for the first time then Mary understood what it was that appealed to people. It was a town in the making. The houses were new, the roads had recently been laid, there was an air about it that made her feel hopeful. Abe had carried Rosie most of the way and she had led Flo, who walked reluctantly, and they were both worn out.

They were ushered into one room to sleep, she thought by nuns but she was so tired that she did not remember, just that they had been kindly greeted and she had never been so pleased to get anywhere. There was a bed for Abe, small, but enough because he was quite tall, and a bed big enough for the three girls.

Rosie had stopped crying and Flo was exhausted too and so they went to bed and slept. It was the best sleep that Mary had ever known except that she had lost both her parents. She was even too tired to think of that now. In the morning she would know huge regret and blame herself somehow for what had happened, but right then she didn't care, she just put her head down on to the pillow, which smelled, at least she thought it did, of lavender, which in past days her mother had always used on her linen in the water and amidst the soap somehow.

In her dreams she thought she saw her parents together and the family was safe and they went to sleep under the same roof and everything was all right.

# *Six*

Isabel Norton had led a very dull life since she had come to the village when her father and mother bought the hardware store. They had lived in Durham City and Isabel had been very happy there with lots of friends around the doors, but her father had worked for another man in the hardware shop in North Road and since his mother had died and left him money they decided to leave the city and run their own business in this little hilltop town where they could live much more cheaply. Isabel was fourteen.

From the beginning Isabel hated it. She was a child of the city. She loved the river and the boats and market square with its church and the winding road which led up to the castle and the cathedral. She liked going to the cathedral services on Sunday and though her father would frown she and her mother went off together.

Isabel loved the choirs, sometimes they visited from other places and she loved the ceremony of evensong and the way that the organ sounded so big and loud and mighty. She loved the different seasons in the city and how the sunlight would fall into blue and yellow beams on the floor of the cathedral through the stained-glass windows as the summer evenings grew late.

She loved how the different coloured autumn leaves dropped

into the grey of the river Wear and how the paths were covered in russet and yellow and brown. She loved the winters when there was snow beside the river, and spring when cherry blossom bloomed pink in people's gardens.

Their house was tiny because her father worked at the shop, but then the little house was just up from North Road and there was a yard in which Isabel grew pots of flowers. Her mother too was happy there but after they moved everything changed.

The weather up on the hilltops was bitter. She left behind the friends in the street whom she had known all her life. The hardware store was vital to the village so her father said, because it was the only one of its kind but the shop itself was very dark and there was only one small room at the back. They were in effect living in the kitchen.

That back room was also dark because there was nothing but a small yard and a rough lane beyond and houses after that, very little light entered the building.

The two bedrooms upstairs were quite big, she had the smaller of the two. From the beginning her father expected her to work all day with him in the shop, she had never had to do more than assist her mother in the house, but now he had his own shop it all changed. She was to wash the shelves down, arrange the stock, put labels on it all and write down each item that was sold.

She thought a hardware store must be the most boring place in the world. It was all nails and tacks and wood and buckets and cleaning cloths and it was mostly men who came into the shop, women would only come for things like pans and cutlery and crockery, and since they were careful with their belongings she rarely saw another female face except her mother's.

She didn't understand what happened to her mother who had always been a sociable creature, inviting her neighbours in for coffee and spending time in their houses doing the same. She loved shopping for groceries but now her father insisted that everything was delivered and even on Sundays there was work to do so he did not encourage them to visit the local churches, especially since there was no parish church here, it was not finished and though people could go into Wolsingham to the church her father thought there was enough to do.

What a bleak place this was, the wind howled up and down the streets and it was so cold that often nobody socialized. Her father would not give her time to read and didn't like her reading the few books which he owned. She could read the Bible on Sundays as long as everything for the shop was already done. Her mother was miserable and Isabel found it hard to help because she felt the same.

It got worse when her mother began to sit over the fire all alone in the back room while she and her father ran the shop. Sometimes now her mother forgot about meals and did not wash up. On a bad day she let the fire go out while sitting staring into the ashes.

Isabel ended up trying to juggle her mother's role and her own since her father said nothing to her mother about her lack of help. So she would make the meals and do the washing and clean, and of course it didn't work. Her father complained about everything.

Her mother didn't sleep. From her bed Isabel could hear her get up and walk the house, the stairs creaked. Sometimes she would find her mother sitting over the dead fire, unaware of what she was doing, not sure that she had left her bed. Isabel thought about asking her father whether he thought her mother needed help of some kind, but there was no way in which she could form the words.

He had never been a talkative man, now he rarely spoke. He had always managed their money carefully, but things were changing. He hid money in various parts of the house, she knew. He had control of what they bought and it seemed to her there was less and less when the groceries arrived. She took her courage and said to him that they could not manage on any less food but he said that he was afraid the business would fail, they would be homeless, and then what would happen.

'I have been homeless before and I have to make sure it doesn't happen to us now,' he said, a fact which Isabel knew nothing about and though she understood him better afterwards it did not help.

The food was reduced to bread, potatoes, and a few vegetables. She made a lot of soup because it all went further but even then both her parents ate sparingly, her mother because she forgot to eat and her father because he would deprive even himself so that the stash of money grew along with his fear.

They all became very thin, and Isabel found that her body reacted against the lack of food. Her periods stopped, her wrists grew skinny, and she had headaches. She was tired all the time and yet her father became more and more particular about the shop, it must be neat and tidy and the shelves must be washed daily and the floors also.

She was not allowed to go out. That had never been the case in Durham, but in Durham to him she had been a mere child. Here she was almost a woman and her father was suspicious of the men outside and even more so when they came into the shop. Sometimes he would not let her serve them.

The shop became a prison. If she stepped outside into the air he called her back. In the evenings she did the housework that her mother did not and she attended to the meals. She did the washing on Sundays. It was a sin to hang out your washing on Sundays, but her father thought nothing of that and very often theirs were the only garments blowing in the wind on a cold day.

The neighbours had long since ceased speaking to her unless they came into the shop for something and that was rare. In the beginning they had been friendly, had offered cake and a stew and gave out invitations so that Isabel and her parents would go next door for tea, but her father always refused on their behalf and in the end she saw few people.

There was one person she liked almost instantly and that was Robert Slater. He was the kind of man she would have liked to know better. It wasn't his smiles because he didn't smile often and didn't say much, but there was just something about his manner or the way he moved that appealed to her.

He was tall and rather taking, she thought when she could think such things and was not appalled at herself. He came in for various stuff he needed because he and his dad made windows for the houses. She didn't think he ever noticed her, and her father for some reason thought nothing of her waiting on Robert and took him for a shy lad she thought, so that now and again she got to serve somebody she felt something for.

# *Seven*

Lydia was beginning to think herself a complete failure, she fitted in nowhere and was very low in mood. In vain had she knelt in the chapel and asked God to help her, to show her the way, to make sure that she would not be sent back to Newcastle in disgrace because there was no place for her here.

In the fifth week at the foundling school she was running an errand at the bottom of the hill not far from where the hospital lay when she saw the horse and trap which she knew held the local doctor, Mr Gray. He had stopped and got out as fast as a middle-aged man could, then he looked around, saw and shouted to her, 'Sister, will you come and help me here?' So she went over to where she could now see a woman had fallen and when she reached the woman she saw that she was very pregnant and was groaning and holding her stomach. Lydia knew nothing of such matters. The three small children were looking dismayed.

The doctor picked up the woman and carried her the few yards to the hospital and instructed Lydia to bring the children. Once inside, and she had never seen a hospital before, it seemed to her very busy. There were women running to aid him.

'Take the children,' he said to one and then turned to Lydia, 'Sister, will you help me?'

She looked doubtfully at him.

'I don't know anything of such things but of course I will do whatever you think I can.'

'Don't worry,' he said, and that was the moment that Lydia learned to love and respect the doctor. He treated her with courtesy, he didn't object to the way that she knew nothing and because he was gentle and undemanding she wanted to help as she had wanted to do little else so far in her short life. He wasn't like the stupid men she'd known, only thinking of himself. It was as if he was a loving grandfather. Her own grandparents had died before she was old enough to know them, but this man was so exactly right for the role that she thought she had conjured him.

He was reliable, somebody who could change things though she didn't understand at the time that he would change her whole life and that Sister Maddy would make it possible. He was almost a magician. That was how people would come to see doctors, although it was such a big responsibility. Lydia felt odd.

He put the woman down on the bed and she thought he would dismiss Lydia but he didn't. Although there were other women around he smiled at Lydia and said softly so that nobody could overhear, 'Just hold Mrs Hope's hand and tell her it will be all right. Can you manage?'

'Yes, of course,' Lydia said and she suddenly knew that she could and that he had known she could and it was the first time in her life that she had felt completely happy. She was surprised at the feeling, she felt heady and grateful and glad. She was taken aback at how happy she felt then, she had had no idea that she could go forward with sudden speed and be where she was meant to be and she thanked God for getting to her to that stage. It could not be coincidence that she had seen the doctor and he had called to her and she had found what she wanted most dearly to have in her life, a real reason for being there.

He spoke softly to Mrs Hope and Mrs Hope nodded and stopped crying and then he washed his hands in hot soapy water and dried them with a clean towel and told Lydia to do the same. Then she held Mrs Hope's hands and he told her when to pant and when to wait and how the contractions moved her on and how she must hold back at some time and give it a chance.

Mrs Hope was sweaty. Lydia learned to wipe her brow with a cloth and cool water, he showed her. She liked how he gave swift sharp instructions and because of his tone which was commanding and yet soft he was obeyed. Lydia longed to sound like that.

She was emboldened, he nodded encouragement at her and she felt thrilled that he put so much trust in her, she told Mrs Hope that everything was going to be all right, even though she had no idea what this was like. She did not know what giving birth was all about. Nobody had told her that it was anything like this. She ought to have been aghast, but for some reason, holding the woman's hands and having the doctor softly voice encouragement, she was thrilled.

Mrs Hope moaned and shrieked and shouted and then panted when he told her to and then she cried and finally she began to voice the pain and Lydia had never heard anything before which had sounded like that, it was so basic, so animal like, all that breath and pain together. When the baby was born Lydia was so excited that she wanted to cry.

It was all bloody and slippery and so amazing. Lydia had never experienced anything which mattered to her so much. He urged her forward to take the child and he cut the cord and gave the baby into Lydia's arms and she was more engaged in this than she had ever known she could be.

He nodded to her to give the woman her baby to hold and that was when Mrs Hope cried and Lydia cried too and the doctor laughed with tears in his eyes.

When it was over the doctor went out and one of the nurses gave Lydia the baby to hold again while the mother was washed and made to feel better. Lydia had never held a newborn baby, she had no idea how complete it was, how helpless it was, how it scrunched together its tiny fists and screwed up its red face and closed eyes and kicked its dimpled knees and bawled. When she was told that she could give it back to its mother Lydia felt reluctant. And that was new as well. She had never thought she would feel maternal and she did and she felt so protective and so vulnerable for the mother.

'It's my fourth,' Mrs Hope said happily, 'what is your name, Sister?'

'Lydia.'

'What a beautiful name. Then I shall call her after you.'

'But I did nothing,' said Lydia, delighted and giving the baby into her arms.

'You were a great comfort to me,' Mrs Hope said.

Lydia could not believe that she had managed to be useful like never before.

Mr Gray came and thanked her and then he would have dismissed but she said, 'Can I do anything else to help?'

He must have heard the enthusiasm in her voice and seen it in her eyes because after a pause he sent a lad off with a note to Sister Madeline, saying that if she didn't mind he would keep Sister Lydia there for the afternoon.

It was the most wonderful afternoon of Lydia's life.

When Mr Hope came Lydia was able to show him in to see his wife and it may have been their fourth child but he was as enthusiastic as though it was the first. The other three, all girls, huddled around the bed. Then Mrs Hope, seeing as she was so well, was sent home.

Lydia very much wanted to go and see how the family was faring but since she was only there for that day she didn't like to ask if she might look in the next day and see if Mrs Hope was all right. She screwed up her courage and went down to the hospital the following day, when Sister Maddy had said she might, and found Mr Gray in his dispensary.

'I'm sorry to bother you—'

'Not at all,' he said, 'just hold that, will you?' That was a piece of paper with some kind of instructions on it like a recipe, she surmised.

Lydia was amazed to see this place, which was full of empty bottles and full bottles with labels. He told her that the bottles had been scalded, cleaned and dried on the outside and put into a low oven so that they could dry on the inside and how he put different coloured mixtures into them according to what people needed. He then seemed to forget that she had come to ask him something and began issuing orders.

She was to wash her hands as she had done the day before and then he gave her a kind of huge apron to go over her clothes and then he began to teach her about what the various mixtures were made of and how they could aid people.

She had gone to Maddy and asked if she might be allowed to go and see the doctor and did Maddy think her going to see Mrs Hope when she was not sure whether she could help at all was a good idea?

'It's a splendid idea. Just for someone to help if she is tired and has nobody there.'

'I'm not much good at these things.'

'It doesn't matter. You were there and she trusts you. You could just offer to hold the baby if she needs to do other things. Go and see her. Spend the time you need.'

When Lydia had gone Maddy was almost euphoric. She had kept on telling herself that Lydia's opportunities to shine here would arrive and she had prayed for it, while despairing that it was not teaching, it was not providing food from the kitchen or the garden, and but for a chance encounter with the doctor it might never have happened. And then she thought no, it was not a chance encounter, it was God, intervening and making things possible when people tried to do something to give them the strength and excitement to take huge steps forward. Lydia had been there so short a time before God put the gift of enthusiasm and possibly expertise into her hands.

At the moment to Lydia it was a small step but although she didn't realize it yet she had told Maddy about the baby and about how Mrs Hope had named the baby after her and how honoured she had felt. So Maddy told Lydia to see the doctor and then if he approved she would go and give whatever help Mrs Hope needed until she felt well enough to go on by herself.

With the doctor's approval therefore Lydia went to see Mrs Hope, who lived halfway down the hill. Nobody went to the front door and Lydia thought it was a good idea for all kinds of reasons. It meant that the dirt did not get into the front room which was kept for special occasions. It meant that the kitchen was where the family lived.

Lydia almost knocked at the back door and then she thought how silly it was. Mrs Hope didn't need people knocking on her door. It was just another thing she had to attend to, so Lydia knocked briefly and opened the door and called, 'It's only Sister Lydia, Mrs Hope, I just came to see how you are.'

She heard the woman's voice and so she came out of the little back scullery into the house and down a step. The stairs went up on the right and the kitchen with its lovely glowing range was there before her. Never, Lydia thought, had anybody been so glad to see her.

'Oh Sister, how very kind of you.' The children were grouped around her and Lydia thought how tired she looked and it was not surprising. The next small child was crying and Lydia could see that she had been displaced from her mother's arms and was resenting it. The other two sat on the settee across from the fire and neither of them looked happy, though neither of them was crying.

The baby was screaming. At first Lydia didn't know what to do. She didn't like to say anything about the state of the house which was in disarray but not dirty, so she just went ahead and did what she could and since Mrs Hope seemed grateful Lydia, encouraged, went on.

She found that she was no longer clumsy. This was different than trying to help in the school. She found bread in the pantry and sliced it and then she got the toasting fork and toasted it over the fire and she slathered it in butter and gave it into the little girls' hands. They were just hungry.

She took the smallest on to her lap and held her and rocked her and somehow the baby sensed that the atmosphere had eased and she went to sleep and the smallest girl also went to sleep. Lydia had never thought she would like having a child go to sleep against her, and the little girl's face relaxed.

She was reluctant to put her down but eager to go on and the child was so deeply asleep that she did not move when Lydia gently put her down on a rug by the side of the fire. Lydia made a pot of tea and gave Mrs Hope some toast, and then she washed up. She found paper and crayons in the front room, brought them into the kitchen and showed the children how to draw various animals.

She had forgotten that this was another thing she was good at and they copied her and were quiet and the whole atmosphere changed. She had done that, she was euphoric.

She even peeled the vegetables for tea which was much easier now than when she had tried to do it under Abigail's critical eyes. She then went to the shop across the road and bought what Mrs Hope needed for the next few days. Having a few pennies on her she bought sweets for the children.

It was fun. Mrs Hope told her how to make mince and dumplings. Lydia was so excited about cooking by then, and she enjoyed making the dumplings and how the flour and suet and water could be rounded into little balls which danced on the cooked meat and carrots and potatoes. Lydia looked at them with a kind of satisfied joy and when Mr Hope came in at tea time she was able to sit him down at the table. Mr Hope told her that she was an angel, which made her blush and disclaim and Mrs Hope was not long in telling her husband that Sister Lydia had made things so much easier for her that day.

'By,' he said, 'you make a mean mince and dumplings, Sister.'

Lydia thought it was the best compliment she had ever been given.

All that week, with Maddy's permission, she went and looked after the family until she got used to them as individuals. She told the children simple stories and she took them out for a walk on the first bright afternoon so that Mrs Hope could get some sleep. Several times she also took the baby and urged Mrs Hope to rest.

'I never sleep during the day,' the woman protested, but Lydia managed to insist and she saw for the first time that her habit gave strength to other women because they trusted in her and in her

God, and in her beliefs and in her abilities. She was so excited and overwhelmed at how useful she could be that it made her happier than she had ever been in her whole life. She had not known that giving, rather than receiving, was the best thing of all.

By the end of the week Mrs Hope had lost that exhausted look and was managing, so Lydia began to go every two days and then every three days and by the end of the month she went once a week and then she stopped going, but she told Mrs Hope that any kind of message would bring her back. She was never more than a few hundred yards away.

This work was what Abigail wanted to do so Maddy almost had a problem. She didn't need two nuns working in the same field, there was too much to do, so all three got together in Maddy's office and Abigail said that she wanted to be there for new mothers and the families and most especially for older girls, hoping to organize them to help in the homes of women who needed extra help.

The doctor had said he would like Lydia to spend time with him at the surgery and at the hospital so that he could teach her what he called 'a few more things about medicine' and when he told Maddy this he solved her problem.

So Lydia spent a week helping him and then she saw that this was what she wanted to do, what perhaps she had always been meant to do. Lydia confided to Maddy that she was not sure she was meant to do such work, she was meant to be humble and work for God. Maddy said that if Lydia had found her passion it was because God wanted her to work that way. Privately Maddy thought that Mother had been right, as she usually was, when she sent another nun to the little hilltop town. Somehow everybody found themselves one way or another when they reached this wild and desolate place.

# *Eight*

Mary could not believe what she was seeing. They had been at the foundling school for three months now and were getting along fairly well. She missed her mother, she missed the mill and the little village which was her home. Here they were just children and there were a great many children, so although they had beds and food and she could go to classes and learn, which she liked best of all, it was hard.

Abe had stopped speaking altogether and although he was in class he sat with his head down all the time. The two little ones were not in the class and had to be looked after and so Mary was torn between wanting to learn and wanting the two little girls to feel safe. She knew that the only time they felt safe was if she was there, so she could not be happy.

She longed for and missed her mother. When she lay down in her bed at night in the long dormitory with a lot of other girls she remembered what it was like when they had been happy before their father had run away. She had slept with the little ones and Abe had had a tiny back room to himself. She remembered them playing in the stream.

Abe never smiled. He ate, she sat beside him and watched him and she hoped that he slept, though she was never there to see it, but she wished they had something else to hope for. And then she was scared. Things had been so awful and now they were a little better and maybe she didn't dare ask for more in case something else went wrong. Don't ask, she kept telling herself in her mind, don't ask or you might have more things taken from you, something more going wrong.

Sometimes people came along who wanted children to take home and look after and she longed for people who looked like her father and mother, in the good days before everything had gone to the bad, to come and rescue her. Sometimes she dreamed that they were near, sometimes she was running and running but they were always out of sight and sometimes she had been playing in the stream, the day was bright with sunshine, her mother was calling her in for tea and she could see her father coming out of the mill for his meal. They would all be together and everything would be just as it had been. The rest of her time here was a dream and then she awoke and it was the past that was a dream and here she was, stranded just as before in an endless nightmare.

The other girls tried to make friends with her but she had to watch for her family and did not know what to say. She wished that she could be like a lot of children and have a house and parents and come to the school to learn and for no other reason. At the end of lessons she would watch girls skip down the road towards their own houses where no doubt their mam would have their tea ready and their dad would come back from work and they would all sit down together and eat and things would be right.

Christmas came and it was the first Christmas she had been without her parents and it was hard. Why was it that you always remembered the best things, the mistletoe her dad used to cut, and how he had once kissed her mother beneath it, the way that her mother arranged holly with berries in her flower jugs. Her mother had always made mince pies and a big cake and the mill house had always been full of wonderful smells.

They would have a chicken and lots of vegetables and her mother made rum sauce, white to pour over each portion of pudding and in her memory it always snowed.

This Christmas was as different as it could possibly be. There was a lot of carol singing, she liked that but she longed so much for her parents that she wanted to cry. It didn't snow, it rained for days and days so that the ground was soggy and every time somebody opened a door huge draughts tore along the halls and rain swept in on to the floor.

They all had a present, Mary's was a book of bible stories, the two little girls had sweets. Abe just grunted and didn't tell her what he had received but she thought he felt as she did, that they were both miserable.

Maddy and the other nuns liked Christmas best, it was such a cheerful festival. Even Lydia tried to sing and Abigail organized parties for the children and showed them how to make paper decorations. There was a big party up at Jay Gilbraith's house because he wanted to show his workmen how much he appreciated what they had done that year. There were huge tables and Miss Proud, his housekeeper, made sure there was enough for everyone, cakes and sandwiches, jelly and blancmange for the children.

Miss Proud played the piano, there was even dancing.

After Christmas the hard weather arrived. It was a Wednesday, Mary never forgot it, she was taken out of the classroom and sent to see Sister Maddy and when she opened the office door her father was there.

She stared at him. He was smiling at her.

'Mary,' he said, 'the job I've had to find you. I went back to Cowshill for you.'

She half expected her mother to materialize beside him but of course nothing happened. Didn't he know that her mother had died and what was he doing here?

'Mr Gilbraith has taken me on as the miller and we will all be together again. Sister Madeline says that you and the girls and Abe can come with me.'

She looked at Sister Maddy and found a small thin smile on the nun's face as though she was being polite and perhaps nothing much more, but she had to do that, so Mary just nodded.

Then Abe was summoned and the two little girls ran to her crying, and their father escorted them out of the school and there outside in the bitter January wind stood Francine Butler, who must have been all of sixteen. Mary had heard of her but not seen her before and to think that she was not that much older than Abe. But she was so beautiful that Mary couldn't help but stare.

No wonder, she thought bitterly, that her father had wanted this girl. Her hair was so yellow that it almost hurt your gaze, and her eyes were the same colour as harebells, a mix of grey and blue. And she was holding by the hand a small child, a boy. That was another shock. Mary had assumed that they had just had the child and therefore it would be a small baby, but the little boy was probably older than Rosie. So he had been carrying on with this woman while living at home with her mother and his four real children, that was how she thought of it.

She wanted to run away but wouldn't let herself. She stood where she was and tried to go on breathing. It had never been a problem before. What did they say, as natural as breathing, except that her breath wasn't coming naturally, it was all over the place and she knew that she was going to cry. She tried to control the feeling but she could not help thinking of her mother dying and of the other three and what this would be like for them.

Her father was smiling. She had always loved that smile. Now she didn't. She wished she could turn and run away but she had to stay and endure it. He stopped slightly short of her and pretended to be upset.

'Why, Mary,' he said, 'I thought you would be pleased to see me. I have been looking for you and they told me you were here, and now we can all be together.'

Mary's throat closed and her breath became even more ragged.

'Mr Gilbraith has given me a house and a job so we can settle down together here. Francine will be your mother.'

'Francine?'

'Yes, you must remember her. We are married and I want to have us all together under one roof.'

The woman had come beside him and was smiling too. Oh yes, Mary remembered her.

She had not seen her close to before. She had to compare this woman to her own mother who had been skinny and pale faced, had lines on her cheeks and worry in her eyes. Francine was already big with her second child. That too was worrying though why it should have been Mary wasn't sure until she thought about it and saw that Francine Butler was making certain of her man somehow in a way that Mary didn't understand but came to instinctively. Mary could have told her that even four children hadn't done that for her own mother.

Francine was beautiful, more so close to. Mary could quite see why her father had wanted her. Men didn't seem to care about anything but what women looked like as far as Mary had experienced in her life. Francine had curves, big breasts and big hips and her face was smooth and creamy coloured and her cheeks had pale pink roses in them like something out of a garden. Mary had never seen anything like her, and now Francine's stomach stuck out. Women would try to hide it, putting on shawls and coats, it was considered unseemly to show you were having a child, but Francine had no such idea, Mary could tell. She was almost blatant, that's what Mary's mother would have said.

Her father was strutting about almost like a cockerel in front of a hen house, Mary thought, warm with embarrassment. He was her father. She couldn't believe that this man had gone off and left her mother to die alone, had neglected his children, and they had all come to this. Abe stood there like a statue and the two little girls howled in dismay and fear at something new coming into their lives.

Francine seemed inclined to make a friend of Mary and came up to her saying, 'Your dad tells me you will help me in the house.'

Mary couldn't stop herself from saying, 'I go to school.'

'Fran will need your help,' he said, and he seemed almost embarrassed that this woman was having his second child. Mary couldn't believe that embarrassment. He had not mentioned her mother and he had deserted his wife and children and yet he did not acknowledge what he had done.

'But you must go to school as well, Mary,' Fran said encouragingly, and Mary thought how sad that her stepmother – this woman was such – was trying to get Mary on her side after how these two people had behaved. Mary said nothing more.

She didn't meet her father's eyes. She couldn't let him see that she was hating him. Before this she had done what was called giving him the benefit of the doubt. If he had said anything about her mother or that he was sorry or that he would try to be a better parent to them she might have tried to forgive him, but now her heart hardened, she could feel the coolness inside her. He cared for nobody, he had left them to starve up in Cowshill and she had watched her mother die while he was behaving like a tomcat.

At the time it appeared to Mary that her new stepmother had given in because she said nothing, but later she saw that Francine was too intelligent to argue and doubtless had other ways of getting what she wanted.

'Don't worry,' Francine said softly, 'I'll make sure you get to school, no matter how much there is to do.'

Mary was astonished. It was exactly how her mother had felt and now Mary had mixed feelings about this woman. She had stolen a man from his wife and four children and yet she was brazen about helping Mary.

'And you can call me "Fran" when your dad isn't about. I'm not your mam, I'm nearly young enough to be your sister and while I'm sure you don't like me I would prefer to get off on the right foot if we possibly can. I think I'm going to need as much help as you will give me.'

Mary said nothing and Fran didn't push her. Mary tried hard not to like the young woman but soon understood why her stepmother wanted her to go to school. Fran could not read, write or add up. She didn't try to hide it from Mary, then took the little help that Mary could offer.

She seemed ashamed of herself but was quite open about it and Mary was inclined to think that Fran had got away from a difficult situation in the only way a pretty lass could, she had picked up a man, the first one who offered. How awful that was, Mary thought, but it could hardly be the only time such a thing had happened.

'Maybe you could learn me,' she said.

'Teach you,' Mary said. 'My mam used to say "you learn" but "I teach".' And then she thought she shouldn't have mentioned her mother but Fran seemed unfazed.

'Teach me,' Fran said and she smiled and Mary smiled too and Fran said that in time they could both do all the things that would help them.

'And this is Burt,' Fran had said about the little boy.

Mary stared at him. She didn't think he looked much like her father but then she thought of Abe and how he didn't look like anybody. At that moment Abe came to her. The two little girls came after him, clinging to Mary at either side and searching out her hands so that they could hold on.

'This is your new mam,' their father said and Rosie hid in Mary's skirts while Flo, who was obviously horrified, let go the wee as she did when things were difficult. The water ran down her legs and sputtered pale brown on the ground and over her shoes.

'Is she still doing that?' was their father's disgusted reply as though Mary should have done something about it. 'I thought she would have got out of it by now. How are you, Abe?'

Abe, larger than ever and moving a little closer to Mary so that there was nothing between them bigger than a breath, stared and was mute.

'Come along, then,' her father said and he turned and began to walk down the hill, expecting them to follow and they did, both little girls clinging to Mary so that she could barely move.

At the bottom of the hill beyond the hospital with several rows of new houses was the flour mill and apparently here her father would reign. It was a good house, much better than the one they had had in Cowshill. Mary could not help thinking of how her mother would have liked this house, about how she had worked, and about how her father had deceived her mother.

Did her mother know about Burt and how old he was? Was that what had killed her, did she find out that her husband had taken up with another woman, or was it his general lack of regard? Perhaps it was the idea of neglect and being left with four children and her body had given in under the weight of such sorrow.

Burt had run off from his mother and was tearing about, firstly outside near the stream and then into the house because the doors were open. Several men were moving about inside and they had been delivering furniture, she could see them bumping around with various objects, clumsy. They went, and Mary felt almost bereaved when the house was empty except for her family and her father and this woman and her child. She felt strange, as though she had stepped into another world which she did not understand.

Her stepmother took Flo into her arms, whereupon the child began to wee again and as Fran lifted her up there was a lovely new stream which Mary was quite proud of. She hadn't known that Flo could wee at will. What a useful accomplishment.

The furniture was pretty and her father's new wife went around exclaiming at how nice everything was. That was her favourite word, nice. The chairs were nice, and wasn't the table nice and oh, look, a nice little settee and matching chairs. Oh, it was so nice.

She turned and tried to take Rosie from Mary's arms and the child kicked and screamed and clung.

'She'll soon get used to me,' Fran declared but she didn't look convinced. Who would, with four children dumped on her just like that? She obviously had no imagination, Mary thought, or she would have known.

Rosie kept up the kicking and screaming for a good while, until Fran stopped trying to take her from Mary, no doubt her second pregnancy clumsy upon her.

Luckily there was a diversion at this point. Burt had fallen into the icy water. He too was crying and he bawled his head off. The sound of all the children crying was like a melody in Mary's ears. Her father had to step in and pull him out while Mary, usually a God-fearing child, could not help wishing that he had not shouted so loudly and had drowned and that her father had gone in after him and been lost. The bitter thought did not linger but she enjoyed the few seconds it gave her.

Abe stood about as though none of it had anything to do with him.

'By God, you've grown, lad,' his father told him in jolly tones. 'You're big enough to carry sacks about and be a good help in the mill.'

Abe was mute. Mary was astonished at how their father was behaving. He was nothing like he had been, but then she didn't really know how he had been, she told herself. She would never have believed he could go and leave his wife and four children, that his wife would die because of his going, and that he already had another child and no doubt had spent a long time planning how he would leave, not telling her mother so that her mother suffered and perhaps thought him dead and had known nothing more when she died.

In her mind Mary had already gone to Sister Maddy and asked whether she really had to live here with her father but she knew what the answer would be. He was her father, he was entitled to do what he chose with his family, and he had come back for them.

'Mary, you are quite old enough to help your mother,' he said.

'I know you weren't much help before but you were younger then. And you have a new little brother. I know you will want to look after him.'

Mary said that she would be delighted. Her father did not notice or did not care to notice her tone.

'We'll get used to it soon,' was all her father said and he called to Abe to go into the mill with him so that he could show him around and tell him what his role would be.

Mary felt like she was suffocating. It seemed to her as if her own mother – she had to call her her own mother because her father insisted on her calling Fran Mother or Mam – had never existed. Her father did not refer to her and had not acknowledged that she had been his wife and had his children and had died after he had abandoned her.

Mary wanted to hate little Burt and tried hard because she could see Abe looking at him and perhaps wishing he was like Burt because Burt was everything a man wanted his son to be, she thought. He was quick and bright and a lovely little boy, smiling all the time and not noisy or troublesome. Abe demonstrated how much he thought of Burt because Burt followed him everywhere and instead of ignoring him Abe took the child to him and looked after him.

Burt spent a lot of time at the mill helping Abe and her father was so glad that his two sons liked being with one another, she could see straight away.

'He's a grand little lad,' Abe said. Mary was surprised. Her brother spoke so rarely and she liked that he had taken to the little boy. Did he, unlike her, want another boy in the family? Why would he not?

His father looked across at Abe and smiled. They were eating at the time and Mary thought it was possibly the first time that her father had seen his two sons together and been pleased.

'He'll make something grand of himself, he won't just be a miller,' he said, and Abe laughed and it was like the sun coming out.

'He will be a gentleman,' their father said, and the three men were in accord, eating their dinner with gusto.

Abe was like somebody new since his father had returned and rather than resenting his little brother, he loved him and was always with him, throwing him up into the air so that Burt laughed and screamed, knowing that Abe would catch him when he came down, and Abe and his father were closer for the new child.

Burt was to sleep in Abe's bedroom, Fran had decided, long before the new baby arrived, that Burt would not sleep with them any more, and he seemed excited by the prospect. Mary could not tell what her brother was thinking, his face had become closed since his father had left and his mother had died. She listened and there was silence and into the silence she heard her brother calling her name, and she went through.

In the gloom Abe said, 'Will you tell him a story? I can't think of anything. Can you remember the stories Mam used to tell us?'

'Can't you?'

'No. Just that it was lovely to hear her tell them.'

She thought about Little Red Riding Hood and then decided it might be too gory for such a small child, then there was Cinderella and Sleeping Beauty, and the princess who slept on the bed and felt the pea under twenty mattresses. She didn't think he would understand that one, and now that she thought about it they were all about princesses and nothing to do with anything real, so she made up a story about a mouse and his family who lived in the mill.

Had her mother sung that to them? She couldn't remember, but then Abe told her sleepily that he had never heard that one before so she wasn't sure whether her mother had read it, made it up or whether she had read it or made it up herself, and somehow she felt closer to her mother because of it and every night after that Burt would climb into bed with Abe and she would go in and tell them a story.

Fran said she was relieved that Burt no longer slept with them as Burt had a habit of kicking out in his sleep and she was worried he might kick the baby, and it was nice for her to get some decent nights where she could sleep and enjoy her dreams before the next baby arrived.

# Nine

Maddy worried about Mary's father and new mother right from the start. She had not missed the look on Mary's face nor the misery on Abe's, and the two little girls had howled and clung.

Now she was worried that their father had found them and that their fate might be worse than before. It was difficult to imagine that a man who had left his wife and four children so that his wife died and his children were made destitute would be any better a second time, but she had at least to think he might have the chance. Jay had thought so and she must accept it but keep watch.

She had asked about their history from the beginning and, though Mary had not betrayed their father, Maddy understood exactly what had happened, it not being the first time she had seen such a thing. She did not understand how a man could go off and leave his family and have his wife die and then pick up where he had left off with another woman and a child who was roughly the same age as the youngest child he had deserted, but at least he had come for them, which a lot of men might not have done.

Perhaps his new wife had persuaded him, perhaps she felt guilt such as Maddy felt certain men did not, at least not many. If there was anything good about the new Mrs Barnfather – and

Maddy always tried to see good in everyone – she might have wanted the children and in some ways wished that she had not deprived the man's first wife of his company and possibly that she could have lived a lot longer.

There was little she could do but she did walk down to the mill after about three weeks of them settling in. She was aware that Mary was not allowed to come to the school any more but for the odd day and sensed her father at work. And though Abe had learned little and the two smallest children did not matter yet in this way, she felt sure that Mary, as an apt and bright child, would benefit from her lessons even more so than she had done previously.

She tried to be hopeful. The second Mrs Barnfather was very young and obviously had not met a nun before or when she had she had been prejudiced as so many people were, because although they had met the day that the miller and his wife arrived, the woman had neither spoken nor acknowledged Maddy in any way.

Therefore she knocked politely on the door to find Mary herself answering it and unable to keep the gladness from her eyes. Mary didn't smile, she looked tired and worn and when she took Maddy inside and into the little sitting room, Mrs Barnfather came in, all hostility.

If she had been a dog the hair on her back would have stood up. Maddy greeted her warmly and asked after Mr Barnfather and how the mill was doing. She was not asked to sit down as she would have been in almost every house in the village.

'Is there something you want, Sister?'

'I just wondered if there was anything you might need help with,' and Maddy tried to smile, but Mrs Barnfather wasn't having any of that.

'We don't need any help.'

Maddy was surprised. She knew that Jay had given this man the mill in a huge gesture when he heard from other people that a miller was available, but he could have chosen someone else.

'I'm sure you're managing very well, it's such a pretty house.'

'It'll do,' the girl said, and Maddy wished she had not behaved in such a rude way. Nobody had taught her manners.

'I wondered whether Mary might come to the school more often. I'm sure you have lots for her to do with the two little ones and need her help, but she was getting on so well with her arithmetic, spelling and writing.'

'We get on just grand by ourselves.'

'I'm sure you do,' Maddy said soothingly, glancing at the door which was shut, in case Mary might be allowed in, but nothing happened.

There was a workbox in the room, such as many of the women had, as there was always such a lot of sewing and mending and darning to be done. Here was a big heap of clothing as though nobody had found time to do it and Maddy could think of nothing to say but, 'Is Mary good at knitting and sewing?'

Mrs Barnfather sighed and turned into a person. She sounded tired and no wonder, Maddy thought, she was so young and with all these children and a difficult husband, her life must be hard.

'I'm having to do it all myself, as though I didn't have enough to do with him and Abe coming in three times a day, wondering where their meals are. Burt is no bother, but them two little girls. Flo, well, I have stopped putting knickers on her altogether but she wets the bed every night.'

'Sister Abigail is good at sewing and knitting. I'm sure she would be happy to come and help or even to take away the extra so that you can still have your house to yourself.'

'We don't need no help, we just need you not coming here with your jumped up ideas. Pardon me, sister, but I'm not a Catholic and I don't like Catholics,' and Fran went back to where more than one child was crying. Maddy didn't wonder why.

She went slowly off up the hill, trying to think of another solution and met Abigail, who was setting up knitting and sewing afternoons in various places but most particularly in Mr Gilbraith's house where Miss Proud had said it was an excellent idea. Abigail was calling in at various houses to see whether the women would come to the afternoons at the big house.

Also she was venturing twice a week to meet Miss Hutton who owned the haberdashery shop, and they had set up sewing and knitting circles in Wolsingham. Maddy was very pleased that Jay had told Abigail she could have the pony cart any time she liked to help her in her new role. She had taken him literally and now went off by herself. She seemed so pleased with it all and so grateful that Maddy was glad her ideas had grown fruit and that Abigail had moved on from the foundling school itself into other things.

These groups were meant to be sociable as well as productive. The women could take their small children, and in the village the foundling school kitchen would make cakes and they all had tea and talked as they worked. Maddy thought the one in this village was a very good addition and Abigail was happy at her work, she could see because Abigail beamed at her now, something which had been absent from her face for some time.

Maddy asked all the right questions and they were back to the school before Abigail stopped her.

'So what is it?' she said.

This was surprising, Abigail not being the kind of person

who understood much about other people's feelings, Maddy had thought before now.

'Why?'

'You sighed, deeply.'

They smiled at one another and then sat down on the nearest wall and Maddy told her about the Barnfather family. Abigail was a good listener and said nothing until the story was finished, and then she frowned.

'I could knit some things for the little boy,' she said. 'He could do with a decent jumper.'

'Now that is a good idea.'

'And I could offer to take the two little girls for her some afternoons so that she could get on with what she needs to do, and she could bring Burt to our sewing afternoons. He is actually quite a nice little boy from what I've seen.'

Maddy was surprised again, she hadn't had much to do with Burt and she didn't know that Abigail was keen on children, having had to do so much for them over the past six years.

'That would be wonderful,' Maddy said.

Mary was therefore taken aback to see another nun at their house a few days later. She had been surprised that Fran hated nuns, but perhaps that was just her upbringing. Also she was becoming more and more bad tempered. She had taken on a man and his four children, and together with her son and another child on the way it couldn't have been easy for her. Mary was now realizing her stepmother's hatred of Catholics, she was always complaining that they had had to come here, where nuns ran the place.

'They don't run it,' her husband replied. 'It's Mr Gilbraith's town. It's a good job, where else would I get taken on? We could hardly go back. Your mam and dad still haven't forgiven us, so Cowshill won't do.'

'Nothing is ever right for you,' his pregnant wife said.

Sister Abigail was very careful when she came, Mary noted with some satisfaction, she hadn't seen this side of the brisk nun before. Abigail openly admired the little boy and produced a lovely blue pullover for him, to match his cornflower blue eyes, she said. Also a hat and scarf and gloves for the bad weather. Fran was rather pleased though she still put up her chin and said she didn't like the idea of nuns in her house. Mary was listening and was therefore astonished to hear Sister Abigail tell what obviously to her was a lie.

'I felt so much the same when I was a bairn, I was scared of them and their weird clothes and then they took me in and made me work, and see what happened.'

Fran actually laughed. Mary was so grateful to Sister Abigail that she could have kissed her. Mary thought that Sister Abigail had wanted to become a nun, you could tell just by looking at her. The idea of anybody making Sister Abigail do anything she didn't choose to was quite funny in its way. And yet Sister Abigail knew such a lot of things.

After Sister Abigail came for the second time and proposed they should all go to the sewing circle on the Thursday afternoon Fran agreed. Mary managed to sneak out and run after her and when she was sure that her stepmother couldn't see her she said, rather breathlessly, 'Thank you, Sister.'

'Well, I don't know what for.'

She was so kind that Mary wanted to cry. That was when Sister Abigail reacted and Mary grew to love her.

'Don't worry, Mary, by the time I've got a bit further with your mam she will be begging for storybooks,' Sister Abigail said, so Mary went back to the mill with a smile on her face until her stepmother shouted, 'And where have you been? The washing's all to bring in before those rainclouds drop their muck.'

As usual her stepmother had waited too long. By the time Mary got the washing in she and it were drenched. Mary knew that Fran couldn't cope with all this. It was too hard and she was clumsy with her baby now. Mary had to ask to go to school though Fran had promised her she would. But the children were always wanting food and there was so much washing and so much cooking, and Mary was not surprised her stepmother had long since lost patience with them all.

'If you'd been a bit quicker this lot wouldn't be in such a state,' and so the wooden clothes horse was set in front of the kitchen fire while the clothes gently steamed and dripped water on to the floor which Mary was obliged to mop up.

Abe was having a rotten time too. Mary could hear her father berating him when he got things wrong and hitting him around the head so that sometimes his ears bled. He said nothing, he knew as they all knew that there was no point in protesting.

Mary wasn't looking forward to the sewing circle which was up at the big house where Miss Proud was Mr Gilbraith's housekeeper. There was a piano. Mary had seen pianos in other people's front rooms but never one like this until she had heard Miss Proud play at Christmas and she was very impressed with this grand instrument.

'Those are upright,' Miss Proud told her, when Mary wandered across to it, 'this is a baby grand, more a piece of furniture if you like. We always had a piano until things went wrong and I had to sell it after my parents died.'

Mary thought it must be wonderful to have your parents die and for you to meet somebody like Mr Gilbraith who had obviously bought the instrument for Miss Proud, and then she felt bad because her mother was already gone but then she had not meant it like that.

The rooms here were big and Miss Proud did not interfere in Sister Abigail's arrangements, she just stood about, smiling. Mary could see that Miss Proud and Sister Abigail were good friends, in the sort of jaunty polite way they spoke to one another. Sister Abigail told Miss Proud that her cakes were wonderful and so all the other women did too. And it was so sort of – Mary couldn't think of the word – the house was so full of light somehow even when it rained, which it did for most of the afternoon.

Mary thought such things cheered up the cold dark winter days and there seemed to be so many of them. It felt never-ending, but this certainly helped her feelings about it all.

Miss Proud had made half a dozen big cakes: chocolate, coffee, sponge with jam, apple cake, cheese, currant and plain scones with cream and jam, and several small cakes for the children with little coloured sweets on top, green and pink and blue. It was a delight.

It was not a women only place either and she liked that. She could see men coming to talk to Mr Gilbraith who had his office there, and they would be offered tea and cake and Miss Proud would take such into the office.

There were also a great number of cats and dogs, including Miss Proud's cat, Tiddles, who liked chocolate cake and could wolf down quite a lot of it. Mary was especially pleased when Mr Gilbraith's favourite (so Miss Proud said), a tortoiseshell called Merlin, sat next to Mary on the sofa so that she could give him cake and stroke his head at the same time.

There was also a striped tiger cat called Pudding who lived outside mostly, but always came in when there was cake, and a black cat called Nettles, a queen, who Miss Proud said was a famous ratter, whereas Merlin would catch rabbits and mice, and then Pudding would seize them from him and bear them into the house as proudly as though he had caught them all by himself.

The dogs were meant to be outside in a kennel in the yard with a big run, but with people coming and going it was difficult to keep them from cake, and Mary liked how nobody and nothing was left out. She liked it best when Mr Gilbraith had gone to his study or library with the other men, and the women were left with the children and animals. Mary was entranced.

Fran had told her that she loathed animals so they didn't have any, but she could hardly express her views here. Also a lot of the women had children with them so Fran could spend hours talking about how wonderful Burt was. The trouble was that he was a completely taking child and she loved the compliments while Mary handed around plates and offered cake without having to be prompted.

It was also quite amusing in that the cats seemed to discern that Fran didn't like them and it was as if one of them had said, 'Hey, lads, Mrs Barnfather's here. Hurry up and get down here so that we can sit on her.'

The cats tried to get on her lap and by her side and at her feet and would even sit beside her on the chair arms and gaze steadily at her for minutes together. It was, Mary allowed, quite funny.

The women also boasted about their men and Miss Proud even boasted about Mr Gilbraith so that Mary wondered why they weren't married.

Several of the women were pregnant and carried on a lot of

conversation about such things but in very low voices, leaning in for fear that anybody was listening.

Mary and Miss Proud couldn't join in, so Miss Proud sat Mary down at the piano and told her all about how the keys were numbered and how the black keys differed from the white ones, how they were named A to G and the black keys were sharps and flats, and that the black keys were ebony and the white keys were ivory, which made a piano like that very dear. When Mary wanted to know why they were named A to G, Miss Proud said she had no idea.

Miss Proud said that if Mary really wanted to learn how to play she would be happy to teach her, but Mary thought she had too much to do because Miss Proud said she would have to go there to practise every day. Maybe when she was a bit older, Miss Proud said, her dad would buy her an upright piano so that she could practise at home and only come to Miss Proud for lessons once a week. Mary was thrilled by the idea but she didn't think it would ever happen. She liked Miss Proud almost as much as she liked the nuns.

One or two of the non pregnant other women, having gossiped for almost two hours, now asked Miss Proud to play a tune. She played and sang 'I know that my redeemer liveth', and to Mary's surprise she had an exquisite voice and half the room broke down, sobbing. Then Sister Abigail pulled what Mary admired as a master stroke.

'We usually have half an hour of reading at the end,' she said, 'and we're all too busy for such things. Mary, you are the eldest child. Do you think you might manage a few pages of Walter Scott?'

Mary appealed to her stepmother, saying that she wasn't sure she could, and Fran, red-faced, said that she was sure Mary would be able to do it. Mary said that she knew her reading was not up to it because she was so busy helping her mother, and when her mother could do nothing but insist she squeezed in beside Sister Abigail who was sitting in one of Mr Gilbraith's leather chairs, and there Sister Abigail helped her and by the end they were all clapping, even Fran.

On the way home to Mary's astonishment Fran said, 'I was proud of you, Mary, I didn't know you were good like that.'

'Thank you,' Mary said and then stood still while Fran burst into tears. Mary was horrified but not really very surprised. She was astonished to realize that she had been waiting for this to come. Fran couldn't stop crying even though the children gathered around her, worried.

'I'm sorry, I've been so awful to you, only I'm finding it all so hard. The nuns make me feel stupid.'

Mary was astonished and watched the other girl weep.

'You must think I'm horrible taking your dad like that, but I got so desperate.'

Mary glanced around but there was nobody near except the children, who did not understand. Nevertheless she coaxed Fran down to the mill and when they got inside Mary put the kettle on, and when the children were happy playing, Fran told her that she had had to marry somebody.

'But why?'

'Because I had a bairn that couldn't be explained. I suppose you don't know about stuff like that, but Burt is my dad's, he took me to him when my mam didn't want him any more and she let him even though I begged of her to help me. Somehow she couldn't and I didn't know how to stop him, so when your dad came along I had to get out of there. I know I'll go to hell because of what happened to your mam.'

Mary's ideas about what men and women did was vague, but having seen farm animals she didn't think it could be much different and if somebody did something like that when the other person didn't want them to then it was awful. No wonder Fran had got herself into such a terrible ravel. To think that a lovely bairn like Burt was from Fran's dad.

It made Mary feel sick and strange. Did Fran not like Burt because of it, and yet it was nothing to do with him, it was not his fault. In a stupid way Burt was Fran's brother. What a mess, what a sea of complications Mary thought with horror, and here this girl was and she was nothing much more than a girl, all these burdens cast down upon her because of men's selfishness.

'Your dad wants a lad of his own,' Fran said.

Mary didn't understand this.

'He's got Abe.'

Fran wiped her tears on her sleeves.

'Abe was your mam's first husband's bairn.'

This was news to Mary.

'He got killed down the quarry or something so your dad took her on and he wanted you to be a lad.'

Yes, Mary thought, he had wanted that, and why wouldn't he? Boys were so much dearer, so much more important. A woman needed a man so that she could have children and a home, and only a man could provide that.

'But now, I'm having your dad's bairn and he knows it's his so I come away with him.'

'Came,' Mary couldn't help prompting her while the tears flowed down Fran's face as if they would never stop.

'I'm sorry, Mary, I'm ever so sorry. I didn't mean nothing. All I thought about was meself. When I knew who he was it was too late by then, and he left you and your mam and . . . I just had to get away and it was the only chance I knew I was ever going to get, what with me dad never leaving me alone. I was so surprised when your dad wanted me, but now, but now . . .' Here the tears overcame her voice and she choked. 'He calls me Fransy.'

'What?'

'Your dad. When we're on our own he calls me Fransy, like I was some kind of flaming teacake,' and then they heard what she had said and began to laugh together, and Mary felt better than she had felt since before her mother died.

# Ten

It was decided by the doctor and Maddy that Lydia should officially become the doctor's new assistant since she had been working with him for over half a year. Mr Gray said he thought that given the chance she might have a good deal of ability. Lydia couldn't believe it.

Also he said to her that spring would soon be upon them, the nights would be lighter, and he had enough faith in her so that she could do small visits without him, but she would need someone with her if she was to go to outlying farms of which there were a good many. The doctor would choose these assignments carefully until she was more practised, but she needed her confidence building now that she was working and reading and he was instructing her all the time.

Also Mr Gilbraith was asked about it and his input was that Sister Lydia needed to have a capable man to go about with her, she could not go to far-off farms by herself especially in the dark, and there were many times when the doctor could not get up here to the village from Wolsingham either because he had too much work to do or because the weather was bad. If Lydia took this on, she must have help and learn to ride.

Lydia was horrified, not only at the idea of having to learn to ride, she was and always had been terrified of horses, but to have some man around her all the time didn't feel right. She had done her best to get away from men of her own age, but she understood that there was no way round it so she agreed.

Mr Gilbraith said there was no road to most of the places outside the village except on horseback. The pony and trap were fine for the dales villages, but often there was nothing but rutted tracks and only horses would do.

Also there must be a private room for her at the hospital since she would often be on duty at night. This was a major breakthrough and Maddy then took Lydia into her office and asked if would she be happy to go on as a nun or did she think she would be better off in usual clothes.

Lydia didn't have to think about it. She looked clearly at Maddy and said that she had no intention of giving up her calling so long as Sister Maddy agreed with what she was doing, and Maddy was so enthusiastic that it made Lydia feel very good.

'The only thing that bothers me is having a man, maybe a young man, around me,' she managed.

Maddy smiled at her.

'I think your habit will protect you, and Mr Gilbraith will choose somebody totally trustworthy so try not to worry,' she said.

The doctor said she had taken a weight off his mind already and Mr Gilbraith said he was proud of her. They mustn't expect too much, but it would make things so much easier for the nurses at the hospital and for Mr Gray to have an assistant he called promising.

So Lydia was to have a room of her own at the hospital and it had a comfortable bed, a big fire, a bookcase which Mr Gray filled with volumes she needed to study, but best of all it gave her a sense of place so that she could concentrate.

Sister Maddy said this was a good idea because there were so many distractions at the foundling school that Lydia would have no peace, but that she must go back there to refresh her mind and to pray for help and guidance when she felt that she needed it.

Looking at that room which she took for hers thinking it was the most wonderful place she had ever seen it seemed strange to her, given that she had been so rich and well looked after before. Her bedroom had been huge and the rooms in the house which she was to inherit were enormous. Now this tiny room which only had in it a decent chair for the fire, a table and hard chair so that she could write, and all she put into it were her few clothes, yet it meant the world to her. She could hardly sleep, she was so excited.

The young man assigned to her was Robert Slater, Jim Slater's son. Jim was Mr Gilbraith's right-hand man. Robert had looked after the goats for Abigail and had helped his father in the window fitting business, but now Mr Gilbraith was offering him something new. He was to be what Mr Gilbraith called her body-guard. It would enable her to go out and see patients at any time of the day or night, and he was totally reliable and trustworthy. He also would have a room at the hospital.

Robert, when Lydia noticed him for the first time – she didn't think they had met before – was a big lad. He was very tall and a wrestler so not exactly skinny, and he became Lydia's. He was typical of this area, a border man, black hair and blue eyes which were very dark.

They were both highly embarrassed to begin with. She wanted to say that she didn't need him though this wasn't true, and he didn't seem to think that looking after a nun would do his reputation any good in the village, she could see by the way he glanced sideways at her. Perhaps his friends would tease him about it, Lydia thought.

The first problem was teaching Lydia to ride.

'But it's such a long way up,' she said, staring at the horse. She had always managed not to ride and tried to convince Robert that she didn't need to, but he was no respecter of such stuff and said frankly, 'Sister Lydia, this horse is a plodder. There is nothing to be frightened of. He will be there for you when you need him and he will not do anything you don't want him to do. He's called Anthony.'

Lydia looked hard at Robert.

'The horse has a name?'

'Of course he has a name. He will look after you. He won't try to get you off or run amok. Mr Gilbraith chose him very carefully for you. There is nothing to be afraid of, I swear it to you.'

Lydia stared at Enormous Anthony.

'He's so very big.'

'Not really. He is totally reliable, like a dales pony only bigger, and they are hardy and capable and clever. You will be glad of him in the middle of winter when he is the only way you are going to be able to go anywhere.'

Lydia knew this, but her heart failed her. Also she realized that her habit was not ideal for riding a horse, but it was what she had and was so she must try. She didn't understand why she was so scared of horses. There was no way she could put this off and so Robert got as close to the big stone nearby with the horse and invited her to try and get on. For this she had to hitch up her skirt and for the first time thought that a side-saddle would have been a good idea or that shorter skirts would have helped. Either way it would not do for nuns.

The horse shied as she waffled.

'Stop flicking your skirts about, Anthony isn't used to nuns,' Robert told her less respectfully than she had thought he would, but she knew it for encouragement and so in the end, Robert, full of apology, got hold of her by the waist and put her on the horse's back.

'Why is he called Anthony?' she said, in desperation, having never had any man's hands around her waist before.

'After that bloke in Shakespeare.'

Lydia stared at him.

'I had this teacher,' Robert excused himself. 'And don't go shortening his name, he doesn't like it.'

'It's a long way down,' Lydia said quivering with fright and looking at the ground, which seemed yards off.

He walked the horse around for a good long while until Lydia took on the rhythm of the enormous creature. In the end she said, 'You can't keep getting hold of me, it isn't respectable.'

'Sister Lydia, do you imagine there is a mounting block at most of these farms and cottages because there isn't and when the snow is pelting at us with a wind behind it you will not care, believe me. It's not as if I'm trying to do owt to you—'

'I know that—'

'Well then. I am not really so desperate for female company that I fancy nuns.'

'It's a good thing there's nobody here,' she said for they had walked up on to the fell.

'I knew there wasn't otherwise I wouldn't have said owt but it's just going to be you and me so you might as well get over yourself. We are going to help people get better, that's the point, isn't it?'

She agreed. The horse smelled good, that was the first thing that pleased her, warm, of hay and stables and the gorse up on the felltop. Robert walked the horse up and down and round and round but it was when he got the horse to speed up that Lydia panicked. Trotting? Bouncing up and down like that, it was hideous and made her feel that her teeth would break they gnashed together so much. She clung both to the horse's mane and to the reins.

'I'm going to fall off,' she gasped, well out of breath.

'No, you aren't.'

'I am,' she said and promptly did.

Luckily she just slid and he caught her and then she was laughing so much that she managed to get on again and conquer her fear of this stupid gait.

It was something else she needed to better, but almost everything was easier than this, until she learned affection for her horse. She got her confidence so that she knew how to canter and then to gallop, though Robert told her that speed was never the point and that there were a great many rabbit holes and pitfalls, especially in the dark. They needed to get wherever they were wanted, and most of the time it had to be achieved slowly.

Robert had never felt as comfortable around a lass as he did with Sister Lydia. He could never think of anything to say to any lass and although his mam was always trying to get him to marry Polly Swift he really didn't want to get involved with anybody. Lasses were bother, he had seen his mates have to marry lasses he would never have given the time of day to because they had taken them behind a hedge. That was not for him, houses and babies and having to worry about all that stuff made him shy away. So far there was only one lass he did like, and it was Isabel in the hardware shop and he knew why that was. He felt safe with her. She was little and plain and skinny and although he never spoke much to her or looked much at her, mostly because she was nowt to look at, she was a person and not just something to get in the way of what he wanted to do in life. And yet he liked being around her. His days when he saw her were somehow lighter. He dismissed this idea as nonsense.

Mr Gilbraith was giving him a chance to get away from the goats and the windows and the awful atmosphere in his dad's workshop, which was boring and the days there seemed endless.

Now Mr Gilbraith had moved him on and although he wanted nowt to do with women, Sister Lydia was a nun. He thought that would intimidate him but for some reason it didn't. And he knew it was because she didn't think of him as a man, she thought of him as some kind of tool that would help her in her work. That loosened his tongue and then she had laughed and by the time he had helped her to sit on the horse without being scared they were good friends.

She was to him like another lad, a very clever lad because lasses did not have minds like steel traps, Lydia did, and she also somehow enabled him to feel as he wanted to feel, capable, enlightened, interested in something other than that which he had encountered before.

He found that he wanted to help people, that he wanted to aid Lydia in helping them. She was clever. But she was not so clever that she didn't need his help, and to need that kind of help was something special to him. He could go forwards with her and have a real place here in the village. He saw that Mr Gilbraith had confidence in him and it gave him confidence in himself.

# Eleven

To say that Jim Slater's wife was unhappy that her son was going to be looking after Sister Lydia would be a huge understatement. Jim hardly dared tell his wife. Mr Gilbraith had seen the hesitation on him, Jim knew, but he couldn't let his boss down.

Jimmy, observing all this, wanted to keep out of the way yet he didn't want to miss anything. He thought it was very funny that their Robert, who hardly ever spoke to a lass and kept running away from Polly Swift, was chosen to help Sister Lydia heal the sick. That was what the nuns called it. Jimmy took to listening at doors and caught most of what was said.

It wasn't that his dad was frightened of his mam, he knew that, but his mam was difficult, and his dad worked hard, and the last thing he wanted when he got home was a row, Jimmy knew, had heard his dad say so. Well, he had had that one, Jimmy thought with some satisfaction. It was a very entertaining house to be in, theirs, you never knew what would happen next.

What with the lasses getting married and now their Robert being more or less kidnapped by Sister Lydia, life was very entertaining provided he could get out of going to school.

'He said what?' Mrs Slater demanded as she and her husband stood in the kitchen, he having not been able to get any further before his wife accosted him with accusations as he announced that Robert was to look after Sister Lydia. 'Well you can go back there and tell him that my Robert is not going to hang around with any fallen woman. If you don't tell him I will.'

Robert, in the sitting room, had so far said nothing. He did not object to Jimmy staying by the door and was pretending to be reading, though reading was not up to now something Jimmy had seen their Robert do a lot. His ears had gone dark red and it was not all embarrassment. Their Robert was like their dad, he wouldn't say anything until he had summat to say and then all hell could break loose.

The girls had gone upstairs, partly to get out of the road, Jimmy thought, but also because they were doing all that daft wedding stuff, with frocks and hairdos and talks about the lads they were marrying and a right pair they were, Jimmy thought. Little squat lads, their dads had been coal miners, so Jimmy's mother had said disparagingly, but only when the lasses weren't there. She had been really glad they were getting married, both in their twenties and at their last prayers. There was to be a double wedding in April.

Jimmy couldn't wait to hear more about Sister Lydia and Robert.

'She isn't a fallen woman,' Jim protested.

'No, well all I can say is that she should be married, not going around pretending to do a man's work and in an outfit like that. And being present when women are having children. It's disgusting.'

Jim didn't seem to know what to do or say, and blustered. He was saved however by Robert, who got up from his chair and went into the kitchen.

Jimmy was quite excited by now. Usually like their dad their Robert did not take part in discussions but this was different and they were in for it. Jimmy watched carefully through the half open door which thankfully Robert had not closed, he was more intent on what they were saying.

'It doesn't matter what anybody thinks, I'm doing it,' he said.

His mother glared at him.

'Indeed you are not,' she said.

'I'm twenty-one. I think I can decide what I am going to do.'

'What happens if you get set upon and murdered and all for a bit lass like that?'

Robert stared at her. Jim was relieved that his son was taking part, Jimmy could see by the look on his face. He would not relish going back and telling Mr Gilbraith that his wife would not allow it. A right turnip he would look and all for the sake of peace in his house.

Jim remembered when their Robert had been born. They already had two daughters, Hester and Kitty, and his wife had been convinced that she would never have a boy so the relief was great on both sides. Had Robert been a girl things would have been awful, but the trouble was that his wife spoiled Robert. He could do nothing wrong whereas the poor lasses could get nowt right.

He wished and wished that Hannah would be another lad and she had paid for not being one. She was the least favoured of the children and her dad thought it had something to do with the fact that Hannah was quiet and self-contained. She had arrived like that. He privately thought she was the cleverest of his bairns, but dared not say so.

After Hannah there had been a long gap and then Jimmy. His wife spoiled Jimmy too and Jimmy was one of those bairns who

made life difficult because he was over-indulged. The times Jim
had wanted to clip his young son around the ear but his wife
would have been horrified, and anyroad, Jimmy had been taught
that he could get whatever he wanted by being difficult so that
was what he did.

There had been a bit of peace the last few months when his
wife, having said she doubted either of her first two lasses would
ever marry they had both found lads. By then Hester was nearly
twenty-five and Kitty twenty-three, and the word 'old maid' had
lingered in the house like a bad smell. Their mother was almost
in despair.

She didn't like either of the two lads, but that was because
nobody would ever be good enough for any of her bairns. But
since both lads asked the girls to marry them their mother could
only stand by and be glad she was not left with them on her
hands. The girls' eyes shone at their new prospects and she
would not deceive herself that they could do better, though she
had hoped against hope that they would marry men who had
some status. The only man around here with any status was Mr
Gilbraith and it was obvious to her that he would never marry,
and in any case he was old enough to be their grandfather.

'We'll have to look around and find a nice lad for you,' her
mother said to Hannah, now that she was going to be the only
girl at home. Her mother said the words with some satisfaction though half the time, Jimmy thought, she was complaining
about the lads her lasses were marrying, how they were not good
enough for her girls and how she would miss having Hester and
Kitty in the house.

Jimmy badly wanted to say something but he couldn't. Most
of the time his mam didn't know he was there and he didn't
want to spoil the impression so that she would stop saying in

front of him things she thought he shouldn't hear. There was little enough in life to be gleeful about and he was making the best of it.

He thought at first that Hannah would ignore this as she usually did but he could see by the determination on her face how strongly she felt.

'What about Ralph McFadden?' her mother suggested. 'He's a nice lad now and he's always coming around here and if not for you then who for?'

His mother sounded so cheerful Jimmy thought, but it was that sort of cheerful which doubted its own wisdom and Hannah must have understood because she said, 'I'm not going to marry anybody.'

'Of course you will.'

'I don't want to end up like—' Hannah stopped there and Jimmy thought she had gone too far. Yes, his mother's face had taken on that crimson hue which meant getting as far away as you could.

'What, like me?'

Hannah backtracked admirably, Jimmy thought.

'Like my sisters. With lads who won't be able to get a good job like my dad and look after their children. You were lucky.'

'Lucky? There's no luck about it, my girl.'

Oh dear, Jimmy thought, Hannah had become 'my girl' and there was no hope for her now.

'I was as bonny as you in my time and your father had no money and no position and who's to tell that your brothers-in-law won't do the same.'

'I don't want any man pawing me,' Hannah said.

'Pawing? You should be so lucky. You've frightened off half the lads in the village with your – your books and your languages and your prayers. I've never seen a lass sitting around with her Bible like you do. It's a disgrace.'

'In some families it would be a disgrace not to.'

'We aren't like that,' her mother said, 'and you would do your best to remember it. And since you are going to be the only lass to be left in this house you had better get some work done or your father will come back complaining that his dinner isn't ready and the floors are filthy.'

That would have been interesting, Jimmy thought, since his father never complained about anything that Jimmy could remember. It just meant that if he said anything his mother didn't like she gave him earache, yes that was what it was. His father would cup his ear as though his mother was an irritating wasp that was in the vicinity of his lugs and buzzing. *Buzz, buzz, buzz*, that was his mother.

Hannah said nothing else but she was unhappy and from the way that their mother looked at the door when Hannah had gone into the kitchen to start on the dinner he could see that his mother was uncomfortable. It was not that she meant to be unkind, she was just trying to steer Hannah in what she would have called 'the right direction', only the trouble was that it was not the direction which Hannah would have chosen and it was going to be a fight, Jimmy thought with some relish, hoping that he would be around when the whole thing blew up.

It was all right for his dad, staying out of the way, but it was difficult to know when to be out of the way and when to be there if the only time you got beyond the doors was to milk the goats. Jimmy had started spending a lot of time in the goat huts and taking the goats for walks down the lane so that they could find something juicy and interesting and new to eat and might therefore leave Mr McConichie's lawn alone.

And then he had an idea. He followed Hannah into the kitchen where she was pulling coal forward to make the fire burn harder and heat the oven so that she could cook the meal.

'I was thinking you know,' he said, and Hannah smiled at him. Hannah was lovely. 'You might like to come and help with the goats.'

Hannah pulled a face.

'I thought you liked going on your own, you take ages over it.'

'I could take longer over it if you were there,' Jimmy said. 'The sisters often call in to see the goats, especially Sister Abigail and you could tell her about what you want.'

'Mam would never let me,' Hannah said.

'She doesn't have to know. It's just the goats,' Jimmy said.

'I couldn't deceive her like that.'

'Well, you could be spending the next forty years in the kitchen,' Jimmy said and then he left her.

After that Hannah could think of nothing else, so it was not many days before she got her courage together and started going with him to milk and water and look after the goats. She therefore saw Sister Abigail and sometimes she went to the foundling school and there was accepted with joy by Sister Maddy, and they inspired her ideas and encouraged her to do what she wanted and told her that God would help her if she really wanted to do something different than the other girls in her family, and so eventually she approached her mother.

Hannah then spoke the unbelievable words, 'I want to be a nun.'

This had been the same week in which the double wedding had been decided. It never rained but it poured, Jimmy thought with glee. He had shut his eyes against that one after he saw his mother's face.

'You what?' her mother had said, going first white with shock and then red with temper. 'You cannot be a nun, we aren't even Catholics and a good thing too.'

'I could go into the convent at Newcastle, Sister Maddy says.'

'You went and talked to that woman before you told us?'

'There wouldn't have been much point in telling you if they wouldn't have me,' Hannah pointed out equably.

'My lasses are too good for a life like that. It's a horrible way to live.'

So Hannah had not been allowed to go to a convent and was now stuck at home. She said nothing and she did whatever her mother asked of her, which was always more than she asked of anyone else as though to punish Hannah for having thought differently than the others.

Not that the girl complained, but there was a hard setness about her, a stubbornness that she would never back down and the few times her mother had got young men into the house she just went on with what she was doing, not raising her eyes or speaking in her soft sweet voice. Jimmy wouldn't have cared, but Hannah was the bonniest of them all and a lot of lads had hung around, but she would never have anything to do with them.

It grieved her mother, and Hannah was always getting to black boots or wash floors, scrub clothes, and being told that there was to be no praying and no reading of bibles in this house.

Jim had always hoped that after he and Mavis married, going against her parents' wishes, she would have a better under-standing of what her own children wanted to do, but it wasn't so. The family broke and would not be repaired and he had brought her to this better place hoping that her ideas would ease, but they were too far gone, too much burned into her mind for such like. Consequently, Jim thought, the nuns could get nothing right for his wife, and Sister Lydia had now blotted her copybook big time.

'She is not getting her hooks into my son,' Mrs Slater said.

'She's a nun, Mam,' Robert objected, 'she's married to God.'

'Then God should stop her from doing such things. It's low and disgusting and you are not having any part of it.'

'It's what I want to do and I'm not going to give it up,' Robert said, which put an end to that discussion.

His mother did go on and on about it, but Robert just walked out each time she mentioned it. Sometimes Jim wished he could do the same and he did when he could find any excuse, but he regretted that there was no peace at home such as he envied other men.


'Do you want me to carry a weapon?' Robert had asked Mr Gilbraith.

'I think you may be getting ahead of us here. It's just the village and outlying farms. I don't want Sister Lydia getting lost in the dark or falling off her horse and breaking an ankle and being left there all day and night because there was nobody to look after her.'

Robert's mam, getting no further, wept. In the past her tears had produced results, but Robert was not going to let her stop him now.

'What about Polly?' was her final effort.

'What?'

'You are going to marry her.'

'I never said anything of the kind.'

'You didn't have to. Her mam and me we agreed it years ago and she spends most of her life here and her mam has been very good to you, especially since Polly's dad is so poorly these days. It would be very ungrateful if you didn't. Everybody expects it.'

'Well, everybody can forget it,' Robert said, 'because it isn't going to happen.'

'You are the most wilful of all my children,' his mother accused him.

'I'm not more wilful than our Jimmy. Nobody in the world is more wilful than him,' Robert retorted.

His mother had learned finally to shut up about it because Robert just didn't go home except to sleep sometimes when he did not stay at the hospital and so the more she nagged the less he was there, but it made things really hard, Jim thought and so he managed to be there less too. He could have said to her did she not understand that she was driving people from her, but she seemed unable to control herself. Her love for her children was being drowned under a sea of bad temper. They all lost because of it.

Sister Abigail did not agree with Mr Gilbraith about how safe Robert and Lydia would be. She groaned when she heard this. They were sitting outside the foundling school, having a few minutes rest, the day being cold and bright. Lydia was already doing good work, Abigail knew, and she thought also that it was when Lydia had to leave the village that there might be trouble.

'It's a pity you can't be like the women in Asia and cover your face,' she said, 'or like these high class types in Newcastle who wear veils when they go outside.'

Lydia smiled at her.

'I am fairly well covered,' she said.

'With a face like yours you can never be sure. Who in your family gave you such a face? The angels in heaven aren't as bonny as you.'

That made Lydia laugh but later that day before she set out to work Abigail put a small silver pistol into her hand. There was no way in which Lydia could ask where she had got it, but they went some way from the school and once up on the fell with the aid of several bottles she showed Lydia how to use it.

'I don't think I should do this,' she objected.

'Don't think, just aim. And low. You don't want to kill the stupid lad. When some man pulls you off your pony or tries to get hold of you when he's drunk you need more in your armoury than an ineffectual thump round the lug. If you have to pull the trigger, aim at his feet and don't hesitate or he will have you.'

Abigail also gave her a small knife which she could carry in the pocket of her skirt and showed her how to flick open the blade with one movement.

'And don't go riding side-saddle however much they encourage you. It's a stupid old-fashioned idea. You're not a lady, you're a nun, and you need not to fall off. The object of your outing is to help people get well, not to go riding around like you look pretty. I'll tell Jim Slater about the saddle because you don't want something too big, and how there must be a place for you to hide a pistol.'

Lydia did not envy Jim his discourse with Abigail, nobody had ever bettered her. Also Abigail showed Lydia various moves in case of attack.

'Despite your skirt you bring up your knee hard between his legs. You can push the force of your fingers into his eyes, and chop him across his windpipe with the flat of your hand, and if you get the chance to be behind him you crack him on the back of the neck like this.'

Abigail demonstrated but Lydia was lost before it.

'Between his legs?' Lydia said, horrified.

'Aye, that'll make his eyes shine,' Abigail said.


Lydia had protested loudly to Sister Maddy but it didn't get her anywhere.

'I don't need weapons or a guardian,' she had said at first.

'Since you have said this is what you want to do with your time we must take precautions. Robert Slater is a fine young man. He will look after you.'

This was all very well, Lydia thought, but she had no idea how to talk to a young man who was always there and therefore in her way. He was totally unaware of this, she realized, she thought that he was most respectful.

She did resent having somebody with her most of the time but he did as she asked him. He did not go into houses with her, but waited outside with the pony cart or with the horses since she had after the first few weeks learned to ride fairly well. There were so many outlying farms and places where the roads were rutted or nonexistent and, as all the hamlets and cottages were miles away and could only be got to on horseback, that was how they went and so she became grateful that she had learned how not to fall off a horse.

'If my lad wants to marry a nun I will kill you,' Mrs Slater told her husband.

## Twelve

Lydia could see from the beginning that Mrs Slater disliked her though they had met only once when she had to go to meet Robert just outside his house and his mother had not spoken to her. The woman's face was pinched and she looked warily at Lydia. Lydia could have told Mrs Slater that none of this was of her doing except that when she thought about it that was not strictly accurate. She had decided to become the doctor's assistant and the rest had followed.

Mr Gray was glad of her help, she could see it in his face. How he had managed all this time on his own she had no idea and she could see his tired look, he was getting old. What they would do when he could no longer work made Lydia panic. Maybe some other doctor wouldn't want her to help because not only was she a woman but a nun, and then she told herself not to be stupid by thinking too far ahead.

He was teaching her everything he knew and there was a great deal to know, Lydia understood, but her enthusiasm kept her working and reading, going out with the doctor and learning from him. She questioned everything and she could see that she was beginning to change. Her ideas were different, now that she was starting to see how people's bodies worked and how she could ease their hard lives she concentrated on that and nothing beyond it. She was barely a nun any more. She was never there for prayers or to do anything to help at the school, but Sister Maddy shook her head and said, 'Your habit will give you some protection and if in time you decide to change it then we will let you go. This is your passion and it has been given to you generously. Unless you tire of the work I think you should give it all your time. You can pray when you go to bed for guidance and that should be enough for the present, I think. Try to live in the moments that you are given. Mr Gray has been alone for so long.'

Lydia therefore took the load from the doctor as well as she could and he encouraged her to do the easier things and watching her, leaving her alone for a few minutes at a time and then letting her out with Robert rather than with himself but only to cases that he told her about, cases she might learn from without endangering anyone.

She was often in the dispensary at the hospital and learned about drugs. During this time Robert could go home. He was not needed there nor at any of the clinics or surgeries that the doctor had set up, though as the days went on he too was always there to help and to Lydia's delight he showed as much aptitude as she did. She thought he preferred the dispensary to anything else, asking questions and taking in information at speed, but he was bright and didn't need to be told anything more than once.

It was when Lydia went to certain houses miles away from the village that she felt grateful most of all for his presence. The roads were uneven and dark and as for the outlying houses, some were so remote that she and Robert had difficulty in finding them after the sun went down.

Also there were a good many country folk who were aghast, not only at finding a woman for their doctor but a nun at that. It was at these times that Lydia wondered if she would have been better off in what were called 'normal clothes'. She didn't want to wear such things and in a way her habit was good for making people stand back and listen to her.

She didn't need their confidences unless it was about the ailment they had, she needed them to respect what she was trying to do and mostly they did, but also she became adept at holding at a distance anyone who tried to obstruct her work.

Jimmy Slater wanted to go to the carpentry shop and help his dad but his dad wanted him to go to school. Jimmy didn't want to go to school and much as he liked reading he would have liked to be a part of something Robert and his dad did, but his dad wouldn't have it. All his dad did was look at you and it was enough to silence your voice. He found his, but only just.

'But Dad—'

'Don't but dad me,' was all his father said.

The nuns liked him, that was the other thing. Jimmy had charm and knew how to use it. Also he was what they called a quick study, he understood everything the first time he was told and he was way ahead in his reading. On good days the nuns just let him sit and read because they were teaching the others stuff he already knew and on really good days Mr Nattrass would come in and bring Dobber and Bonny, his sheepdogs. Mr Nattrass taught the older lads about farming, they stayed at other farms round about because Mr and Mrs Nattrass had not been long married and couldn't take on everything, so Jimmy had overheard Sister Maddy saying. The lads went to the Nattrass farm to learn to milk cows. Jimmy knew all about milking goats so that was one thing he wouldn't have to learn if he could just persuade his parents to let him go and live at some farm. They also learned all about pigs and hens and how to grow crops and how to plough fields and making hay and harvesting corn. He had already read so much about it that was almost like he was good at such things before he got anywhere near. Also he had heard that Mrs Nattrass who had been a nun before her marriage was a wonderful cook and baker, which was something his mother certainly wasn't and up at the school the meals were awful, watery soup and hard bread and goats' milk. Jimmy loved the goats, but he couldn't stand the taste of the milk, he thought it was weird. Jimmy saw himself shearing sheep and having dogs like Mr Nattrass did and training sheepdogs with a whistle.

Jimmy longed to be allowed to go there, he was tired of his home, and bored at school where he just didn't fit in. The other lads wouldn't talk to him because he wasn't good at football and was always reading. They were wary of folk who were good in class. That meant that Jimmy hated classes because he knew the lads of his own age despised him, and he had no time for lasses even when they tried to make friends with him. Having three sisters at home he had far too much female company already.

When he talked to his dad his dad just looked sorry and said that he was far too young to go anywhere. His mam was scandalized and said she wouldn't let a son of hers go into another woman's house to live and she certainly wouldn't let him go to the Nattrass' farm. Mrs Nattrass had been a nun which was an unnatural thing to do. Mrs Nattrass, Jimmy thought with a sigh, had blotted her copybook big time as far as his mam was concerned before she had ever got married and gone to live with Dobber and Bonny. So Jimmy went on going to school just to get out of the house.

When he could he managed to be ill and stay at home and

his mam fell for this one almost every time, but also he thought she liked him being there because she could spoil him, making him nice things to eat and talking to him about the books he was reading even though she was always telling him off for not spending enough time outside in the fresh air. His sisters ignored him, but his mam was always there for him and she was warm and kind and made him fried eggs on buttered toast.

When the two lasses were away to their lads everything would change and maybe after that things would be different and his mam and dad might let him do something he wanted to do, though he wasn't sure what he could do that would make him feel happier. When things changed in a family, he thought, sometimes it kept on changing, so that everybody was different and everybody went on to something new. He would live in hope because he was getting impatient and needed something else to face.

Part of him wanted to run away but he knew that it wasn't sensible and that his mam would have fits and his dad would be ashamed of him. So he made the best of milking the goats because it meant that he could spend more time with Robert, though of late Robert was very often unavailable because he was always with Sister Lydia. She was a big nuisance Jimmy thought, causing rows in the family and making Robert do so much stuff away from the house that Jimmy missed him all the time. And then a horrible thought occurred to him. Did Robert want to marry Sister Lydia? After all Mrs Nattrass had been a nun.

Robert was hardly ever there any more and even the workshop where his dad's men built the windows and doors was not the same without Robert. Sister Lydia was getting in the way so much and Jimmy couldn't like her. He still liked the atmosphere of the workshop even when Robert wasn't there though: the way that the men talked and sawed up wood and smoothed down and then fitted the pieces of wood so that they made up and completed a shape so that it became something useful. Jimmy liked that. He also loved the warm smell of freshly cut wood and the way that the sawdust was inches deep on the floor. He liked how something new and real came out of the workshop at the end, but without Robert it was not the same and in any case his dad didn't think he should be there, he was getting in the way and he was not allowed to touch anything in case he sawed his finger off, his dad said. Jimmy knew that his dad was only making a joke, but it didn't make him feel any better. Therefore if he ventured in there his dad always came in and found him and sent him home. Could things be any more boring, Jimmy wondered.

The first time Lydia was called to the Slater household professionally she was all alone. The moment she got there she could see Mrs Slater looking past her.

'I thought the doctor was coming,' she said.

'He is busy with a patient at the hospital but he will come if I find that he is needed,' Lydia said.

'If he hadn't been needed I wouldn't have asked for him,' Mrs Slater said stiffly.

Lydia managed to get up the stairs to see the patient and then to get rid of Mrs Slater, she asked her to go and boil some water. Lydia sat down on Jimmy's bed.

'I feel awful,' he said.

He had no temperature, his eyes were bright and if he was hot it was only because he was still in bed when his family was not.

'Where does it hurt?'

Jimmy said vaguely that it hurt everywhere. Lydia paused and that was when Jimmy said, sitting up and looking at her, 'Are you going to marry our Robert?'

Lydia thought she had got to the stage in life where nothing surprised her but it was not so.

'I am married to God,' she said. She was starting to understand what was going on here. This clever little lad had told his mother he was poorly so that he might get to give Lydia some advice. She had to try hard not to smile.

Jimmy frowned.

'Is that why you look like a pigeon? My mam says that pigeons are vermin. She doesn't like nuns and she especially doesn't like you.'

Lydia was not going to contradict his mother so she just smiled.

'Our Robert had a lass before you came,' Jimmy said. 'Polly Swift. She's gone off with another lad. Me mam wasn't half upset and so was hers. They thought he was going to marry Polly and gan on working with me dad cos she says he needs our Robert's help and Polly and Robert would have bairns, that's what me mam says. Now he can't marry nebody because you're always there.'

'Nothing is for ever, Jimmy,' Lydia said.

'What do you mean?'

'I mean that he may very well get married when I can manage to do my visits by myself. At the moment he's there because it means I get time to see and help more people when they don't feel very well. He looks after me.'

'In case you get set on and murdered?'

'So that I don't fall over and break a leg or get lost in the darkness or go to the wrong house.'

Jimmy smiled at that.

'Robert is like the light in the Bible,' Lydia said, 'he lightens the darkness for me.'

'Like a star then or the moon or at least a candle.'

'Something like that,' Lydia said.

Jimmy's mother came back at that point with a bowl of hot water and a towel.

'So what's wrong with him?' she said when Lydia needed neither of these offerings.

'I think he needs a week in bed,' Lydia said when they had left the bedroom. Mrs Slater closed the door firmly behind them.

'He's wrapped you round his little finger, Sister Lydia, just like he does with everybody,' Mrs Slater said with a modicum of pride.

'Is he a bad scholar?'

They had reached the bottom of the steep stairs, Mrs Slater looking pleased that Lydia was about to leave her house.

'That's the daftness of it, he's really good, much better than the others. He learned to write, read and add up in a matter of weeks when he first went to school.'

'Then maybe he's bored.'

This was obviously not a concept that had occurred to Mrs Slater.

'If he's so far ahead of the other children his age he may be ready to move on. You know that Mr and Mrs Nattrass have taken several boys to their farm recently and they go on to other places and learn all manner of different skills.'

'He's little for that,' Mrs Slater said, having seen the idea of her youngest child taken from her and become afraid, Lydia thought.

'You could give it a try. I could talk to Sister Maddy about it. Then if Jimmy doesn't like it we will think of something else.'

'He's nothing like the others. Now my Robert is what you call a good lad, at least—' Mrs Slater stopped there, having recognized her mistake.

Lydia, however, caught on straight away.

'The doctor is going to ask Robert if he will learn chemistry,' she said, 'it is a very difficult thing to do. The doctor thinks that Robert will shine there.'

Robert was obviously the diamond in Mrs Slater's crown. She could not help but smile with pride at her favourite son.

'Maybe then he'll settle down and marry Polly Swift. Her mother is very keen on it and so am I. You won't find a better lass than Polly in all of County Durham.'

It so obviously did not occur to Mrs Slater that Robert might have to go away to learn such things, and Lydia was not about to enlighten her.

## *Thirteen*

Isabel was now almost eighteen and was beginning to think that her life would go on forever as it had since she had reached the village three years before. She was restless and dissatisfied and longed not to have to work as she did and to be able to go out and meet people her own age. Her father would not allow it and neither would he give her time to read or do anything that she wanted to do.

It was as though her mother was not there. He expected everything to be done, his meals to be on the table exactly when he chose, and her mother was silent and rarely moved and did not sleep. Isabel knew, because she did not sleep either. She dreamed up various ways of leaving, but she had no money and although she did suspect the various places where her father hid his money she found that she could not take it. She had not been brought up to do such things, she had been taught her duty and that was what she did.

Also if she ran she would be leaving her mother and although she barely recognized the woman her mother had been in Durham, laughing and open and rather proud of her cooking and baking, she could not endure the thought that this sad skinny woman who had lank hair and grubby clothes — this poor creature — should be left here alone to the mercies of this mean man, so she struggled on.

She did see people in the shop and her father watched her carefully if any young man should come in, but he seemed to view Robert Slater in a different light now that Robert was helping the doctor and Sister Lydia.

Robert had changed, Isabel thought, he now smiled as he came in and it was not for window things any more, no wood or paint or tools. He needed special things ordering from a supplier of chemist's drugs, and other things, which Isabel needed him to spell for her. She ordered bandages, liniment, bottles, medicines. The doctor did not have enough time to do such things and besides it was easier for Isabel and her father because they ordered so much from the various wholesalers and her father was used to doing business with them and knew which ones were reliable.

Isabel liked Robert. She liked how he had become someone almost of importance. He wore nice suits now, she thought, and he stood taller and spoke confidently and he was always so pleasant. Other young men of his age were shy and fumbling and did not speak clearly.

Sometimes if her father was out of hearing she would talk to Robert. It was nothing special, nothing that her father could not have overheard without getting upset, but she liked that it was just the two of them and how Robert was eager to talk to her though he was not allowed to discuss any of the patients. Afterwards Isabel could never remember what they did talk about, but he managed to make her smile about the horses, especially Enormous Anthony, as Sister Lydia had christened her horse. Robert's horse was called Shylock. That took some explaining. Robert coming into the shop always lightened her day.

*

Robert didn't realize at first that he particularly liked Isabel and could not imagine why, just that she had a sense of respect for him, she didn't do daft things with her eyelashes or thrust the top of her body towards him as Polly did. Other girls also noticed him now that he had been elevated to such a place in the village. They saw a future with money and perhaps they saw that he would in time become a chemist or even a doctor.

This had become Robert's dream and no daft lass was going to stop him. He kept out of danger, but the hardware shop was not dangerous. Isabel liked talking to him and she asked the right questions and she laughed at his little jokes and she was so open with him. He didn't have to be careful with her. It was a good feeling, she was somewhere between the way that the other lasses looked longingly after him and his sisters who dismissed him as an idiot. Not Hannah of course, Hannah was kindness itself.

It was a shock for Isabel to go downstairs early one Thursday morning just before Easter ready for whatever the dull day would bring when she thought she saw someone in the shop. She knew that her father locked up carefully each night, back and front doors, he was always thinking that someone would break in and find his various stashes of money. There was however somebody in the shop. She could feel it rather than see anybody, and she was inclined not to say anything, she would tiptoe back up the stairs and rouse her father from his bed.

She was scared now. Silently she closed the door into the kitchen and climbed the stairs as softly as she could, aware of the odd creaking step until she let go of her breath and opened her parents' bedroom door.

She never went into that room. The curtains were closed and since it was barely light outside very little shadow came through on to the walls so that she couldn't see much except the bed. She didn't even know which side of the bed was her father's, so she waited until her eyes became accustomed to the gloom and even then it was difficult to see, but all she could distinguish was one shape in the bed and it was her mother, so small but at least she was sleeping. Was that then her father in the shop before her and if so why didn't he greet her as he usually did by giving her instructions for the day?

Could he be hurt? Could he have fallen? She had not heard any noise, and her hearing was good. She therefore crept out so that she would not awaken her mother and went back downstairs just as carefully, and then she went back into the shop.

She soon saw why her father was not in bed and why he was not moving. He was lying on the floor. She whispered to him, but he did not respond, and when she got down to him she could feel no breath and no pulse. He had slid to the floor, she surmised, in a faint presumably, and then he had died.

She went back upstairs, pushed open the curtains so that she could see. She spoke to her mother, who lay still for a few moments and then Isabel sat down on the bed and her mother sat up, her pale scared face told Isabel that her mother no longer hoped for anything. Perhaps neither of them did.

What should she say? She didn't want to put it too bluntly but then it was possibly the hardest thing she had ever had to deal with.

'Daddy is down in the shop on the floor and he isn't moving,' she said, and so her mother got carefully out of bed as though he was still there and she didn't want to disturb him, she put on her old woollen dressing gown and followed Isabel into the shop. She stood there looking at him as morning sunshine began to make its way into the front of the shop, and then she said to Isabel that she must go for the doctor.

Isabel unbolted the door and ran. Why she ran she wasn't quite sure. It was the not knowing. She thought her father was dead, but she had no experience of death and needed some help as soon as possible.

When she reached the hospital the doctor was not yet there. The first person she came across was Robert and she was so glad. She didn't know Sister Lydia, had just seen her from time to time and had the impression that Lydia was powerful and difficult, so explaining what she thought was happening to such a person would be so much harder. She even managed to grab hold of Robert's jacket for a few seconds before she became aware of what she was doing and then she stumbled over her words, but he understood her straight away and he picked up a bag and followed her up the street and into the shop.

There she watched his grim face and the way that he shook his head as he got to his feet.

'I'm so sorry, Mrs Norton,' he said to her mother, and her mother burst into tears.

# Fourteen

Things got better at the mill so that they could actually enjoy Easter. Sister Abigail told them that it was the most important part of the year for them. Mary preferred Christmas, but she liked how the mornings began to get lighter and the leaves started to bud on the trees.

Fran boiled eggs with onions for the children so that they looked like marbles and they rolled them all the way down the bank towards the mill. She also made special cakes for them such as Mary had not seen before, and the children responded to the kindness. She made sure they had sweets for Easter Sunday, and Mary helped her to cook a big meal.

Mary was astonished. She had thought that they never would be friends but she was managing so much. Fran was kind to her and it was as if the sun had come out on their mill house. It was, Mary had to acknowledge, a very pretty house. Sister Abigail kept coming back to see them until Fran got used to her and she was another pair of very capable hands.

The meetings at Mr Gilbraith's house were now weekly until everybody knew everybody. Mary liked the cake best but also showing off at her reading. When Sister Abigail came to see them she got Mary to read to her so that her reading was coming on very well. She encouraged Mary to write stories and they would sit around outside when the weather was fine or over the fire when it was not.

Sister Abigail turned up with a pretty pink covered notebook which she had found in a shop in Wolsingham on one of the trips she and Sister Maddy took down to the little haberdasher's that provided wool and silks and cottons.

Sister Abigail told Mary that there was a newspaper shop which sold stationery, art materials with cream coloured paper for sketching, oil paints, water paints, and people in the dale, she thought, must be very artistic because they would come in to buy all these things. Also paintings by various artists in the region were displayed upon the walls and they sold, not for a fortune, but at least she thought it would keep the painters enthusiastic, eager and able to afford what they needed.

She thought too that the skies here in the dale were large and the people who did the paintings thought so too because the sunsets were painted again and again, but also there were wonderful pictures of farmhouses and rough winters, sheep and horses, sheepdogs and farmers, and all the birds and animals that were found there.

Sister Abigail bought coloured pencils for Mary and encouraged her to illustrate the little stories. The children cooed over them and Flo was learning to read and write. It seemed that with Sister Abigail around the housework was done more quickly and if it wasn't finished she would take a broom and sweep up and do the dishes, and she also brought what she said was a recorder which Miss Proud was teaching her to play, so she brought music as well as expertise and joy into their house.

She made yellow curtains for the windows to let the sun in, and showed Mary and Fran how to make clippie mats, and they began a blue mat for in front of the fireplace in their sitting room. Mary missed Sister Abigail when she left to help other people with their homes and children, she wished she was there with them every day.

Things at the mill seemed to be going well too. Mary could hear her father whistling. It didn't last long and she watched him carefully now, his moods were so changeable. She thought also that he grew less and less patient now that Fran's baby was almost due. Was he worried about her?

Burt was eager to spend time in the mill, but her father said it was too dangerous. As he had grown a little older he was the kind of child who rushed about, so Burt would stand by the door watching for when Abe, his idol, came home for his meals and then Burt would run to him and Abe would catch him, throw him up very far into the clear blue sky, and Burt would scream with delight and then Abe would catch and secure him and hold him tightly in his arms as the child came back to earth.

Mary was learning to cook in a more adventurous way and she made special cakes for her father, but he did not seem to notice. He did not see the sunshine which came through the yellow curtains or the way that his home was sparkling clean because his womenfolk had made it so. She thought it was so welcoming, like no place had ever been before. She was desperate to make him happy, to keep him so. Sister Abigail never stayed for when he might come in, she was too clever for that, Mary thought. She instinctively knew that the miller would not like a woman who was given to God.

'A waste of a good woman,' he said one day when he saw Sister Lydia with the doctor in the village.

It was not a waste, Mary decided, people were talking about how clever Sister Lydia was and the women liked her being there. Perhaps it was difficult for them having a man to see to them, but Sister Lydia was always there now and it made them feel a lot more comfortable and relaxed, Mary felt sure.

Sister Lydia was with the doctor when he came to see Fran. She had not called him and was surprised to see him, it was just a courtesy call, he said, but he sat down and talked to her. Unfortunately the miller came in and asked him what he thought he was doing when he felt sure his wife needed no help in this matter and he was not about to start paying doctor's fees.

The doctor, who had been talking to Fran, got up and was as tall as Mary's father – she was glad of it, so that the doctor could look the miller straight in the eyes – and he said that nobody in the village paid for medicine or the doctoring – it was Mr Gilbraith's responsibility and it covered everybody and since the miller worked for Mr Gilbraith the doctor must come and see her.

They had been so lucky to come here. Mary's only wish was that her mother could be there, which she knew was a stupid thing, but she missed her as only a mother can be missed. Fran was too young to be her mother, the relationship between them was so different. There was nobody holding up the very walls as her mother had seemed to, and although her father could be said to do that he was the grumpy part of the family and nothing seemed to please him, however hard they all tried.

Mary noticed that her father had begun ignoring Burt completely as though he did not exist. She couldn't understand why such a taking child should be treated in that way even if Burt was not his, he was the only father Burt knew. Like a persistent cat Burt was always going to him, to show him a flower he had found by the stream or a drawing he had just made, but her father told him in a voice of disgust that such things were for lasses.

'Yes,' Mary said, 'why doesn't he cut up a worm or torture a toad?'

Her father glared at her. She wished she knew why her father was so unhappy, they had so much now, they should be happy. The children were thriving and Fran sang in the house. Mary got to go to school sometimes and she helped as much as she could because she did not want to give her father anything to complain about.

Burt gave up taking things to his father and took them to Abe, but Mr Barnfather didn't seem to like that either and was always ordering Abe back to the mill and Burt was not allowed in there.

It was perfectly understandable, Mary knew, there were dangers in the mill and the stream, and he had to be watched because he was also quite an adventurous child. It was just as well Mary was there because Fran could never have managed alone.

Flo was happy now and had stopped wetting her knickers, which meant less work. Mary would take her along to school. That left Fran with the two toddlers to mind and Mary felt sure it was more than enough. Burt would not sit still and Rosie just didn't seem old enough to attend to anything.

There was always too much to do. Her father appeared for meals, ignored the children, ate and went back to the mill to smoke his pipe when he sat outside. He made no conversation nor joined in with anything the others were talking about. The children were afraid of his loud voice so they repressed their needs until he went back out. It seemed to Mary that when he was not there the whole house relaxed.

He worked every day but Sunday. Mary and Fran took the children to church. Fran told Mary she had never been to a church like this one and Mary was surprised that Fran wanted to go, but they went. He did not go. Mary liked going to church, she liked seeing the nuns, and everybody went unless they were Methodists – Mr Gilbraith had built them a small chapel too so that everybody had somewhere to go, except that there was no parish church, which at the moment was half built, being a big and complex place.

Those people crowded into the chapel at the foundling school, but since the nuns had in all kinds of ways helped them there seemed to be little division and if people were keen and the weather was clement they could walk the three miles into Wolsingham where the vicar, Mr Brunswick, and his wife, accepted them gladly. Also now Mr Gilbraith had put on a pony and big cart to take them there and back unless the weather was so bad that they could not go.

Mary liked nothing more than to hear the singing in the nuns' chapel. Sister Maddy was getting up a choir and when Mary asked her father if she might join he laughed and told her that her singing voice was like the croaking of a pheasant, which dampened her feelings. She had been used to singing quite often, but his criticism though idly meant, she thought, had hurt her so much that she could not manage words or sounds.

Mary might have gone anyway but she was aware that Fran started to slow down, the baby in her womb seemed to take up all of her energy. She was tired. Mary therefore began to do so much that she was tired too. She wanted to suggest that they have help, but she didn't dare and was only glad of Sister Abigail's visits, which were at least once a week because she was visiting other people as Fran grew near her time. Mary was astonished that they got so much attention and worried that somebody was getting less than their fair share, but she was too tired to wish things otherwise.

The weather was cold and wet which meant that washing was a burden because everything had to be dried indoors. Her father complained that he could not sit over the fire. In fact sometimes in the evenings he did not come to the house at all, but when Mary ventured across to the mill he was always about, it just seemed that he did not want to be in the house with so many people, she thought.

Fran started to be in pain one morning at the beginning of May. She ignored it at first, she had had pain before and it had gone away but this time it didn't. There was a woman halfway up the bank who helped with such things and had said she would come when Fran's time was due. She was called Mrs Summerson. At dinnertime, noon, Fran was in more pain.

Mary's father came in for his dinner and said it was ridiculous, that his first wife had had four children without any help and that it was natural and she should just get on with it, it was her second after all. Mary had the feeling that her father was not only nervous but was afraid either that something would go wrong or that the child would be a girl. That thought, which had been sudden, made her gasp with comprehension and fear.

When he went back to the mill Mary begged Fran to let her go for Mrs Summerson. She could see that Fran was white faced and not coping alone but she said it had been like this before and she had been all right. By teatime she was doubled up with the pain. Mary decided to go for Mrs Summerson anyway but she was astonished that her father didn't go back to the mill after his tea, he put on his coat and made his way up the road.

Mary hung back. She didn't know where he was going or what he was doing but she worried about it. However he turned in at the Golden Lion so he was probably just going for a couple of pints. She backtracked to Mrs Summerson's house and Mrs Summerson turned out to help.

She was a reassuring sort of person and Fran seemed pleased to see her even though she had told Mary not to bother Mrs Summerson, as it was a Saturday night.

'Bairns arrive on Saturdays and Sundays just the same as other days, they don't care for day or night,' Mrs Summerson said cheerfully.

Fran's pain went on and on. Mary's father came back singing and fell asleep on the settee. Mary and Abe put the children to bed and Abe stayed with them while Mary remained with her stepmother and yet by morning there was no baby and Fran had sweated her way through two nighties and two lots of sheets by then.

Mrs Summerson said that they would need the doctor, she tried not to look worried but Mary was undeceived. It was Sunday and unlikely that the doctor would be in the village, Mrs Summerson said, and then she did sound worried.

She was frowning and her mouth was turned down at the corners and Mary knew then that Mrs Summerson did not like to be beaten but at least she knew when she was. Mary was so relieved when daylight came. She thought it had been a very long night.

Mary left Abe to manage and ran up to the school. She could hear the nuns singing and didn't know how to interrupt, but as she hovered in the hall she saw Sister Maddy coming towards her.

'There is something wrong?'

How did Sister Maddy know?

'I didn't mean to disturb you on Sunday, Sister Maddy but my – Fran, my mam – is in a bad way and Mrs Summerson wants Mr Gray but I don't suppose he is here.'

'Don't worry, you go back and I will get Sister Lydia to come to you and I will send for the doctor.'

'Thank you, Sister.'

Mary ran all the way down the hill and was in time to hear their father shouting in the kitchen and to see the children frightened and crying and standing back against the wall. Abe had taken them into the shadows so they could barely be noticed. As Mary went in she saw that the shouting was directed at her.

'So there you are,' he said. 'What do you think you are doing?'

Mary wanted to back away but she made herself stand her ground even though he seemed as tall as a house and she wanted to flee.

'I went for the doctor but he isn't here, it being Sunday morning.'

'She doesn't need anybody, she didn't need this stupid woman. Your own mother had four children without any help. I don't want strangers in my house.'

Burt had run upstairs by this time, Abe went after him, no doubt to keep him from the bedroom, the two little girls stood stock still and Mary badly wanted to go to them but she had to stand where she was, she didn't want him to direct his anger at them too.

'There's nowt wrong with her,' he said.' It's a lot of bloody fuss and nonsense about nothing,' and then he walked out, clashing the door behind him. Mary was shaking and to her dismay cold tears chased themselves down her hot face. Neither of the two small girls was crying now, she thought they were too afraid to do so as his voice had got louder and louder.

It seemed to her a long time before Sister Lydia appeared. Mary opened the door gladly and saw the nun upstairs. She was praying now that things would get better, something had to.

*

Lydia had also seen Mary and she came out of the foundling school guessing that it was about Mrs Barnfather. Lydia was worried. She was new at this. She had attended several births, but always when the doctor was there, so she sent somebody off with an urgent note. Even then she didn't hold out much hope. If he was not busy or at church it might be hours before he could get up there. She would have to do the best that she could.

Lydia took comfort in that this was not Mrs Barnfather's first child. If she could have one she could have another and everybody said that second births were easier, but if they had been then why did Mrs Summerson need her? Lydia knew that Mrs Summerson was practiced and rarely got anything wrong.

She was a huge asset to the overworked doctor and it was not the first time that Lydia had been glad of her, but then if things had been going well Mrs Summerson would never have asked for a doctor. She hurried up the stairs.

Mr Gray respected Mrs Summerson probably a lot more than he did Lydia, she kept telling herself and she saw when she turned up Mrs Summerson felt the same way. Mrs Summerson looked hard at her, drew her out of the room and on to the landing and enquired none too gently, 'Where is he?'

'Sister Maddy has sent for him. What would you suggest?'

'I have no idea. I have the feeling that she was very young for having a bairn when she had her first and I don't think it's done her insides any good.'

Lydia examined her patient and since she had already had one child all Lydia could think was that it was lying wrongly – she had seen something like that recently and although she knew what was going on it didn't make her feel better.

'It's in the wrong position,' she said to Mrs Summerson in private.

'Oh dear.'

'I'm going to try to turn it.'

'Oh dear,' Mrs Summerson said again, almost in tears. 'I have done it but never with any success and once I had a lassie who died as well as her bairn because there was nobody there but me and there was nothing else to be done. It was when I lived up at Rookhope and the winter was so bad that nobody could get through and they said afterwards to comfort me that she would have died anyway, but I couldn't forgive myself and I have had to live with it ever since.'

Which was not terribly helpful or encouraging, and Lydia was already sweating. She felt, and when she was fairly certain what she was doing she attempted to turn the baby. It was not an easy or pleasant experience for either the nun or the patient. Mrs Barnfather screamed and Lydia was not very surprised. She wanted to scream herself and wished heartily that the doctor had been there because she didn't know whether it would work and if she lost mother and child she would leave a man and five children and it would be all her fault.

She could not stop now, however, and so despite Mrs Barnfather declaring that she could bear no more and screaming and screaming, she turned the baby. Mrs Summerson held on to Mrs Barnfather's hands. Blood from Mrs Barnfather's nails was now dripping down her wrists. Lydia noted it in passing but it did not make her stop from what she was trying to do. The baby had hopefully, she thought, turned. Mrs Barnfather's screams were running one into another but her body was completely dilated and the baby was coming. If Lydia hadn't got it right she felt that she would never forgive herself, as Mrs Summerson had not been able to, but she'd feel more guilt and a sense of responsibility because she had had training which she well knew Mrs Summerson had lacked.

She thought how brave the woman was to carry on because nobody else would do it, nobody else would take the care, she was the only woman in the area who was trying to help in such difficult ways.

She wished she could delay until the doctor came, but she didn't know how long he would be. She knew how stupid it was, that there was nobody here who could have done better but she was more afraid than she had ever been in her life.

Lydia talked gently to Mrs Barnfather and then by slow degrees they worked until Lydia could see the baby's head. She thought she had never been more happy to see anything. Half an hour later the baby was born. Lydia was exhausted. The tears ran and ran down Mrs Barnfather's face, yet all she could say was, 'Is it a boy? It is a boy, isn't it?

They drew the child from her. Mrs Barnfather had had a very healthy girl.

Abe had taken Burt downstairs, but the little boy still clung to him so Abe sat down in the chair where their father usually sat and they waited and waited. Fran screamed. Mary turned her gaze towards the stairs but she hesitated. Sister Lydia and Mrs Summerson would take care of whatever it was, she couldn't do it, not knowing anywhere near what they knew.

She thought she had heard a child cry and Fran had stopped screaming. Perhaps the baby was dead and that was the root of the agony. And then she knew that it was a different kind of cry. It was not physical pain, it was mental anguish and once the screaming stopped Fran let out wails and she and Abe stood there and listened and were horrified. The noise above turned into helpless sobbing.

And then Mary knew what the problem was.

'She's had a baby girl,' she said.

The three children were wide awake now, nobody within earshot could sleep through that and all three began to cry, not knowing why they were pulled out of their first deep sleep. So Abe and Mary began to quiet and reassure them, but the horrible wailing from upstairs went on and on until it sounded like despair.

# *Fifteen*

'I can't have that thing near me,' Fran said. The snot and spit and tears were mingling on her shiny flushed face. Lydia had never seen anything like it and Mrs Summerson stood back and gazed at her.

'But it's a perfectly lovely little girl,' she said, cradling the baby against this vitriol from the mother. 'There's nothing wrong with her.'

Fran's eyes were full of despair.

'She was meant to be a boy. Don't you understand anything? He has girls, he has three girls and no son of his own. Oh God.' She lay back on her pillows and sobbed.

Neither woman understood completely but they were beginning to and both of them knew that men wanted sons. It did not seem to occur to people that if they did not have men and women there would be no children. It was so obvious and yet to some men it was not and in some cultures it was not.

What they would end up with would be villages of men with no women to marry and give them children, Lydia could not help thinking, and with that thought she wished people were not quite so stupid. She prayed at that point so that God would forgive her for such thoughts, but having brought this young woman through such a difficult birth, Mrs Barnfather was not just ungrateful but catatonic with despair and grief.

Mrs Summerson looked exhausted, Lydia thought, and yet she went on holding the child, rocking it slightly against its mother's rejection.

'Mrs Summerson, you must go home now. Thank you for being here when nobody else was, but I think you must go back to your family,' Lydia told her.

Mrs Summerson hesitated.

'I don't like leaving you here, Sister—'

'I will be fine.'

So Mrs Summerson passed the baby over to Lydia and made her escape. Lydia half wished she could do the same and then the door opened and she saw Mary.


Mary watched Mrs Summerson leave the house as though she could bear no more and then she trod up the stairs, warning Abe to keep the fireguard up, not to touch the fire, and to watch the bairns. She'd told them all that they were being silly and everything would be all right as she ventured up the steep stairs and into the bedroom.

She knew exactly what was the matter and so she got to the bed and she said to her stepmother, 'For goodness' sake, shut up. You are frightening Burt.'

The wailing stopped, Fran gulped down the tears.

'You've forgotten what Mr Wales used to say,' Mary said.

Nobody spoke. Sister Lydia still cradled the child and even though it was crying a little it was not making a huge amount of noise.

Fran stopped wailing and she stopped crying and then she said, 'He will never forgive me.'

'That's daft,' Mary said. 'Don't you remember what Mr Wales used to say?'

'I didn't know him.'

'He was the biggest farmer in the area. He said that if you don't get the calves you want you have to change the bull.'

There was silence for several moments and then Fran laughed and she said, 'Oh Mary, how would I ever manage without you,' and as Mary bent over, Fran put both arms around her. 'He will leave us now, like he did before. He will leave. I don't want this child,' Fran said and she wept afresh.

'Well that's really bad, because you have just given birth to it. Why would women not want to have girls, because it's what they were once?' Mary said, trying to be brave and practical.

Fran attempted to smile at Lydia.

'If you have other things to do, Sister, you must go.'

'I really think I should stay here,' Sister Lydia said.

Mary had never been more grateful for anything in her life than she was when Sister Lydia said that she would not go. She would have tried to take this on without her, but she was glad that she did not have to.

She was aware of Abe downstairs with the children, she was worried about her father, and she did not have long to wait. She could hear his voice, loud and drunken, and so, the baby being safe in Lydia's arms, she trod down there and it was just as well.

He stood in the middle of the room, feet planted carefully. Abe was disabled by the children so Mary came forward to take them from him so that Abe stood as tall as her father. At that moment the baby above them cried and he lifted his gaze to the ceiling and he said, 'My son,' so reverently that Mary had to urge herself to say it.

'Your daughter.'

He did not hear her at first but when the crying went on he became incoherent.

'My son.'

He cried now, a cry of keen disappointment and disillusion-ment, and then not being able somehow to gain the stairs, he staggered towards the door and was outside in seconds.

Lydia thought she had done what she could the moment that the baby was born and the afterbirth came and the child and the mother were all right. Mrs Summerson had cleaned up baby, mother and bed, and had left, but the trouble was that it did not end there.

She couldn't go and leave Mary to manage and she heard the sound of Mr Barnfather's voice and then the door slamming. Lydia wondered how many women had been glad to hear the outside door clash like that and how many of them dreaded the moment that it would open again.

Meanwhile Mrs Barnfather would not take the child, even after Mary was so straight with her. She turned her face to the wall and Lydia didn't know what to do but go on. There was no way in which she could leave the mill house, she just prayed that the doctor would get here soon and that he would be able to sort this out.

In the meanwhile the baby moved in her arms, crying just a little until Lydia instinctively began to rock it. She had never held a newborn in her arms for this length of time. Sometimes the doctor would hold it for a few moments and so would she, but usually the baby was given to the mother as soon as possible. It was what Mr Gray called 'bonding', and Lydia understood perfectly but she did not think she would respond as she did though it had happened to her before. She must try to put such things from her mind if she were to succeed as a doctor. She could not be wife, doctor and nun.

The mother so obviously did not want the child, and Mr Barnfather did not want it because it was a girl. Lydia was ready to run out of the door. She thought of the old Chinese saying, 'There are forty ways to avoid conflict, the first of these is to flee.'

That was what she wanted to do now. She even half turned towards the door before she knew that she could not go. Her instincts shrieked at her to run with the child in her arms as if somebody who would kill them was close at hand. What an over-reaction, she chided herself, but she was now crooning softly and rocking the baby until its eyes closed and for a few seconds she felt as though it was hers. She didn't want to give the child back to Mrs Barnfather, her senses as well as her mind knew that the baby was unwanted.

Mary, in a fit of conscience, she thought, went downstairs and several minutes later came back with hot sweet tea and when Mary offered to take the child Lydia gave her up, even though she wanted to turn her back on Mary and hold the child herself for evermore.

She let Mary sit down on the hard chair in the bedroom and then she took the tea and stood by the window, drinking it. She had no idea what more she could do and was half glad and half sorry when she heard the doctor's voice. She thought his voice was musical, it was the best sound in the universe. Ever since she had entered this very small world of medicine his voice had been more reassuring than anything else. With him there she felt she could manage almost anything.

She turned to the door as he came in. He looked so tired. Often now he was up all night with an accident, a childbirth, or some old patient on a deathbed whose last request was that Mr Gray should be there.

He said very little and when he did he spoke first of all to the mother until she turned to him so that he could see how she was and then he smiled and told her how brave she had been and how she had a wonderful baby, and then she turned from him again and said that she wouldn't have it, neither she nor her husband wanted another girl. They must take it away.

Lydia thought this was a first for the doctor, he looked surprised, frowned, and then he took the baby from Mary rather clumsily and as he let the baby down on the bed at its mother's back the child began to cry and that was when Lydia knew he was being clumsy on purpose. The child opened its mouth and screamed.

Lydia thought no woman on earth could resist the sound, she wanted to grab it herself and had to stand back a little and let it scream and scream. It screamed until it was almost purple. Mrs Barnfather began to cry and then she began to scream too, saying, 'Take it away, I won't have it, take it away.'

Nobody moved. Lydia glanced across at Mary and saw the look on her face. It was bewilderment and pain and then she wished she could hold Mary to try and ease some of the pain, but movement was not the right thing so she just waited. Gradually Mrs Barnfather turned over. She took the child into her arms and looked down on it with distaste, but she didn't let it go.

# Sixteen

Her father's death changed Isabel's life and it would have been farcical, she thought, to pretend that she was unhappy. She could not remember what happiness was like but she welcomed it when it arrived so suddenly.

The dark shadows had gone, the summer light was the brighter for it, the flowers seemed to have more colour, the rain felt warm, she could say what she wanted and do what she wanted. She tried not to seem too cheerful because her mother was so shocked, and Isabel had to organize the funeral and see to the running of the shop and everything else.

She even thought that her mother might recover, but she didn't. She was just the same, as though even now that the weight was lifted it was still there on her shoulders. Sometimes Isabel could tell she thought that her mother heard her father's foot-steps and shrank even more into her chair by the fire.

She seemed cold all the time and so even when it was a fine day Isabel put the fire on in the kitchen. They needed it for cooking. Isabel no longer felt that she had everything to do even though she had even more now, but she got up with a song in her heart and a lightness that went through her whole being.

She now had total control of her life. She found the money that her father had hidden around the house. The frustrating thing was that her mother barely altered even when the days went forward and the meals were plentiful. Her mother could not or would not eat, and she would not change her clothes.

Isabel longed to talk to the doctor about it. She became so worried, but when she ventured to the hospital at the bottom of the hill she saw Robert before she saw anybody else, it was like he was everyone's first port of call, being less official than the doctor or less scary than Sister Lydia. She could not help blushing when she found him just inside the door, but he was reassuring and took her into a little room where there was a desk and two chairs. He closed the door and asked her what he could do to help and he frowned and said that he would talk to the doctor about it. Isabel began to warm to him, and not just her face, she could have spent all day there with him, she was so interested in his voice, in his eyes, in his confidence. He made her feel better in so many ways.

In the end it was Sister Lydia who came to the house. She confused and worried Isabel, she was so unusual and Isabel felt disappointed that Robert had not come by himself. She hadn't really expected the nun and was rather afraid of Lydia's brisk manner, but Lydia was not brisk at all the moment she got inside. It was just after closing time, Isabel was grateful that Sister Lydia had cared enough to understand it was the best time, but she couldn't take Sister Lydia into the back because her mother was there.

'Your mother is grieving for your father,' Sister Lydia said.

Isabel didn't like to say it but she couldn't help herself.

'He was a bully, a very nasty sort of man and he treated both of us badly. Why would she feel bad now that he's gone?'

'He was her husband and a lot of women feel these things are their fault.'

'But it wasn't. When we lived in Durham we had a perfectly lovely life. It was only when we came here that he changed. Once he had his own business he was like a different person. We weren't allowed to go anywhere, we weren't given enough to eat, and we were both afraid of him. I'm so glad he's dead. I know I shouldn't feel like that but I do.'

'Perfectly understandable,' Sister Lydia said. 'Let me see your mother. I'd like to try to help.'

They went into the back and there Isabel saw her mother afresh through the nun's eyes. She was smelly and wizened and shrank as she sensed somebody new. Isabel thought her mother would have run away had she been able, but she sat there and shook and began to cry.

Then Sister Lydia did the most extraordinary thing that Isabel thought she had ever seen. She pulled forward the chair which was Isabel's father's – she hadn't been able to bring herself to sit in it so far, and instead sat on the little stool she had used as a child. Then she thought of how little time she spent in that room and that it seemed tiny with so much furniture in it. The blue settee, which was shabby and worn, was pushed against the back wall under the window, the table and three chairs dominated the room, but the chairs were pushed in so that they didn't take up too much space, and then there was the fire and the two easy chairs. Sister Lydia had had to squeeze between things to get to her mother and then she got down and took Isabel's mother into her arms.

Mrs Norton broke down and then she sobbed hard into Sister Lydia's shoulder and Sister Lydia stroked her hair and told her that it was all right to be sad, that she should just let it all out, that none of this was her fault, that she had always done her best, that she was a good and kind woman and that things would get better.

They sat there like that for a very long time but it did not seem long to Isabel, and in that time she made plans. She would change things. She would make life better for her mother, she would make sure her mother had some joy. It was only when her mother had quietened that Sister Lydia let her go, and even then she traced her fingers down Mrs Norton's cheeks and smiled at her. Isabel thought that she could not remember her mother being held or hugged before, and then she felt the same about herself, she was never shown love, never had been from her father, and her mother had long since given up any form of affection.

She saw Sister Lydia out and then she went and got down the bathtub from the yard and she helped her mother take off her clothes and wash. Isabel soaped and gently washed her mother's body and her hair and then helped her with a big towel and into a clean nightgown and dressing gown. Tomorrow, she promised herself she would go out and buy new clothes for them both.

That Sunday, in their new clothes she accompanied her mother to the nearest church which was the Methodist church. She was astonished at how many people spoke to them, it did not matter that they were not Methodists, people were so welcoming, so kind. Then she urged her mother to lie down, and after that she made them a huge dinner, lamb with new potatoes and mint and peas with lots of gravy and Yorkshire puddings. Her mother ate and then went to bed, and Isabel sat in the little back room with one of her father's books and drank tea and thanked God for sending Sister Lydia to them.

## Seventeen

There was a lot of rain that summer and to Lydia it felt more like October. The hard wind blew rain through the country and many a night Lydia and Robert were called out to farms, but Lydia never doubted Robert and she was right. He was devoted to her service, that was what the doctor said. Mr Gilbraith paid the lad very well for his services so Robert himself said.

'If it gets to be too much, Robert, you must say so,' Mr Gilbraith said to him, 'and when you need time off I will find somebody else to be there instead.'

'I don't need time off, sir, with your leave.'

'Yes, well, just remember that she is a nun.'

'Men do not fall in love with nuns,' Robert said.

'Believe me, it happens.'

'Not this time,' Robert said comfortably.

'Do you have a girl?'

'No, and I don't intend to. Women are more bother than they are worth.'

Jay laughed.

'Just be careful. And look after her.'

'She is very talented,' Robert said, already worshipping. Jay just hoped it would be all right. 'Very clever. I like being around clever people.'

'You are clever too, don't forget that.'

The lad blushed but laughed and disclaimed, and Jay thought he had got the right person for the job.

In his own way Robert adored Lydia, but it was more admiration than anything else. He didn't want to get near, he didn't want to hold her. Her uniform such as it was would have deflated the boldest lover. It was not that she wasn't comely, he thought she was the most beautiful thing he had ever seen, but it was just that she was beyond him, like the church and Mary and Jesus were beyond him. This woman had been given special powers. It would not have surprised him that she could do anything, and he was just so pleased that she needed his help.

Despite how hard it was, Lydia was the happiest that she had ever been. She did not go back to the foundling school very often, but she did see the children in the surgeries and at the hospital and she saw the nuns when they weren't feeling well because everybody came to Mr Gray for help.

Robert, being such a large person, he was tall but also broad as wrestlers needed to be, was great for moving and lifting people. Lydia asked him whether he minded at first and then she began to take for granted that he would be there for her. He was always within earshot, no matter where she was.

She wished she could tell him how grateful she was to him, but she didn't know how to say it and the one time she attempted to he went all awkward and said that she needn't think he was doing this for nothing, Mr Gilbraith was paying him handsomely or else he wouldn't have done it, but Lydia knew it wasn't that. In his way he was as dedicated as she was.

She soon saw what he had said about the roads, most of which were dreadful, and a lot of the farms had nothing but a rutted track to them and sometimes these were so long that she despaired of reaching anyone who was ill. They seemed to go up and up into nowhere and nothing, or down and down until she thought she and Robert would soon be in the river. Beyond the village here the road could be hard and bend off at angles, but at least it was on the level.

The dale was narrow and so everything was up or down or twisted and turned and was here and there, and so often invisible that when there was no moon she had to rely on Robert's keen eyesight and his knowledge of the area. There was nothing wrong with her eyes just that she had not had to employ them this far before now, but she loved that she did have to.

One night they were called to an out of the way farm where a woman was having her first baby. The rain and wind had not stopped for several days and Lydia was tired though she would never have admitted it. Mr Gray could not even get up to the village, the road had washed away at one point on the second hill and there were houses on one side and an almost sheer drop on the other.

By the time Lydia and Robert got to their destination the baby was born dead and the mother swiftly followed. It was the first time that Lydia had seen a failure like this and she could not contain her distress. She insisted on telling the young husband, but his mother looked accusingly at her and said, 'You were too late in coming. I sent a message hours ago and now look.'

Lydia held up until they were outside and then she started to cry. She was disgusted at the fact that the mother and baby had died, she was disgusted with herself that she had been too late and that she had not been able to help them, she felt disgusted with God for letting such things happen. She tried not to weep, but the feelings bettered her.

Robert stood there for a few moments and then he put her

on to her horse, told her that everything would be all right, and they went back to the village very slowly, the weather was so vile. He had not wanted to be there, he had already told her that they should not go, the weather was the kind that hurt your face as it whipped against you with a savage wind behind it, and seeing anything was hard, but she had insisted that they should go and he had obeyed her. He was not happy about it but he had gone with her, and yet the woman and the child had died, but then Lydia never gave up. It was the thing he most admired about her, and he could not stop her. He had to be there for her and with her and do everything he could to make it right.

When they got back she just sat there so cold and soaked through, barely able to move and so cast down that she didn't want to dismount. In vain did Robert urge her to, and in the end he lifted her down.

She said, 'The doctor could have done more.'

'No, he couldn't,' Robert said, 'he says himself he knows no more about these things than you do, and there is too much to do so you can't both be there. Come on Sister, bear up. We're home now and you shall have tea over your fire and I will see to the ponies and then I will have tea over my fire and if you need me I will be there.'

He urged her inside. Lydia duly sat over the fire and Mrs Waltman, who was one of the head nurses at the hospital and understood very well, gave her tea and a large ham sandwich and told her that everything would look better in the morning, she was not to fret.

'We lost the baby and the mother and it was her first. We were too late,' Lydia said, and Mrs Waltman, being a sensible woman, told her that it was not the first time nor would it be the last, and they had done everything that they could.

Notwithstanding that Lydia was a nun, Mrs Waltman told her that she was a brave lass for doing such work. When the doctor had been longing for somebody to help him, she had appeared like a guardian angel and she had been there and had done her best when there were so many calls upon her time. She must try to think that she was doing more than any nun had ever been called upon in the entire area to do.

'And Jim's lad, by he's a good 'un is that. You are a fine pair,' she said and that comforted Lydia. Whatever would she do without Robert?

She was too tired to cry any more. She managed somehow to eat her sandwich, drink her tea, and then she just went to bed, fell asleep and didn't dream. Mrs Waltman made sure the fire was kept up in Lydia's room all night so that she was comforted by the blaze and warmth of the flames.

That week Lydia and Robert were called to Polly Swift's house and it was a most unusual kind of call in that there was no explanation of the ailment. It was late and dark. Lydia wanted to go on her own but Robert would not let her go without him. When she tried to argue about such things he always brought Mr Gilbraith into the conversation so the best she could do was to say to him that he must wait outside in the back lane beyond the yard.

She had never met Polly Swift or her mother. Polly was an only child, most unusual in the village, but the minute that Lydia got inside she could see why. Polly had been a child of her mother's late age. Her parents had been old enough to be her grandparents. Lydia sensed that Mrs Swift did not like her and she now understood why, even though it had not been her fault, Mrs Swift was seriously worried about Polly, she perhaps even thought that Lydia had blocked her daughter's chance to marry Robert. She would not be the only one in the village.

Mrs Swift said that her husband had recently died so it was no wonder she was feeling bad, Lydia thought. Polly was upstairs and although her mother thought she was in bed she was standing by the window, turned away from the room. It was the back bedroom and she had a lamp lit so she would have seen Lydia come in by the back lane and across the yard.

Lydia had insisted on going in alone, suspecting that Robert would not want to go, knowing that his mother and her mother wanted them married and she thought he did not. For once he seemed glad to stay outside, even though the night was cool and windy. She knocked on the door and heard Polly's voice and went in. There was a fire on. A fire upstairs, even though they were in a coalfield, was most unusual, and signified the gravity of the illness and the turn of the weather.

Polly must be pretty when she was well, with her long dark red hair, creamy skin and generous form, and it was not that Lydia thought the girl ill now, she was more distressed than anything else. When she turned, her face was white and tear-streaked and yet her cheeks were red with some emotion. The way that she lowered her dark eyes almost at once told Lydia quite a lot.

'Miss Swift, Polly,' she said, 'I'm Sister Lydia.'

'I know you are,' the girl said. 'I don't want you here. I told my mam there was nothing wrong with me but she wouldn't have it.'

'I can ask Mr Gray to call if you prefer.'

Polly let out what was meant to be a scornful laugh and would have been a lot more effective if she had not sobbed at the same time, catching her breath so that she would not break down completely in front of her unwelcome guest.

'I don't want that old man here telling me that I was evil. This is all your fault. Before you came along I was going to marry Bobbie.'

Lydia almost winced. She had never heard the doctor spoken of so disrespectfully and it showed how upset this girl was that she didn't care or wanted to hurt somebody, anybody other than herself, mentally flailing around at anything or anybody that would make her feel better.

It was a second or two before Lydia saw that Bobbie was Robert. Even his mother called him Robert, but perhaps this showed how close they had been that she had this baby name for him. She wondered how he had referred to Polly, though the name in itself was sufficient. Bobbie and Polly, they were names for caged love-birds. She upbraided herself for a frivolous thought, but she had realized she was being blamed here for something which she had not intended but had unwittingly caused.

'He would have married me, but oh no, you arrived with your clever ways and your – your flouncy skirts and your bonny face. My mam and his mam, they had the wedding all planned and where we would live and that he could go on with his dad's work. It pays well, you know, and I was all ready to be a bride and to settle down and be there for when he came in from work. I was all ready to—' she stopped there, her voice hoarse and almost giving in but it was only to take a breath. She was still standing by the window in nothing but a thin nightie and must have been half frozen, but Lydia could hardly tell her so and she did not notice it. Lydia had never heard of a habit being called a flouncy skirt. She swore that she would remember it and how it threatened some women.

Polly now looked Lydia full in the face, all accusing.

'I went to Laurie Hargreaves I was so – so upset. '

She must have been, Lydia thought, he was foul-mouthed and ignorant and the last lad any mother would want her girl to have anything to do with.

'And he – he did what I wanted Bobbie to do. He did it and I was scared because I knew that I didn't really want him. It was nothing like I thought it would be, that was the most awful thing. It wasn't that, it was that Bobbie had left me for you and I didn't care. I just wanted somebody to hold me and he did more but it was nothing like I thought it would have been, it hurt and got in the way and spoiled everything. It was so disgusting and messy and nothing but a few seconds.

Then I was scared cos I thought we would have a bairn out of it, a baby.' She broke down at this point. Lydia wished that the curtains had been drawn across the window or at least that the net curtains had enclosed them because the moon had most unobligingly come out at that moment and she could see Robert there beside the gate, lounging against the wall, half hidden by what moonlight there was.

Lydia wasn't quite sure what was so special about Robert from a romantic viewpoint. He was trustworthy and depend-able, which was why she needed him, but he was not 'such stuff as dreams are made on'. And then she tried looking at him as Polly might and she thought that it was just that she didn't look at men as suitable partners. She never had. She thought of Clive Laidlaw and of David Welcome and of all the other young men she could have married, and she knew now that she was different and perhaps that was her luxury in life. She had found another way or the way had found her. She felt lucky, she would never pine after a man who didn't want her, or be bullied by one who thought to tell her what to do, but the young women here had no such advantages, it was marriage or nothing. She would have to adapt to the way a man looked at life and bear his children and put everybody's needs before her own.

Polly had got lost in the limitations of what she might aspire to. It made Lydia shudder.

'I didn't bleed for two months,' Polly said, 'and I was getting scared because I couldn't tell anybody and my mam would have had a fit and we would have had to get married and I don't even like him and I don't even think he likes me.'

Here she broke down again so noisily that Lydia feared her mother's tread on the stairs and the sound of her voice, but nothing happened. And then she thought that perhaps Polly's mother knew, as mothers did, what had been going on, despite having had her husband die or because of it she was more acute in feeling.

'I love Bobbie. I love him.'

Lydia had no idea how to handle this. She sat there silenced, guilty and horrified and yet full of relief that she could watch this, help this poor girl, and stand apart. She knew now that it was what she had always wanted.

'And now there isn't going to be any baby. I couldn't tell my mam, I couldn't tell anybody. It hurt so much.' She drew her arms across her stomach in remembrance. 'I told my mam that it was a heavy bleed, but it wasn't. There was a great big lump that came out of me. It went down the netty.'

Lydia wanted to ask obvious things, such as had she stopped bleeding, but she had, that much was plain. You could not wear a white nightgown even with big knickers underneath as this girl had if you were still bleeding. Lydia had the feeling that her knickers were stuffed in some way so that if she was bleeding nobody could see it, but it must be very slow and therefore was not going to kill her.

'Don't you want to tell me how bad I am, Sister, how much I have sinned and therefore will go to hell?' and that was when she broke down properly, falling on to the bed and sobbing. Lydia didn't know what to say. If she told Polly that Robert did not think of Lydia as a woman Polly might be insulted, and if she said that he did then it was a bigger insult, and all of it untrue.

When Polly had cried herself to sleep Lydia went downstairs very slowly and told her mother that Polly would be well but it might take a couple of weeks. Her mother looked relieved.

'I was so worried about her. Since – since – she was heart-broken.'

'I think that with her dad dying and the way that things have gone with her life it has all been such a lot for her to take in. I am sure that it's been hard for you too,' Lydia said.

Mrs Swift nodded and smiled, but Lydia could see the relief in her eyes.

'As long as you can get her to eat and sleep, and I'm sure you are the same.' She could see the strain in Mrs Swift's face. 'You need to be gentle with yourselves and with one another. Things will get better but they take a long time. How are you off for money?'

Lydia was amazed that she said such a thing. It was all very well telling this woman and her daughter to rest, but if they were short of money then they did have problems and of late Mr Gilbraith did not pay everybody. Some folk worked for themselves, some of them worked there part time or in other villages, and a few folk, like the milkman, had a dairy herd or a small farm and his own business.

'My husband was a stonemason and Mr Gilbraith is looking after us. I'm so grateful. In a lot of places we would be left on the street. Polly was working up at the house.' The house was Jay's fellside house. 'And he said to take as much time as we needed.'

Lydia could hardly get outside quickly enough, so she half fell over the step down into the backyard. She barely knew how to go on. Robert unfurled. They walked together down the back lane.

'Was it Polly?' he asked.

He didn't usually ask, so Lydia could hardly tell him not to.

'Yes, but she will be all right.'

He walked her back to the foundling school. She was not needed that night at the hospital. There he hesitated.

'They wanted me to marry her, you know, my parents and her parents.'

He didn't say, 'But I didn't want to marry her', or that she had wanted him.

'I don't want to get married yet. I want to do other things. Mr Gray says I might make a chemist, do you think that's right?'

'I'm sure it is, but you are so good at a lot of other things,' Lydia said.

'I was hoping that in time I might go to Edinburgh to study. I would like that more than anything. I talked to Mr Gilbraith about it and he said that he would pay for it, but it means I have to leave here and that's a hard thing to do, and my mam wouldn't be keen to let me go.'

Lydia knew that too, but she thought that if women wanted their sons to go on and do the things they chose to do they must learn to let go of them, but she was also discovering that Robert was strong and despite his mother's ideas he would get beyond them and probably not too far down the line. She would miss his strength and ability.

'I think it's an excellent idea and that you will be very good at it and enjoy it and it might help you to get away.'

He looked almost satisfied.

'That's what I thought, Sister.'

He wished her goodnight and Lydia was relieved. It was not

her fault. This young man had ambition. If he burdened himself with a wife now he would never get beyond the village. The doctor had seen his potential and so had Mr Gilbraith. He was not thinking of her, he was not thinking of any woman, and when he did it would be because he was a mature adult with skills and knowledge, but she could not stop thinking about Polly and how hard it was for her. She could not get beyond the village. The only way it seemed to Lydia was to become a nun and it was not a path that many women would choose to follow.

Also she thought that Polly's mother knew more than she was letting on, as people said around here. Her mother was grieving for the marriage that could have been and yet she must be pleased that her daughter was not marrying the man who was strange and unusual.

She could not be pleased that her daughter had lost a child, but she must be relieved that at least her daughter didn't have to marry in a hurry the kind of man she did not want in her house because he was dirty and ignorant and stupid.

There was also at the bottom of Lydia's reasoning an idea that Mr Gilbraith had deliberately put Robert Slater into such a position so that he was no longer at the mercy of the village lasses who were looking for a husband. Perhaps Mr Gilbraith had done them a service.

She wasn't sure that Robert Slater would make anybody a good husband; he might be the kind of man who was so absorbed in his work that he had no time for anything else. There was a way about him as such that he sought things differently than what was apparent to others. She had long since suspected it, that his mind had but a single thought at once, unlike a woman's mind, but such determination might make him the kind of man who made important discoveries, you could never tell with these things.

# *Eighteen*

Things did not get better at the mill. Since the new baby had been born and nobody named it, nobody looked at it, things went down and Mary could feel how they did. Everybody was so cheerless. Fran fed the baby because she had to, but she didn't hold it or bother with it and everything was left to Mary.

Her father no longer came into the house, she was obliged to take his meals to the mill and since she was trudging there with one meal she took Abe's as well. He had nothing to say, neither of them thanked her for what she was doing. Mary expected nothing. Her father did not come in to sleep either, he said he was sleeping at the mill and so more and more Abe slept there with him.

Burt was now confined to the house with the other children, and Mary was forever having to stop him from going there because he rarely got to see Abe, his idol.

Fran had no energy and lay in bed most of the day, staring out of the window so that Mary no longer got to go to school or to see Miss Proud. Her dreams of playing the piano disappeared under the weight of what there was to do.

It was several weeks after the baby was born that Sister Abigail turned up at the mill house. Abigail had called briefly several times and Mary knew how busy the nuns were so she tried to refuse once again, but Abigail wasn't having it.

'I'm going around all the various houses and offering just a little help,' she said.

She didn't ask what she could do, she was very polite at the door, but when Mary tried to get rid of her she said, 'I'll just go and get your washing in for you before the whole lot is soaked.'

Mary didn't think it was raining that hard but she could not refuse. By the time Abigail had the washing in her arms and in the basket the rain had come on so Mary could hardly complain and had to allow Abigail into the house.

Without saying more or giving Mary the opportunity to refuse, Abigail did all the things Mary had been attempting to do. To begin with Mary resented it, but by the time Abigail had been there two hours she was rather pleased, things were so much easier when there were two of you.

Even though the miller scowled and left the mill for the house when he saw a nun go in, Abigail just smiled brightly and thanked him, though Mary wasn't quite sure for what, but he could hardly complain about his dinner because Abigail had the knack of making a little go a long way. So for once they all sat down to dinner and it tasted twice as good as it would have, had Mary had to do it while she was trying to do everything else.

That afternoon Sister Abigail spent time with Fran and eventually managed to coax her downstairs. She even put on the sitting room fire so that Fran could nurse the baby while sitting there, and she asked what the baby was called.

'She doesn't have a name,' Mary said, while her stepmother didn't look up.

'Then we must find her one,' Sister Abigail said. She asked Fran for a good name but Fran just shook her head. 'What about Bridget?' Sister Abigail said. 'Saint Bridget's favourite flower was the dandelion.'

'Too Irish,' Fran said.

'What about Daisy?' Mary said, instantly transported into wild flowers.

Fran said nothing for about a minute and then her face cleared.

'That's a nice name,' she said, so the baby was called Daisy and Sister Abigail said she would baptize the baby while she was there, anybody could do it and so she sprinkled the baby's forehead with water she had made the cross over, while the three of them plus baby and children sat over the fire and Mary felt better than she had felt since the baby was born.

That afternoon Sister Abigail and Mary made cakes while Daisy and Fran nodded over the sitting-room fire. It was much easier with two rooms, as the three children alternated between them, and Sister Abigail was not above giving them the bowl which had held the cake mix so that they could put their fingers in and scrape out what was left.

They were also mystified by how the cake baked and came out of the oven smelling hot and sweet and it was such a positive thing to do that Mary felt better. Before Abigail left at tea time the clothes were half dried so she ran an iron over them as she called it and hung them up so that the creases fell out, and they looked better than they ever had.

Mary liked the help but she didn't like having somebody else in the house because she knew how much her father hated even the very idea, so she thanked Sister Abigail but said she would manage in future.

It was Mary who sensed the miller's restlessness. The first sign was that he didn't leave her as much money. Usually it was on top of the dresser in the sitting room, but it was short. The first week she thought he had just made a mistake, but when it happened for the second week running she knew that there was something wrong.

Surely beer wasn't that expensive. Abe knew nothing of it, he did not do the money side of things, he was the man who lifted the sacks and saw to things physically, her father had always been the man who dealt with the buying and selling, but the more she asked about it the more impatient her father became until she had to cut back on the quality of the meals, and then he complained.

'We haven't had meat in a week,' he said as she offered him vegetables, and Yorkshire pudding. She gave them Yorkshire puddings as often as she could, they too filled people up and were cheap. Rosie liked them with treacle after dinner. Mary concentrated on the children and said nothing.

# Nineteen

Isabel's mother died. It was as unexpected as her father's death had been, and almost as quick. She had been happy with her mother, but then her mother caught cold and coughed and coughed. Within days she just lay down and didn't get up again and this time Isabel understood what grief was like.

She had loved her mother, had such good memories, and felt desolate. At least her mother could have what she thought of as a proper funeral because her mother had loved the little Methodist chapel and had even begun to make friends. Isabel did not know how to carry on. She had no friends, she had been too busy with the shop and caring for her mother since her father had died, and now everything seemed so bleak.

Sister Lydia urged her to get out when the weather was fine and talk to people, but Isabel couldn't manage it. By the time she had seen to the shop she didn't even want to eat. She didn't sleep, the house was so empty, so odd, and she found herself crying hard and constantly for her mother and wondering if she should go back to Durham, but there was nothing to go back to now. That life was gone and she must make the best of things, though how to do so she had no idea.

It was all she could do to keep the shop open and not go mad. At night by the back-room fire she blamed herself that her parents had died. She tried to think what she had done and whether they had died because of her. She lay there in the darkness, worrying and blaming herself and sobbing into the bedclothes. She had not understood how silent the nights were.

So it was something of a relief when Mr Barnfather came to the shop and spoke kindly to her. She had seen him before but not talked to him and he had not been back in since her father had died. At first she didn't know what to say.

She had never met Mr Barnfather, though she knew of the miller, he was such an unforgettable figure. He was a big man, tall and muscular, and he had bright orange hair and penetrating green eyes and when he spoke to Isabel she thought she could see that he liked her.

He seemed to enjoy making her laugh. Some men did that, she saw now, they loved making you smile, so she began to look forward to his infrequent visits. He had a lot of children, she knew, and yet he was not old like her father had seemed.

The miller was perhaps only thirty-five. She liked the way that he looked at her though she was inclined to blush, and it was not that he was slimy and lecherous like some older men who came in and kept looking at her body. She ignored them, she had to, but he was always looking into her eyes and making her laugh. She often kept him longer than she should have when there was nobody else in the shop because she enjoyed talking to him so very much.

He would start out trying to leave and would gradually ease out of the shop while they were talking, but he would not shut the door until the conversation had come to some natural close or a new customer walked in, and she found herself looking at the door when he had gone and wondering if she would ever find a man like that, somebody she might care about. She did think of Robert, but he had not been into the shop since her mother died and she thought that he might be under the impression she was trying to make up to him as other girls would be doing now that he was becoming important. She wished he would come and they could go on. It was the only thing that resembled normality.

For so long she had thought that her life would go on the same as always, that she would be the daughter and live with her parents. It seemed strange to her now that she should think so. The fetters were broken, her life and thinking had changed so much and when she thought of the miller, which she did from time to time when she had time to think her own thoughts, she found that she was interested in him and excited as to how her life might work out. She no longer felt lonely, she did not cry, she felt in charge and capable and almost happy again.

Yet when the younger men came in she was not attracted to them. They seemed like boys, so silly and frivolous, and she felt superior to them and older even when she was not. One or two were not like that, they were serious and said nothing or as little as they could manage for their errand, but she found these were too much like her father had been.

When Robert Slater did come into the shop he barely spoke and she saw then that like other men he was afraid she might want to marry him. She began to wish he would take more notice of her, but he went on just the same and Isabel grew frustrated, but there was never any chance that he would look at a plain thin girl in the way that she wanted him to.

He didn't make her blush any more, it was as though he was cautious now that she was alone. He was so far beyond anything she could ever have thought of in her life, he was as distant as the stars. And she could tell that to him she was nothing more than another shopkeeper. He did not make conversation as he had done. He was civil, polite, and even smiled, but it was just because he had been brought up like that. She would never aspire to thinking that he might like her in a special way.

She started to dream about what it was like when you had a home and children and somebody who came back to you at night, as far removed as possible from what her parents had had. She would never settle for something like that. When she looked into her glass she was dissatisfied with what she saw, and yet there was nothing wrong with her. Her hair was glossy and these days her dark eyes were bright, but she had no special features, nothing that would attract a man. If any of them did like her it would probably be because of her shop, and that was a horrible thought.

Robert did not like going to the hardware store. He had not understood why he felt like he did, but he would have asked other people to go had not the doctor encouraged him to take on the task of ordering the medical supplies they needed. Somebody had to be discreet and so the task was given to him.

Somehow he hadn't minded going when Isabel's parents were alive, it had seemed harmless. Now he saw her differently. He understood that she liked him and he did not want anyone to like him in that way. It was not part of what he was going to do with his life. He did not intend to get stuck here with a plain little lass from a shop. He had liked talking to her. Now it was different and he began to understand that she saw him as a way out of a difficult situation. He understood that she must be lonely, but there were things she could do about that. It was nothing to do with him and he began to resent her.

He would have given a great deal to be able to approach Mr Gray with the truth, but he felt stupid about it, that Mr Gray would laugh or say that there was no reason he shouldn't marry, but Robert had no intention of staying here once he and the doctor agreed that he could learn no more without leaving.

Robert felt that that time was coming soon and he would have been an idiot to have compromised himself now. The trouble was he soon saw that he was hurting Isabel now that he got himself in and out of there with as little time or conversation as he could, and she went pale in the face and it was not embarrassment any longer. He had upset her, a little lass with no parents who did not make friends. She was shy and clumsy. She dropped stuff and became confused and then withdrew as much as she could, seeing as how there was nobody else to serve.

He wished she would take on an assistant, it would make life easier for both of them. This didn't seem to occur to her so he actually introduced the subject himself. She seemed taken aback that he spoke other than asking for what he wanted or handing her the list. All he said was, 'Don't you think to have any help now that you're all by yourself?'

She looked alarmed and went even paler so that he thought she was going to faint.

'I don't need any help,' she said brusquely and that was that.

Then he liked her the better for having said it, for looking straight at him, and after that she never blushed when he went in, she said the little she had to say and then turned from him before he left. Robert began to think that he had gone too far and she was offended. He minded that he had hurt her, perhaps he was imagining that she liked him. Maybe she didn't like anybody, maybe she was really unpleasant when it came down to it, maybe she was as uncouth as her father had been. He would not think about her any more, he told himself, and then spent half the afternoon, when he was meant to be reading as he did when he had time, thinking of her and how alone she was and whether he had upset her without real cause.

Mary did not think so very much about her father leaving the mill because he rarely did so, but she was surprised to find him inside the hardware shop. She wished now that she had not thought so much about blessed cake tins. It seemed such a stupid thing to want and yet the children were fond of cakes and the only tin she had had started leaking the mixture through so that it dropped on to the oven floor and burned, smelling awful.

Cake was cheap and so she was now making cakes every day. She liked the miracle of how you beat up eggs and flour and milk and sugar, mixed it all together and put it into the tin and the oven and then the wonderful smell of sweet baking emerged as they rose into peaks like she imagined mountain tops to look, before they were taken from the oven and allowed to cool only until the children could devour them. So she needed a tin and could not let a day go by disappointing the children, so she duly made her way up there.

The shop was deserted except for the lass who ran it and to Mary's surprise there was a large good-looking man in at the back in the shadows and he was talking softly to the lass and making her laugh. It was her father. Mary felt herself go cool but they had heard the shop door and her father altered his tone somewhat and asked in polite tones for whatever tool he needed for whatever job he was busy with.

Mary waited and it was not long before he left the shop without even acknowledging his daughter, as though he couldn't wait to get out. Mary concentrated on her cake tin, not looking at the girl, not sure what she felt, confused probably. She told herself when she was back on the street that she was being stupid and perhaps her father was nice to every woman he met, unless they were nuns. She was quite content at that and sure he could be the polite man he had been when she was small and they were happy.

Seeing him as an attractive man and not just as her father was weird, Mary thought, but then she had always seen him only as her father, first being there and then not being there and how hurt she had been. Looking at him as a person was not very nice somehow because she did not think he was constant, he was like some large will o' the wisp who could not be contained. Or like some enormous butterfly banging on the window pane to be let out, and when the window opened there she stood, watching him leave. The whole thing made Mary feel sick and she did not understand it. She had thought that grown-ups were parents and teachers and even nuns now she had met them, that they were old and handled things.

However, she did not think that her father was interested in this girl. After all he had Fran, and Isabel Norton was plain and sallow faced and skinny, and she had a small whining voice, so Mary went home feeling better and hugging Daisy to her. Her father was a busy man with a large family and a good respectable job. And also she loved him very much and somehow that was the hardest thing of all.

# Twenty

That was her first mistake, Isabel thought, to be nice to the miller, but it was difficult not to be when he was so soft voiced, unlike most of the men who came in and were abrupt and barely spoke and rapped out what they wanted and then hovered impatiently when it took time to find what they needed and then didn't want to pay and were slow in taking money from their pockets or tried to get her to give them credit.

She followed her father's rule on that and for once she thought he had been right. If you couldn't pay for it you didn't walk out of the shop with it, and if you had to order it you had to pay half up front. She had had a few nasty remarks, but it didn't get them anywhere. There was no choice unless they wanted to go to the hardware store in Wolsingham and that was impractical, so she won every time.

She didn't realize until later that she had made a mistake. Her second mistake was that she was so lonely she encouraged the miller to stay when he went in just about closing time. She couldn't help wishing he would be there. She had nothing to look forward to but her room in the back, nobody to talk to, and nowhere that she felt she could go. There was nothing now but her own company and the shop, and she felt sick and cheerless.

When she went into the back room to see if his order had

come he waited patiently for a few minutes and then followed her as far as the door saying that it didn't matter, he could come again.

Isabel told him that she would find it, but in the end she had to admit defeat. She wanted to keep him waiting, she would have done anything so that he did not leave her there by herself, so when the object had not come to light and she had to admit that the order had not arrived he seemed barely perturbed and told her that it didn't matter. She couldn't believe how she was acting. She was usually so efficient and knew exactly where everything was and which order had come in and which had not. She could not understand what she did and said next.

Since the shop was closing she had popped into the kitchen and put the kettle on so now she hesitated slightly and then said, 'I was going to make some tea when I close up and the kettle's boiling. You must have worked so hard today and be thirsty.'

He admitted that he had, so she turned her back on him, her face burning and her feelings down at her stomach where they plunged back and forth like waves on the beach during an October tide, while her hands shook over the kettle and it took her ages to get water from the kettle into the teapot. She was flustered, she couldn't locate the sugar or the milk, but finally she made it, she got the mixture into a cup and saucer, and then urged him to sit down since he towered above her almost as tall as the ceiling. He sat down.

He stayed for about an hour and had two cups of tea but he didn't make polite conversation. He asked her about her parents and how she felt. Nobody had done such a thing and she could not but be grateful. Nobody spoke about those who had died. Nobody thought about her being alone or how afraid or grief-stricken she was, at least about her mother, and it soothed her feelings and brought her comfort just to hear him say her mother's name.

Then she was able to tell him that her mother had been shy and didn't speak to anybody and never went anywhere. She told him how hard it was when she and her mother had been almost on a level and she had begun to forge a feeling of affection with her mother for the first time in years, since they had moved from Durham City, and then she had found her mother dead.

She couldn't believe she could speak so to this man she barely knew, and why was he so understanding? She told him about how good her life had been when she was a little girl and he confided to her that his mother had given him up when he was a very small child because she didn't want a son. Isabel was astonished and horrified that anybody could do such a thing, but then she couldn't imagine having children and it was only when it became a reality that you could know what it involved. She had only just learned what her parents were like when they had died. How on earth could she know what being a parent was like?

'She gave you away?'

'She didn't like boys apparently,' he said, looking down into his by now second time emptied teacup.

'Why not?'

'My father ran away and left her and she couldn't bear the idea of any kind of man in her house, so she gave me to the nearest woman she saw on the street. I never met her, and the woman didn't want me either so I ended up in a place like the foundling school, they told me what had happened and I ran away, it was so bad. And then I got taken in by the couple who ran the mill up in the dale and after that things got better, they treated me like I was theirs.'

The miller fascinated her with his talk and she couldn't wait to see him again. She wanted to go on telling him her thoughts from then onwards, and he came in twice a week since they always had so much to say. After that she could never remember what they talked about, just that she waited for him coming and it was a much better day when he was in it.

He made her smile and then laugh. He made her feel warm and important and that her company was wanted. The days when she didn't see him were endless and she longed for his conversation or even a sight of him on the street. She would go to the door and stand just outside when she had no customers, and her eyes would search for sight of his tall figure with the fire-coloured hair and the sharp green eyes.

She had finally made a friend. It had not occurred to her that when she did it would be a man, a married man who had a family, not a woman of her own age, but then she was not certain she had anything in common with other young women. They rarely came to the shop and all she saw of them was when they were out in the street with their younger siblings or with their parents going to church.

What would it be like to be part of a family who attended some kind of service each Sunday? She thought of Mr Bunting, the Methodist minister, and how kind he had been, but she did not think she could turn up there by herself, she had barely been beyond the doors and had no idea how to go on, but the miller came to her and she was so grateful to him and so proud that somebody wanted to spend time with her.

He encouraged her to tell him more about what her life in Durham City and since these were her best memories she spent a lot of time talking about the city she loved so well and what a good childhood and upbringing she had had. It brought back all the sunshine, all the Christmases when her mother had bought her ribbons and hairslides shaped like bows, and the Easters when she had new clothes for the coming better weather and chocolate eggs from the best sweetshop in the city.

She remembered playing with her friends outside the house, hopscotch on the pavement, and the toffee which she was allowed to buy with her Saturday penny at the shop on the end of the street. His presence and the patient way he spoke to her and seemed interested brought it all back and gladdened her heart.

When her mother had been dead for about six weeks things changed and Isabel did not know that she had been waiting for this. He took her hand. Isabel could not remember being touched before. She liked the pressure, the feel of his fingers. She liked that his hands were so big, and he teased her a bit about what tiny hands she had and how white and fine they were and then he turned over her hand and he caressed the palm with his thumb and then he kissed the inside of her wrist.

After that it seemed a short way for his lips to find hers, and that was when she knew how starved she was. Her body was urgent, she needed holding, she craved his mouth. The more he kissed her, the more he held her, the more she wanted him. He was so big, so capable, so much hers. She had never had anything or anybody for herself, and so they moved forward. All he did was come to visit and kiss her and hold her, until the night several weeks later when he put his hands inside her clothing and after that her body went wild for him.

She wasn't ashamed, it couldn't be wrong, except that she had the idea it was. When he finally divested her of her underwear and did disgusting hurtful things to her she was somewhat surprised and swore never again, but he came back and she did not know how to turn him away. By then she could not stop herself. He knew exactly what he was doing, he had so much confidence and he knew how to make her cry out again and again though he would laugh because of the neighbours and put his hand over her mouth and then they would giggle together.

She had a lover and the autumn seemed so bright, the leaves were like copper and golden coins, even the rain ran silver on the windows while she felt so good. She even thought that she could be happy like this, it was private and she didn't think a little happiness was asking so much. It made her feel so powerful. She felt like a woman for the first time, and it was nothing like she had thought it would be. She had not thought she would ever have any kind of man who would take an interest in her.

She was proud of him. He was so tall and good-looking and so funny and kind and warm and he knew exactly what he was doing so that the pleasure she gained from what she did lifted up her whole life, made her able to endure the rest.

During the day she found a smile on her lips, at night she dreamed of him, and she found that she could work. It was only when the shop closed that she waited for him to come to her. When he did she felt like she had the whole world in her arms. When he did not she was disappointed and it was like blackness had come down and she had begun to cry herself to sleep when she did not see him, and to find life bleak behind the counter in the shop. Nobody was like him, everything which was not about him was boring. She wanted to run to the mill and grab him and hold him. She wanted to ask him to run away with her and leave everything behind and never ever come back to this place she was beginning to loathe.

*

It was during this time that Mary sensed things had altered, and since she thought she had gone through these circumstances before and remembered them well she could not stop herself from watching what her father did. She went to the mill one cold evening when she saw the miller leave, she went and asked Abe about when her father was there and when he was not, but Abe had nothing to say so she watched for when her father left the building and then she followed him.

She went carefully through the main street because the nights were long and the evening sun went down quickly at this time of year. He turned down and into the back street behind the shops and then in the middle of the street he opened a gate and went into a backyard. Mary was almost sure it was the hardware shop, but she couldn't be certain. Having seen him in there she felt she was perhaps judging him unfairly and it was nothing to do with either him or the ugly girl who ran the place, but she couldn't tell because the back of the street seemed to her not to look anything like the front, so she was confused and unsure.

They were almost all shops, a line of them but broken up here and there by the odd house, so she could not tell one way or another, just that he let himself in and the door closed and after that she could see nothing.

She wanted to tell somebody what her fears were, but so far there was nothing to tell. Just because her father was being civil to a young woman did not mean anything, at least she didn't think so. Surely he had more taste and sense than to go after somebody like Isabel Norton.

It couldn't be a public house as she had hoped because although there were several around the town all in among the houses and the shops she didn't think there was one nearby. She walked back home worried that Fran would have missed her and asked questions but she obviously hadn't and didn't notice.

Mary didn't sleep. She saw everybody to bed and the house quieten, and then she lay awake, wondering whether her father had another woman and if he would leave his family as he had done before. However would she manage, burdened with Fran, Daisy and Burt, as well as the others, and if he did leave they would lose the mill and it would be the same thing all over again only worse somehow.

If Fran would just get over herself it would make all the difference. Also Mary worried about the baby. Sometimes the baby was left to scream because Mary had so much to do and Flo was not old enough to take charge of the baby. Mary was terrified that Flo would let Daisy fall and she couldn't manage anything more.

One night she did hear her father come home, but it was almost daylight when he walked softly into the house and up the stairs, which was odd. He had not slept there in days and came back only to change his clothes and wash his body as far as Mary could tell.

There was no conversation between Fran and her father, she doubted they had spoken to one another since the baby had been born. They could not forgive one another, she knew that now. They were so hurt and misguided and stupid.

When Abe and her father went off to work the following morning she persuaded the children out with her and then she led them up the main street and tried to determine whether he had gone into the hardware store the previous evening. She couldn't be sure, it wasn't easy. The front street to her looked nothing like the back street, and both men and women ran the shops, so perhaps her father wasn't doing something wrong.

She longed to have some kind of basis on which to confirm this so that she could believe it. Maybe it was cards or billiards or darts, maybe it was a pub that she had missed, but there had been no noise and nobody going in or out, and anyroad folk usually went into the pub by the front door.

She could see no pub anywhere near. The children grew restless as she paused and went forward and then back up and down the street. There was definitely no pub close by, she even checked the other side, which was ludicrous, she knew. Maybe it was just that he had made friends and was so fed up with his family that he longed to spend time somewhere else. She wouldn't have blamed him, she often felt the same herself had she been able and had somewhere to go.

There were lots of shops, including a drapers and a shoe shop. The drapers was run by a very old lady and the shoe shop was where the cobbler lived and he looked very old to her too. There was also a hat shop and the woman in there looked a hundred, Mary thought, and the hats looked awful, so dark, so dingy. They were grey and black and navy and brown, the kind of thing women would wear to go to church in, nothing colourful, nothing which might bring any joy or lightness to the wearer's day.

The only place she felt differently about was the hardware shop, and she didn't know whether her suspicions were getting the better of her because she was so worried or nervous that she could be right. She didn't want to be right, she couldn't bear the idea. She thought of her father in there with Isabel Norton. She liked the shop. There was all sorts of stuff inside: hammers and nails, but also things people bought for their kitchens, such as pans and pots and cutlery. As somebody came out she remembered that it was not that long since Isabel's parents had both died and how hard that must have been for her.

Mary was convinced by this time that something was going on and she went inside, trying to ask for something which she didn't think they would have, though the children made it impossible to buy anything, they were so restless and wanted to run about.

Isabel Norton did not look anything like a young woman who would attract a man like her father. She couldn't remember how good-looking her mother had been, but Fran was stunningly beautiful and this girl was just a wisp of humanity, and Mary could not reconcile the two.

She looked pale and worn and almost fragile in her grief and loss and loneliness. Her dark hair was tied back in a scraggy way. She wore an old dress, and there were marks under her eyes, making her sallow skin look even worse. She had a harsh voice, she was attending to a customer and ignored Mary, only saying when the customer left, 'Can I help?'

She was smiling just a little as though not used to children. She was not much older than Abe, Mary thought.

'No, no, nothing,' Mary said hastily and when Mary looked back she felt much better. The girl had a long sharp nose and a narrow forehead and a short neck. She was not exactly ugly, she was just plain. Mary was so pleased.

Her father came home in the evenings for the next week and the time he did go out after that she followed him to the pub and, while resenting that he could spend money on beer but would not give her enough for their needs, she was relieved that that was all he was doing. Mary slept.

# Twenty-one

And then one day Robert Slater came into the shop and Isabel's eyes were opened. She had thought she no longer cared about him and she saw that it wasn't so. She was taken aback and suddenly realized with a horrible sick feeling that what she did with the miller was not love, whatever else it was. It was need and loneliness and desperation, but she loved Robert Slater. She felt that she had always loved him and she was aghast, ashamed, horrified not only that she had done what she had done with another man but that she could feel so differently and yet so much the same about a man of her own age. She did not know what it was about Robert that made him different, but she saw that these feelings differed very much from the way that she felt about the miller.

After he left the shop Isabel shut up the place and went to bed and howled. What had she done?

Robert was not hers. It was rumoured that he was going to marry Polly Swift, she was sure she had heard this from women talking on the pavement outside the shop. Isabel was taken aback at this revelation. It was like the shutters lifted from her eyes. She was of an age when young women married and so she needed a partner, and biology had decreed that when you needed something so badly you would do almost anything you could to make it happen.

She had made it happen, and with a man she did not love. She wanted Robert though. Her face grew hot at how much she wanted him. She did not know what to do. Robert Slater did not even see her any more as a person she felt sure, there was no chance she would ever have him to herself. There was not much chance she would have the miller for herself and she could think now of his wife and children.

She remembered Mary and the little ones at the shop. She remembered how Mary looked suspiciously at her as though she thought something might be going on. She couldn't know that, she was just a child, but then Isabel thought she had been nothing much more than a child before her parents died and she was certainly not one now.

Perhaps the circumstances rather than the years had done their work on Mary too. And then the guilt set in. She thought of the miller's wife and how she had not long since had a child, and she was so ashamed of herself that she wished she could die, that she wished she had never seen the miller, that she could not believe she had acted in such a selfish and stupid way, and it was too late now.

It was Robert coming into the shop that altered things for Isabel, but she had to admit to herself that she was already wavering. Her conscience was getting to her and telling her that she was doing the wrong thing. In vain did she attempt to tell herself that it was understandable she was not getting things right, her parents had died one after the other and she told her-self that she would have gone nowhere near the miller had her mother still been alive.

She had enjoyed those few weeks before her mother had gone. Isabel had not been lonely then. She had not known how cruel loneliness was, and that silence had its own sound and how much she hated it. She didn't know what to do, she had no one to go to and she had to mind the shop. Sometimes she thought that she might sell up and leave, but then wherever would she go? This was the only safety she had left, but then it had dealt with her badly, the loneliness and the grief together brought the miller to her and her to him. She craved kisses, her body was young and needed holding and although each morning she was ashamed of herself each evening she waited for him to come to her.

The evenings were wasted without him, she had nothing but the fire and the silence before she went to bed. She would lie there and imagine him with her, how they could be together, how he would give her somewhere to go. He did sometimes talk of his life up in the dale and how pretty the villages were and how they could have a cottage together and a garden full of flowers by a slow moving stream. She longed for those times, but she was also aware that he was married with a responsible job and several children.

Just when she thought things could not change, Robert came to the shop again and she so much wished he had not. She had taken the miller because she had no choice, and now she saw how foolish she had been.


Robert's father had not completely given up on him and when he needed anything would ask Robert to go. Robert understood that it was the only real connection he had with his father because he almost lived at the hospital and the requests gave his father an excuse to see him, to spend a little time and have a small conversation, so he tried not to begrudge his father the few minutes, which didn't happen very often. He knew that his father, despite saying nothing, was proud of him and of what he was doing and that just the sight of him pleased his father, so he let it go on.

That particular day he was almost late, Isabel was about to close the shop, and then she smiled and let him in. That was when he remembered that he had heard rumours about her, that she had a man, that she was seeing someone. The talk was all over the village. If it was true then she didn't look happy about it and he could see straight away that only loneliness would drive her forward. She was just a slip of a thing, small and rather like a frightened animal.

Although she was polite there was a look in her eyes that he had seen in rabbits and other small animals when they were in pain and fear and had no hope. He could hardly bear it and kept up chat such as he never did, while Isabel hunted for whatever stupid thing his father had sent him here for.

He wished to be away, he could do without that look. She got on a stepladder and then stumbled, the stepladder rocked a little and gave. She ended up on the floor. Robert got down to her. He did not believe the rumours, she was lost and alone and scared.

'Are you hurt?' he asked her.

She disclaimed and laughed just a little in embarrassment.

'No, of course not. Just a bit tired I think. It's been a long day.'

She scrambled up even before he did and whisked herself away in search once again of the stupid tool which she so obviously didn't have.

'I'll order one,' she offered, going to the back of the shop and hiding behind a notebook in which she wrote her orders. Then she swayed.

'You are hurt.'

'No, no,' she disclaimed, going backwards and therefore banging into the wall. 'I haven't eaten all day.'

'Let me get you something.'

'No, really, I will be fine.'

He hesitated.

'Please don't stay,' she said, and her voice was so low and her eyes were so pleading that he couldn't have moved had somebody been dragging at both his arms. What was it about her? He didn't know. And that was when he kissed her.

He wanted to protect her, he wanted to own her, he couldn't stop the feelings or his actions. He hadn't known he was going to kiss her, but somehow she was all vulnerability and hurt. At first she hesitated, pushed him away, but very gently. It was a momentary thing and then she found her voice under his mouth and her lips parted and her body yielded.

Robert didn't think, couldn't think of anything but how he felt and how she was so close to him. Afterwards he called himself every name he could think of, but now he could not even remember his own name. His world was small and getting smaller every second as he got hold of her.

The kitchen door was open and in it there was a settee and there he drew her down and for the first time in his life knew what a woman really felt like and how it made him feel, and it was exquisite. Her body was so smooth under his hands and he had not known that women also took pleasure in such things. He thought it was when they had children that they so liked, that the children were the most important thing about this, but it wasn't true.

It was only when it was over and the room came back and the fire was low and her body was no longer part of his that he saw what he had done, that he remembered who he was and who she was and that this was not what he really wanted. He had promised himself that no woman would trap him and now he was falling into that trap, and he had to get away.

He fastened his clothes and got out of the shop as fast as he dared say he had ever got out of anywhere in his life, and stood there panting for seconds, and then he got away. He didn't run, it would have looked conspicuous, though there were few people about, it being teatime, and it was dark, the cold night was closing around the little village. It felt so strange, so alien. Usually he thought the cold nights were like a hug and in some ways he liked them best, but everything had altered and once altered like that there was no going back.

He didn't want to go home. His father would understand that the item he had wanted which even now Robert couldn't bring to mind was not in the shop. Robert went down the hill as fast as he could considering that he didn't run, and then he tried to shut himself into his little room next to Lydia's, but it was not to be.

The head nurse banged on the door and called his name and he had to gather his wits as best he might and carry on. There had been a fight, such things were uncommon in the village but sometimes they happened, and one man had been hurt with a knife so Robert had to go and assist Lydia because at this time of the day Mr Gray had gone back to Wolsingham. Robert could no longer think of what he had done and he was glad not to be able to dwell on it.

He was so tired when he went to bed that all he did was blame Isabel for being a loose whore because had he let himself be blamed he would not have slept, and sleep was important now, it was the most important thing of all.

He also remembered what people were saying. Could it be true? Did Isabel really do such things?

*

Mary had no idea when it occurred to her that she was sure her father was carrying on with Isabel Norton. She didn't even know why she knew it, she just did. It came to her that he looked different, that in some ways the atmosphere in the house had eased and that meant he was in a good humour again. He was never in a good humour now and so when he smiled over his dinner and left more money on the mantelpiece Mary took it as a bad sign. She had learned to read them and in particular him, by now. She earnestly wished that she had not been able to do so.

She just wished she had somebody to talk to, some person who was on her side. She didn't want to take her problems to the nuns, she didn't want them in her way, she didn't even want them to know, she felt as though the shame would fall on the whole family. She had the feeling that she and Fran between them should have been clever enough to stop him from going to somebody new, but she knew also that he was always – and perhaps even more now after Daisy's birth – obsessed with the idea of having a son. The nuns could not know that he had no son.

Mary spent many hours worrying about it, hours that she did not have. She was so tired when she went to bed that she longed for sleep, but often the night held so many terrors of the future that she could not rest. Whatever would they do when her father got Isabel Norton pregnant and there was yet another child, and what if he went on like that and never had a son? Her mind boggled. Did he not think that he had bedded two women and neither of them had had his son, for they'd had their sons with other men, and it could be his fault? No of course not, it could not be anything to do with him.

She couldn't even leave the children long enough to go to Isabel and try to talk to her, there was so much to do and as they got older they took up more and more time and Daisy had taken to crying each time she was put down. Whatever was Mary to do? In the end she waited until Abe came in from the mill and, urging him to keep the children from the range, she ran after her father, baby on hip as he made his way from the mill.

'Father!' she shouted. When she had shouted it for the second time he stopped.

'What is it then?' he said, obviously keen to get away.

'Don't go.'

His eyes gave him away as he lied, they wavered.

'I'm only going—'

'No, you aren't. I know where you're going and no good will come of it. Haven't we got enough to worry about? Please don't.'

He looked impatiently at her and then at the road before him.

'You don't understand, you're just a bairn.'

'While you are behaving like a daft lad.'

'Don't say things like that to me, Mary.'

'It's true. You go around like somebody of seventeen who cannot resist the first lass who looks at him. Don't do it. Things are so hard at home.'

'It isn't like that,' he managed, and his voice shook a little and he lowered his eyes.

'You have a wife and half a dozen children.'

'They aren't mine.' He looked confused, almost mad, and nothing like her father had been.

'I am.'

'Not Abe and not the lad.'

Mary was surprised and rather pleased when he acknowledged the truth. 'You don't like that lad. Would you like him better if he was yours? How could you not like him when he's the loveliest little soul in creation? How can you not?'

'He isn't mine.'

'And you think Isabel Norton will give you a son?' He looked taken aback. 'She won't. You can't have a son.'

He glared at her, and Mary took a step back.

'Don't you say things like that to me.'

'Two women and no son? Does it not seem to you that you can only have daughters?'

He stopped glaring at her, he stood his ground for a few moments, and then he turned and strode away. Mary, defeated, adjusted Daisy on her hip as the child, sensing the dispute and hearing the raised voices, began to cry and then to scream. Mary saw nothing of him for the rest of the day.

The following day he was there at the mill as usual and came in for his meals. He was silent and did not raise his eyes. Mary waited on him and the others and worked, but she said nothing. She could not manage cheerful as she usually did.

He did come to her, awkwardly and with something of the boy about him, when she was as by herself as she could be, hanging out the clothes, for it was a fine almost spring morning, cold but bright.

'I'm sorry, Mary, I know how you feel and I do even sort of understand, but I'm your father and I am doing my best, no matter how it looks to you. You have no right to say such things to me when there's nothing else, nothing more that I feel I can do.'

Mary said nothing, she ignored him. What was the point? He would not listen and she would not excuse him. Having done what he thought was his best, Mary saw, he went off back to the mill.

That day when the shop was about to close she took the children with her and then she said to Isabel when time told her she was about to shut the shop, 'I have something to say to you.'

'What, me?'

'Yes, you. You know who I am, don't you?'

'I can't say I do.'

'I am Mary Barnfather and you have got to leave my dad alone.'

Isabel stared at her. Then at the children, but they weren't taking any notice. They were enjoying looking around at the shop, and Flo was running about and was soon joined by the other two who thought it a great game.

'Here, they can't do that,' Isabel complained.

'Can't they? If you don't leave my dad alone I'll bring them here every day until they wreck your shop.'

Isabel eyed them and then said uncertainly, 'You're just a little kid.'

'Watch me,' Mary said, and then, despite having Daisy on her, she went down a whole line of pans and made sure they hit the floor hard, and then she threw everything she could find, a box of nails, a box of screws, a whole load of crockery and cutlery on to the floor. Some of the plates seemed to spin before they landed, and after they smashed Mary stood over them. By then the children had stopped what they were doing and watched her, aghast, and Daisy, disconcerted, had begun crying in a low scared way with her fingers up to her mouth.

'You leave my dad alone,' Mary said, and then she stamped out and the children ran after her.

Robert discovered who the man was that Isabel had taken to her before him and he was horrified. His dad had said so to him, had told him that people in the village were worried, and Mr Gilbraith wondered what he could do now that the miller was behaving so badly once again. Robert called himself a fool for caring about her and he felt justified in not wanting her, in not going back to her. She had played him for an idiot and did not really care. Anybody would do for her, and she was sleeping with a married man, a man who many people respected. What on earth did she think she was doing? He would never see her again.

The next time the miller came to Isabel's back door he found it bolted. He would not dare to hammer too loudly, she knew. It would alert the neighbours on both sides and people would be in the back eating their tea at that hour. He went again later, but she had gone to bed. No light burned upstairs or down and there was nothing else to do but go home.

She did the same thing the following day and the day after that and in the end just as she was about to shut up shop the next day he pushed past her and slammed the shop door behind him.

That was when Isabel saw that he had played her, used her against his own disappointments, his letdowns. She saw him differently now, but she also saw that he cared for her in his own way, and she could see the sorrow in his face and the need. He had been married before when she had let him have her body, her truthful self said, and she resented him and herself. He could not therefore marry her had she ever wanted such a thing, but she saw now that she didn't. She loved Robert Slater.

She needed to get rid of him so that somehow she could make Robert Slater love her in return. She needed him as she had never needed anybody in her life. In her dreams now she saw them married and living above the shop, or perhaps if he did well she could sell up and he could buy her a beautiful house, perhaps in the dale by the river, and she would become a lady.

For the first time now she was afraid. The miller was looking almost kindly at her, as though he did not understand.

'Are you poorly?' He asked her so tenderly and she wished he wouldn't.

'I just can't see you any more like this.'

'Like what?'

'Well, you know. I can't. You are married, you have lots of children.'

He smiled, rather like a boy who was saying he had not kicked his ball through a broken window.

'They aren't all mine,' he said, 'my wives were engaged with other men before me. And besides, you knew that when I first started coming here, surely.'

'I didn't understand.' She wanted to excuse herself by saying that she was lonely and bereft and grieving, but it sounded so lame, so pathetic.

'Have things changed?' He still spoke kindly, and she thought he was not a bad man, he was just weak.

'I have changed.'

'Indeed you have, you have grown up. I love you so very much Isabel, you are everything I always wanted.'

Isabel shook her head.

'No,' she said. 'You must go away and not come any more.'

'But what would I do without you?' He looked so lovingly at her, and she could swear his eyes filled with tears. 'I've never felt like this about anybody. You mean the whole world to me.'

Isabel shook her head. She could not let him near now or she would never get rid of him. She didn't love him. She had never loved him. She had wanted somebody near, somebody to assuage the terrible loneliness, and that was all. She had somehow felt sure of him, secure when he was there, and she could see that it wouldn't do.

'You must go. You must not do this.'

'You have somebody else?'

'No.' It was true, of course she had not, and was able to shake her head. She didn't think Robert Slater had ever thought about her but that one time, that one impulse which had led to such a rash act. She had hoped and hoped that he would come back but he didn't.

Why would he? He was clever, good-looking, important. He would never think of her again. She felt sorry for herself. Perhaps the miller was the best she could do. But she did not want him. This strange friendship would not do, she knew it. She could not hold him, nor did she want to.

'And is that to be it?' he said. 'Just like that, I can't come any more? You can't do that to me, Isabel, I need you. You can't stop me.'

This was a new way of thinking about things but Isabel caught on straight away. He was threatening her even though his voice was cloaked in gentleness, and she thought it was just stupid.

'Oh yes, I can,' she said. 'If you won't leave me alone I will tell Mr Gilbraith that you molested me.'

The good and tender look disappeared and so did the threat. He gazed at her in disbelief.

'That would be a horrible thing to say. I've never done such a thing in my life.'

'I know that, but if I had to I would do it. Then what do you think would happen to you?'

She knew that this was not the right thing to do but he was

not behaving the way that she wanted him to. She had to get rid of him any way that she could.

'Isabel, you can't do that to me. All I think about is you. I long for you all day and I can't sleep at night. Please don't send me away. I will give up everything for you.'

'That's ridiculous. You have children and a wife and a new baby.'

He shook his head.

'It's not mine,' he said, 'I never wanted it.'

Isabel stared.

'Not yours?'

'It isn't my son, it isn't mine.'

Isabel had no idea what gender the child was nor did she think about it. All she knew was that she had to make him leave, one way or another, but he was still leaning hard against the shop doorway.

'You must go. If you don't I will scream and scream until the neighbours hear me.'

So he went, without a word or further protest. She was so relieved to get rid of him that she didn't think any further, she just went to bed, worn out with all the changes, exhausted with her new life and its mistakes.

# Twenty-two

There was talk in the village about Robert and Lydia. Lydia was half expecting it. The nights were shortening, and folk stayed up later and sat outside their houses so people noticed more than they would have done if it had been dark and cold. She and Robert spent so much time together that people began to think that something was going on between them. They had particularly at that time a lot of night-time calls and some lasted well into the morning. Being seen riding back in the village streets with Robert did not go unnoticed and Lydia was too sensitive not to see it and not to care. She was aghast, but when she looked carefully at Robert she also could see that he had changed. She didn't understand why, but it was not helping. She didn't think anything had changed between them but other people seemed to think that he cared about her as a man cared about a woman. She knew that it wasn't true but there was something happening with him which made folk suspicious.

She wanted to talk to him but every time she tried there was a patient to see to or a discussion which was much more important so it was a long time before she managed to say something and even then she hesitated to try and find the right words and decided to be brisk and light.

'Is there something the matter with you?' she asked when they were in the pharmacy together one afternoon, taking advantage of the fact that Mr Gray was not about to hear her.

He jumped in surprise.

'With me? Course not.'

He spoke too quickly and Lydia was now seriously concerned.

'It's not me, is it?' she said.

He looked blankly at her.

'Folk will talk you know, if you go around looking that gormless,' she said, unwilling to explain, but she could see that he did not understand what she meant. She thought a little humour might help. It didn't.

He looked away.

'It's not you,' he managed finally, and Lydia was somewhat reassured by the sound of his voice, so definite.

'What is it then?'

'Things just alter that's all,' he said.

'What things?'

He didn't answer and at that moment the doctor came in so she could say no more. It didn't make her happy but they went on as usual, they had no choice, and as the talk grew the local women would cross the street when they saw her and the men looked at her as though she had done something wrong, something that a daft village lass would do. What did they call it? Being no better than you were. It was a stupid idea, but it made Lydia cringe and turned her cheeks to crimson and to a lot of people it showed that she was guilty of lusting after the young man she was working with and that he had taken her to him despite the fact that she was a nun or perhaps even because of it.

She tried to carry on as usual but the thing came to a head when she was called to the Slater household. She went by herself and was glad of it until she got there and encountered Mrs Slater's dark and wrathful face.

'You've got my Robert in your clutches, my girl.' Mrs Slater, incensed about what was happening, no longer cared that Lydia was a nun, Lydia could see. They were standing in Mrs Slater's kitchen, Lydia having been called for what she had assumed was an important clinical matter.

Lydia stared. It took her several seconds to work out what Mrs Slater was talking about and then when she understood she felt guilty even though she had done nothing wrong. Trust his mother to put it into words.

Lydia was so angry that she couldn't speak for a few moments and even then she tried to say nothing, but she found her voice and it would not be silenced. She had stood enough during the past days. She had done nothing wrong and she would endure it no longer.

'Have you called me here for such a thing as this, when I have patients to see to?'

'When you are behaving wickedly—'

'Wickedly? I have been working for my patients and you have no reason to criticize what I do or how I do it. Your son is helping me to look after people and there is no other reason for us to be together. I am married to God and your son is not married to me nor will he ever be. Now, perhaps you should respect my calling and my way of living and leave me alone.'

'Have you any idea what folk are saying about my Robert?' Mrs Slater said. 'The lads are sniggering and no decent lass will take him now.'

Lydia wanted to retort that Robert was so clever that he would not be there much longer and that she was glad he could get to Edinburgh.

'And who are you to endanger my Robert's reputation in that way? Who do you think you are? Well, you think on this, my girl. Our Robert is going nowhere with you any more. I'm going to speak to Mr Gilbraith about your ideas and your behaviour, and if you think you can cast off that stupid outfit you wear and get our Robert to marry you you can think again because it isn't going to happen.'

Lydia had gone there to see Hannah because supposedly the girl wasn't well, but she could see now that she had been duped and that Mrs Slater had wanted to give her what the local women called a piece of her mind.

Lydia had to stop herself from giving Mrs Slater a bigger piece of her own mind, but Hannah came into the kitchen in the middle of the row and told her mother not to say such things, that it wasn't right and wasn't true and how on earth did she think folk would manage if it wasn't for the work that their Robert and Sister Lydia were doing.

'How can you say such a thing to her?' Hannah admonished her mother, 'After all she's done for the people here, after all the work and effort, you cannot believe such things. It's nonsense.'

'Don't tell me what I say is nonsense,' her mother shouted, and Hannah stood back and all she said then was, 'I'll see you out, Sister Lydia. My mother got you here under false pretences and considering how very busy you are she ought to be ashamed of herself.'

Lydia went and when they were outside Hannah said to her, 'I do so want to become a nun.'

This was not news to Lydia or to the others, Maddy was just waiting for Hannah to say the word before Hannah went to the mother house in Newcastle, but in a way Lydia could not help feeling sorry for Hannah's mother. She was to lose her children, one to religion, one to medicine, her two daughters had got married, and newly married women did not want their mother unless there was a problem, which so far there had not been.

She tried not to wish it on them so that Mrs Slater would become once again important. Lydia could see that soon she would have nobody left but Jimmy, and a lad like that would not be waiting around to grow much bigger before he threw out both arms towards freedom away from his home and parents. Lydia felt sorry for Mrs Slater though Mrs Slater would not have appreciated the sentiment had she known it.

There was a disaster up the dale in a limestone quarry at that time so that Mr Gray was absent for many days and just as it is an ill wind that blows nobody any good as they say, Lydia benefited from it. Luckily nobody was killed, but there were a great many injuries at the quarry in Stanhope and Mr Gray was absorbed with it so people could see nobody else but Lydia.

Having had an empty surgery, within a few days she had a lot of folk needing help. Nobody said anything, though they hesitated, but those who were sufficiently ill were in no position to object to her and she did the best that she could. They soon stopped looking askance at her and it was nearly always women, when their babies and children were ill.

Best and worst of all was Mrs Slater, whose youngest child, Jimmy who had caused no end of problems, came in with a bad leg. He had just tripped and fallen, but Lydia had to determine whether it was broken. She ordered his mother outside while she did it and Mrs Slater, stiff faced but obedient, went.

Lydia couldn't decide whether this was the moment to ask Robert to come in and watch how she did it since she was busy teaching him, as the doctor had taught her how to do such things, and so now while his mother was standing outside she sent for him and he came wordlessly into the room, having had to pass his mother sitting outside the door. He was very pale when he came in and had nothing to say, but Lydia felt it had been the right thing to do.

And she thought it very good that she should teach him about limbs by having him work on his young brother. She was sure he would not knowingly hurt Jimmy and he was very deft in everything he did, but even so while she was instructing and Robert was helping to ascertain that the leg was broken Jimmy cried quite a bit and didn't look at anybody.

Lydia hoped his mother could hear the soft reassuring words that Robert said to his brother while this was going on, and when it was all over and Jimmy was still in a lot of pain he took the boy to his shoulder and hugged him. Lydia felt that such things did not often happen in the Slater household, she doubted that Jimmy had been cuddled like that for years and was even more sure when Jimmy clung as if he would never let his brother go. It had already formed a bond between them, Lydia felt sure.

Also, Mr Slater, having no doubt heard that his child was hurt was waiting just outside with Mrs Slater, and while Mrs Slater was not crying though she had her face turned away, Mr Slater thanked Lydia profusely for her deft work and she said coolly, 'It was Robert who did most of it. He excels at such things and you should therefore thank him and not me. Mr Gray could not do without him, none of us could.'

Mr Slater wrung his elder son's hand and then carried his younger son off towards his home. Lydia was rather pleased with her afternoon's work.

It was then that Lydia began to let Robert sit in on all her sessions with the patients and sometimes they were keen to see him because he was one of them. Men would come to him when they would not come to her, and she often saw Robert stopped in the street by various men because they were too shy to come to the surgery or the hospital, and he encouraged them or sometimes even went out by himself to see them. He would report back to Lydia and then take medicine to the house on her advice. Lydia was glad about what she had done, it made life easier both for her and for Mr Gray.

Neither of them talked any more about Robert leaving as he became further and further absorbed into the practice, and Mr Gray did not have time to be there at the little village. If Robert had wanted to leave, she thought, he just had to say so and he could be helped.

Lydia, without asking anybody, dropped the doctor a note, and then with Mr Gilbraith's blessing, the doctor doubled Robert's wages. He deserved it for what he did, knowing that he had their lives in his hands when they were ill. Robert went everywhere with her and was now officially doctor's assistant, and sometimes when she was dealing with women's problems and even at births she would let him stay as long as the woman in question did not mind.

He began to shine at women's problems. Lydia would never have thought it, and far from the women being embarrassed, they had never come across a woman doctor so because he was a man and spoke gently to put them at their ease he became invaluable so that Lydia, far from wishing Robert would leave, became glad that he was still there. His voice was soft and appealing and now had a touch of authority about it which women understood and trusted. He was the man in charge, she thought with a slight smile, and to them it made all the difference.

Lydia taught him everything she knew about women and their physical forms, the problems in their lives, about childbirth and menstruation, how before and after birth sometimes their mental condition was low, and how difficult it was raising children. He seemed to understand these things without effort, though how she had no idea, but then men had been doctors for hundreds of generations so perhaps it was some kind of given in certain cases or was it just that they had opportunity? Whatever, the women talked to him as they did not talk to her and she was glad of it.

He was no longer just a young man to them, they called him Mr Slater and took him seriously, whereupon he learned to take them seriously, and their conditions. He and Lydia would sit over the fire talking about the kind of painkillers women might be given so that birth and periods were easier.

The Old Testament might talk of women bringing forth their children in pain, but Lydia knew that the writers of this were men and also that it was a stupid idea that pain improved people's souls since it was only women involved and men could know nothing of such things.

Lydia also wanted women to be able to talk about their problems rather than hiding them, so that they might cooperate amongst themselves and lend aid and an ear where necessary, especially when they bled. It shouldn't have to be a secret. And she wanted them educated in such matters so that they understood what was happening to their bodies, but it would take some doing to get that far, she knew.

Secrecy pulled women down, it meant they had a harder time looking after their families, and because there was nothing to stop them giving birth each year it killed them. Their husbands could marry again, well, wonderful, Lydia thought, but she was not having women on her watch being in pain, and if she could help them avoid having more children than they could feed and bring up without poverty or death, then she would.

The doctor was teaching Lydia and Robert about ether and

chloroform, but they had to be administered with care and Lydia soon realized that Robert had better instincts and was lighter handed than she was.

He could even relieve pain by getting pregnant women to breathe differently, teach them when to breathe and when not to and when to push, and they believed in what he told them, but he soon learned to give them something to help when things got difficult.

It was a pact between the two of them that nobody should endure more than she could bear, that the pain should be as little as possible so that the woman giving birth could see to her family and also do other things with her life were these offered, and where they were not offered she might seek them out.

Robert saw that everybody was unique, that each birth was different, and yet they had enough in common so that he soon recognized what should be done and what should not. When he had to turn a child he did it more easily than she had done even though he was much bigger. He had fine hands, that was what Mr Gray said, the fingers were long and slender and the day that he said it was Robert's proudest day.

Instead of puffing up like a turkey cock he then worked harder so that he became indispensable to both of them and to a great many of the people in the village. Mr Gray also took Robert with him when there had been an accident of any kind because he was a great help just by talking and being reassuring and telling everybody concerned that it would be all right, even when they knew it wouldn't be. And he was young and strong.

Best of all, so Robert said to Lydia, he was learning a great deal about bones, the structure and how they broke, how they could be mended, and when to make people walk and when to ask folk to rest, and he was as excited as she was about all possible aspects of medicine, it filled their whole lives.

# Twenty-three

It seemed strange and rather pleasing to Mary that summer that her father stopped going out. He no longer went either to see Isabel or to the pub, and she was so grateful for this happening and tried to forgive him his bad temper, but it was difficult to deal with and she knew why. He was not convinced that he could have a son without a new woman, without Isabel Norton.

Mary ignored him as best she might and the other children took their lead from her. Abe, still working in the mill with his father, was silent. Her father came to bed where Fran lay, but Mary made sure that Daisy stayed with her. She did not trust her father with the child because she felt he was in a much worse place than ever before.

She had no doubt that when she was small and her father still thought he could have a male child he did love his little girl. That time had gone. It was as though he noticed nobody. Fran said nothing, but Mary could see how disillusioned her stepmother was. She grew thin and wouldn't eat and didn't even ask to hold the baby.

Mary therefore did everything with help from Sister Abigail when Abigail could spare the time, and sometimes other women were sent from the convent to assist but she knew that there was a lot of work for them to do everywhere they went in the village.

Also Mr Gilbraith would not have people called servants, everybody was well paid and nobody was coerced into anything. They had to be willing, so between his ideas and those of the sisters everybody found something to do which they liked, at least as far as could be managed, Sister Abigail told her.

Mary had seen how Robert Slater's sisters married and came to live nearby. They would nod and say good morning but after the first flush of being married the two sisters became friends with Fran, and Mary was so glad of it. They were older than she was and rather made the best of it, bringing cake and talking about their husbands and their lives, but best of all they would come in and hold Daisy and tell Fran what a wonderful daughter she had and there was envy in their tones. Burt of course was always there and they loved Burt too and sometimes took him to stay with them for full afternoons which was easier on Mary's part.

They were very sociable women and Mary was pleased because it was almost as though they had become attached to the mill house. Her father of course did not speak to them, neither as far as Mary could tell, did he speak to their husbands, but since the men were nearly always out at work and the miller was almost always in his mill it did not make a lot of difference.

Also Mrs Slater came to visit almost every day. On Sundays she brought with her her youngest child, Jimmy, and Mary liked Jimmy. He was the only boy she had ever met who enjoyed books, and soon they were reading the same books and talking about them so that Jimmy would often come to the mill when his mother was not there. She was forever taking him home as though he was some precious object she could not let out of her sight, but Mary's life was much better because of the Slater family.

Jimmy was not interested in the mill, and she was also glad of that. She did not trust her father's temper, and although Jimmy and his sisters were often in the mill house, the miller would send to have his meals at the mill so there was no conflict as he was not around to complain.

Fran began to bloom. Both sisters were wonderful bakers and they were always making cakes and bringing them for Fran and the children, so almost every day there was coffee cake or chocolate cake, or Victoria sponge, and the sisters made bread at least twice a week and since they were making it, they said, almost as one, that it was too good not to let everybody have some, so Fran and the children gorged themselves on good bread, butter, and various kinds of jam which Mrs Slater had taught her daughters to make.

Mrs Slater was not the kind of woman who said much, but Mary could see that she had brought up her daughters to be useful. They could sew, their houses were immaculate, and Mary could often smell dinner for when their men came home.

They also confided in Fran, and Mary heard when she was moving with Daisy on her hip from room to room that they were both desperate to have their first child, and each month their mother had taken to enquiring and they felt as though they were not really married and settled until there were babies, but the weeks and months went by and nothing happened.

Mary could not help being secretly rather pleased at this since she liked having all the attention and felt sure that when they had babies they would be too busy to come to the mill, but thankfully nothing happened and life at the mill settled down a lot and she became happier.

Also there came a time that summer when Fran picked up Daisy from the rug on which Mary had left her while she mended clothes. Mary was stunned since it was the first time Fran had seemed to want anything much to do with the child.

The lads were always tearing their clothing and also Sister

Abigail was showing her how to make dresses for the girls and even shirts for her dad, and she was really pleased with how much more successful were her efforts at what had seemed incomprehensible just a few weeks ago.

Sister Abigail was really good at finding material cheaply on Wolsingham market and she would bring this back so that she and Mary could fit out the little girls to their satisfaction, and Mary also began to make pretty frocks for Fran who had never had such a thing, but she was so bonny that blue made her look even more beautiful. Not that the miller noticed. Mary doubted he noticed anything these days since he absented himself more and more from everyone around him.

Mary did not want Daisy anywhere near needles of any kind so she put Daisy down when she was sewing, but she was astonished when Fran came into the sitting room where Daisy was lying in a pool of afternoon sunshine on the hearthrug staring at and murmuring sweet nothings to her own fingers, which obviously fascinated her. Fran stole softly into the room, hesitating at first, and then she went over and took the child into her arms.

Mary prayed that Daisy would not object. She was used to nobody touching her beyond Mary but the little girl looked straight into her mother's face and smiled. It could not have been better. Then she put one fist up to her mother's face and suddenly the tears slid from Fran's eyes so that Mary wanted to get up and help but she made herself sit still. Fran was seeing her child as if for the first time, and to the baby she smelled good.

Mary was convinced that animals and small children distinguished different people by what they smelled like, and Daisy could smell Mother on this woman. Fran took the child to her shoulder and began to sing to her and Mary thought that her heart would burst with joy.

# Twenty-four

It was late summer when Isabel went to the surgery complaining of feeling ill and of her stomach being bloated.

'You're having a baby, Miss Norton, I would say,' Lydia said, having got Isabel to lie on a table to examine her. Lydia was aghast but had long since learned to hide her feelings and kept her face impassive. Unmarried mothers were practically unheard of here, but also Isabel was young and orphaned and was having such a tough time getting by that she had quite obviously done something stupid and once people found out it would go hard with her. Lydia had heard the rumours which had lately died down about Isabel and the miller. Being a subject of much talk herself she was sensitive to such issues.

Isabel gazed at her. Her faced was so white that Lydia worried she would faint. She was horrified. In such a small place as this Isabel had to marry.

'But I can't be.'

'I'm afraid you are. I would say that you were well along the way, so not much time before the baby arrives. Did you not notice the difference?'

Isabel shook her head. Lydia barely knew what to say.

'Are you about to get married?'

Isabel gazed at her and said nothing.

'I don't mean to pry, Isabel, but you cannot have a baby in a place like this unless there is a father. Is he in a position to marry you?'

'No.'

'Then how will you manage? Can you talk to him, or can I?'

'He's – he's already married.' Isabel's voice shook.

'You're going to need help and support. Do you have friends or family who would look after you?'

'Nobody.' Isabel's voice had almost disappeared. Lydia was not surprised. What a shock for the girl, and such a lot of problems to come. There was no point in telling Isabel she must rest, she lived alone and had the shop to look after, but she was obviously finding things hard already, Lydia could tell by how tired and wan she looked.

'Would you like me to try and help?'

'I don't want any help.'

'You will nearer the time,' Lydia said. 'Have a think about it and if you like I will find someone to be there with you.'

Isabel went home. She wanted to shut up the shop so that she could try to get used to the idea of a child, but typically, in the days which followed, she had people in all the time, more than one at once, sometimes three. She was scuttling around trying to find things for them, some of which she needed to order, and people were impatient and cross that they had to wait, but she had what was it – oh, yes, a monopoly – they could not buy the goods anywhere else so they were obliged to wait however long it took for new products.

Her thought was that if some of them were less mean and ordered what they needed before the tool broke or wore out they would fare better, but she wasn't sure they could afford to do so.

The strange thing was that she kept forgetting what Sister Lydia had told her. At first it was a relief that at least she was not dying. Then she felt sick and ill and heavy and tired and when she looked in the mirror in her bedroom she could not believe that she had not gone to the surgery sooner. She pulled her old slack frock close against her and stared.

Her stomach felt huge and was starting to head down towards her knees. She stared, willing it to go back to where it had been, and then she thought about the miller, how she felt about him and how she felt about Robert Slater, and her face burned. She tried to excuse herself, that she had not known, that she had been ignorant about her body and a man's body, that she had not intended this, that she was lonely and griefstricken, but none of it made her feel any better.

This was her fault, she had let a man do things to her, not slight things, not kisses and cuddles. She ought to have known better. The trouble was that she had liked what was done to her and what she did to him, she had enjoyed it, but she felt that decent women were not meant to do such things. She was wanton, low.

She was a fallen woman, a disgrace to the village. Whatever would it be like when people realized what was happening? However would she live with the knowledge that she was having a child? That also made her panic. What was it like giving birth? What could it be like when she was all alone with the shop and had nobody to help? How would she go on? Would she be hounded out of the village?

The end of the day when nobody came to the shop was the hardest time she had encountered. She sat over her fire, unable to eat and feeling sick, and worse than that in total panic, her back aching and she began to cry. Crying had up to that point alleviated her grief, but this time it did not. She didn't go to bed for a long hour, but she let the fire die down and when the warmth and what comfort she could gain was finished and over she went wearily up the stairs and wondered what it would be like when she was run out of the village.

Where would she go, what would she do? She had nobody to go to, nowhere to run. Eventually she had worn herself out and then she slept, waking up almost too late to open the shop. She was glad of the work and that she had money saved, because there was nowhere she might be able to go and the loneliness came down upon her like the world's largest rain cloud.

That night was even worse and since she had eaten nothing for two days she fainted in the kitchen, only just not knocking herself out on the edge of the kitchen table as she slid gently into an ungainly heap on the floor.

# Twenty-five

Lydia couldn't understand the way that Robert reacted when they were called in to see to Isabel Norton.

'It's her first baby,' she said, and was not pleased when he looked beyond her. Was he going moral on her and did not want to attend to an unmarried mother? The village had been rife with gossip for months. The miller had been seen on more than one occasion going into the backyard at the hardware store, and people were convinced that the baby was his.

Lydia did not dispute this, in fact she and the other nuns were horrified, but understood how lonely this girl had been, how ignorant of such matters she was, and had they not been nuns would have blamed the miller for such immoral behaviour but they thought that they understood him.

Also she had told Isabel that she would get help for her, but Isabel would not listen. She looked dreadful, Lydia thought, skinny and hollow cheeked. She had put on no weight even though the baby became huge, and Lydia was most unhappy that she was so upset and so physically ill when she was about to have a baby, but if she would not consent to having help then there was nothing Lydia could do about it. It was, she thought ruefully, the only kind of respect that Isabel was left with, as people knew that she was pregnant and not married. Only men now went to the hardware shop, and that was because they were obliged to, Lydia knew from the other nuns.

Trying to get further with the problem and feeling that they were getting nowhere the nuns had sat over the fire in Maddy's office.

Maddy had not forgotten how Mr Barnfather had turned up with his second wife, a small child and another on the way when his first wife was barely cold in her grave and his children had been left to starve. He was so cheerful, and she told the others that a man that cheerful after what he had done was somebody to be worried about.

Lydia also told them about Isabel and they had sat in a circle over the fire and groaned in unison. People created such huge problems, but then they were beset by ignorance, being what Abigail called 'daft happorths', and the fact that a lot of them were set in their ways. Also their religion made them capable of judging other people's behaviour rather than trying to help when people were stuck.

In such a small place everybody knew what had happened to the hardware merchant's daughter and many a matron shook her head and said that she had gone to the bad, which again according to Abigail was tantamount to hell, and no good would come of it.

'I just thought that Mr Gray would go. He was here earlier,' Robert said in some discomfort, Lydia didn't know why.

'Isabel was not in labour then,' she said. 'He thought she would be later, maybe even a few days, so he asked me to go and see her, and he had to go back to Wolsingham. Are you quite well, Robert?'

She was brisk with him, it seemed to be the only way. Even now that he was so knowledgeable and useful she deemed it better to treat him not quite like an equal because at heart he was a village lad and perhaps retained some of the prejudices of this place and of the towns where he had lived before. It was hard not to become entangled in what she would dismiss as a lot of old wives' tales and unsubstantiated superstitious nonsense, so they set off for Isabel's back door.

She thought she had cut through his reticence and that he must know Mr Barnfather had taken up with Isabel Norton, everybody in the village was aware of the scandal and the state of Isabel Norton's huge stomach, which to be fair to her she did not display.

Lydia doubted Isabel had been beyond the shop doorway and her backyard since she had known of her condition, but Lydia also was aware that women must have noticed because they did not go to the shop if they could help it, they sent their sons or their husbands, and even here she had the feeing that the men were reluctant, they were not used to setting eyes on such a Mary Magdalene. Much as the nuns thought differently than the people in the village about such an iconic figure, they knew also that to people such as these she was a prostitute and sinner, yet she had washed and oiled Jesus's feet and been with him when he was crucified and he had appeared to her first after his death when he was resurrected. Abigail could be got to lecture on Mary Magdalene for hours would anybody listen. She equated Mary with herself, badly done by and to, so woe betide the person who said anything against the woman.

'None of the women will let their daughters go anywhere near her, like it was contagious,' Lydia said.

'There is another way round it,' Abigail said.

'And what's that?'

'We could have Jimmy Slater to help in the shop, and having a young lad there will encourage others to go, if his mam and dad would let him. You have said yourself that he needs something to do since he doesn't like school, and his mother is suffocating him at home now that his leg is better.' Lydia had made sure Robert kept an eye on Jimmy's leg, she had no intention of going anywhere near Mrs Slater if she could find an excuse not to. Broken limbs took a lot of healing and Jimmy must be frustrated by his mother's close attention.

'I'm not going in there to fight with Mrs Slater, she already drives me round the bend.'

'I think it could be the answer,' Maddy said. 'If Jimmy won't go to school and his mother keeps him there like that, it can't be good for him. The two girls are married and live at the bottom of the hill, Hannah spends most of her life with us when her mother doesn't know, and Robert of course is turning into Lydia.'

Here Lydia allowed herself a slight smile.

'You're right,' she said, 'the poor lad needs to get out of there, but his mother will not allow it.'

'I could talk to Jay about it,' Maddy said.

'Oh dear,' Lydia said, 'how to pass on the problem. Ouch.'

'You're kidding me,' Jay said, sitting back in his chair in his office. 'You think I'm Mrs Slater's equal? Why don't you send Abigail?'

'They would kill each other.'

Jay sighed.

'You want me to ask Jim? Do you know what his wife is like? She scares me.'

'Nothing of the sort. Go there and insist. I don't think you should leave it to Jim. He'll never manage it. And Jimmy needs to get out of there before his mother has him painting paper doilies from sheer lack of anything else to do.'

Jay said nothing.

'She doesn't approve of him reading,' Maddy said.

Jay sighed and then he said, 'We've already stolen Robert and his father. If I go in there and suggest that Jimmy goes to work in the hardware store she will throw a poker at me.'

'Have you a better idea?'

Reluctantly therefore Jay, who would never put off anything that worried him, went and bearded the woman in her lair as his mind mocked him. Mrs Slater was alone with Jimmy, and the sisters had been right as ever, Jimmy was bored and sitting by the fire and he was skinny and pale and resentful, Jay could see. He had become a problem and this was a way of solving it if only Mrs Slater could be persuaded.

Jay gave Jimmy some money and told him to go and buy sweets at Dick's shop, Dick had apparently come back from some skirmish or other with a limp and thereafter taken to running a shop just up from the hardware store. For the most part it was sweets, the children loved it.

He kept lucky bags in various barrels so that you could dig around until you came out triumphantly with a small white bag filled with various goodies, and he had jars of sweets on high shelves behind the counter, lemon drops and rainbow sherberts and bullseyes, and so you chose what you fancied, and Dick would weigh them out and put them into a bag twisted around to a cone shape where the sweets could be seen beguilingly before you started to eat them.

Mrs Slater looked disapprovingly at him but Jimmy, face full of relief, skittered off so fast that Jay was almost encouraged and happy that Jimmy was so much better.

'I don't know what to do with him,' she said, gazing after her younger son with great affection and slight dismay. 'He won't go to school, no matter how much we threaten, and if I let him he would just sit there all day reading books and never helping with anything.'

Mrs Slater could do with a job too, Jay thought, to get her beyond the house and her endless concern over her family, but she would never manage it, she would never allow herself. She had brought up her family and there she was, clinging to this boy, when she needed to let him go and for them both to move on. Most women moved on to their grandchildren, so he only hoped that Mrs Slater would have some soon.

Jimmy was not the sort of boy who would do well at the farm, in fact, Jay thought, Jim Slater's lads were both very clever but only in certain ways, which he felt sure had nothing to do with milking cows or feeding stock, and Jimmy had not looked after the goats since he hurt his leg so it would be a very good thing if he could move Jimmy on. Abigail had been tending them while Jimmy could not walk, and she loved them.

The Slater children were a mix of the two parents and yet the parents couldn't see it. They thought only of loss. When would people ever learn to let their children go? He was convinced, though he had said little of this to the doctor because they were so busy, that Robert should go to Edinburgh to train as a doctor or a chemist or whatever, because the look on his face these days was not happy.

The doctor agreed, Jay knew, but also they needed Robert badly, more and more, so it could not be any time soon. The doctor was always looking for more skilled help, but there was little to be found in this area and all his general enquiries had yielded nothing so he was more than glad for the two young people who were there to assist.

The glow of a new and original way of spending Robert's life was not sufficient, Jay thought now, and though the doctor and Sister Lydia felt that they could not spare him, he must get out of here before he ended up marrying Polly Swift, it would end him, Jay felt sure.

Polly was not one of Jay's favourite people. He tried to be sympathetic because her father had recently died, but she was one of those girls who stood on street corners waiting for lads to come past and she would shout out to them and turn up her eyes.

Jay wanted to smile at himself, he had turned into a Puritan and looked at these things only through the eyes of the older man trying to run the village, and Polly had already caused more than one headache as far as he could see. Robert was a scholar in effect, and Jimmy was very like him.

'So,' he said, having not been asked to sit down and not daring to suggest it, 'Robert is doing very well.'

Mrs Slater, who was not stupid, shook her head. 'I worry about him.'

'But it's good to think that he can achieve something which is rarely done. He is very clever.'

She sighed and looked beyond him as though if she gazed enough at the window her family would crowd into the house and never leave.

'I wish he hadn't been. I wish Jim hadn't been. To be honest with you, Mr Gilbraith, I preferred it when Jim was making windows. When my bairns were all asleep in their beds, that was the best time. Now the lasses have gone, my Hannah spends all her time praying, for goodness' sake, and Jim is never here.' Her voice shook.

'And Jimmy?'

'I need somebody here with me,' she finally admitted.

'But doesn't he need something more?'

'He has me and his dad.'

Jay said nothing.

'There is talk of our Robert going to live with the doctor in Wolsingham. He will never come back.'

So she hadn't heard that the doctor wanted what Jay wanted and between them had plans for Robert to leave home and go to Scotland. The poor woman. If she thought Wolsingham was far enough, whatever would she do when her boy effectively left not just the area but in her eyes the country, as he was convinced she would think of Scotland that way. Many people thought Durham City a long way.

'I think I may have found something which Jimmy might manage. The hardware store needs an assistant.'

Mrs Slater stared at him and then, understanding what he wanted, she glared at him and held his gaze so hard that Jay wanted to break his own, but he had to face her down and eventually she looked away, but her voice showed him her fury.

'That – that lass is – is evil. I will not have my bairn anywhere near her.'

'She is unfortunate,' he said steadily, 'her parents were not there to look after her when she needed them and she did what many a girl has done and took whatever affection she was offered.'

'Affection?' She glared at him again, though her face was shiny with tears.

'Mistaken affection?' Jay said, voice hard. 'Doesn't everybody need somebody?'

'Well, you don't.'

They had moved into new realms, Jay noted, she was abusing

him, perhaps even trying to bully him he thought in some admiration, and he felt sorry for her.

'I did try to marry, twice. Nobody would have me,' he offered.

She almost laughed.

'It's true,' he said. 'First Sister Maddy and then Eve Gray as you probably know—'

'Sister Maddy?'

'She was Madeline Charlton then. I asked her father if I could marry her but he wouldn't have it. And isn't she glad now. Look at all she's achieved. Maybe Hannah will be like that.'

'I'd rather she married a decent man.'

'Isn't it about what she wants? Haven't you had what you wanted? A good man and five healthy children who have grown up to make you proud of them, at least four have, and I've no doubt Jimmy will do the same. He is too young to be judgemental about what is happening to Isabel, and she must have help. This is the only way for it to work and Jimmy will do very well. It's just a few doors along. I'm not asking you to see her or have her here, and Jimmy can come back for all his meals. It's just a shop job, and I think he would really like it. Isn't his arithmetic good?'

She nodded, wordlessly.

'If he says he doesn't want to then I'll understand,' Jay said. 'If he thinks it might work he could go for a week. He doesn't even have to see Isabel. I could ask that one of the men goes with him and shows him what to do. It's a question of taking money and giving change. That's all. It's four doors away and he would only have to be there on Wednesday and Saturday mornings and the other days from nine to five with dinner off, so it's a few hours a day. Even if he could just manage the mornings it would make such a difference. It is the only hardware store we have, it was left to her by her parents who wanted to make sure she had something to keep her. It's essential and it's hers.'

Why Robert was behaving as though he thought Isabel disgusting was a mystery to Lydia and she thought less of him for it as she led the way towards Isabel's house.

'Mr Gray prefers to leave it to us when he is able, you know that he has far too much to do. We've both got so much better at this and no woman has objected to you being there. If Isabel doesn't like it you can stay outside. Besides, I need you, it's hard doing these things by yourself and you've got better instincts than I do.'

She thought this admission might cut through his reticence, but it didn't seem to. Wordlessly he followed her in by the back gate to the hardware store. Isabel was alone. How horrible of her neighbours not to help her, Lydia thought. She was little more than a girl. Somebody had gone to the hospital to say that she thought Isabel needed help but that was all. What Isabel had done was called 'the dirty' around here, so nobody would bother with her. Lydia was determined to be there and to do everything she could to make it right.

She had no idea how hard it would be. The week before she had brought a new mother through no more than half an hour's labour and before that there was a mother with painless contractions. Isabel had not been that lucky, Lydia could see as soon as they got there. The poor girl was hanging on to a chair and doubled over. She looked gratefully at Lydia, but stared at Robert.

'Robert can stay outside if you like,' Lydia offered. Isabel just shook her head. Lydia thought she was in too much pain to care if the whole village should be watching.

'Can you walk about? Would you rather be upstairs?'

Robert carried her up the narrow stairs when she said she would rather have her bed. Lydia sent him back downstairs for cool water for Isabel's sweaty forehead and she got Isabel to sit up and asked how long she had been in pain, and then she needed to see how far Isabel was dilated and it was clear that she had a long way to go. Isabel was, she said, hoping it would go away soon.

That was what every woman wanted, but Lydia was going to do her best so that she would not be in more pain than they could help. When Robert came in they gave her pain relief and she lay back and sighed and thanked them.

It was a long night and Isabel was soon in a great deal of pain, try as they might to contain it. Robert was usually a good help, but he was white and quiet as he had been when he first helped at births, but perhaps he was seeing something she wasn't, Lydia surmised, she hoped not. He kept turning away as though he could sense something in the shadows, which quite unnerved Lydia. She had a religion which didn't believe in ghosts, but she had to keep reminding herself because very often now she feared the shadows in her own life and was half convinced there lay the people she had not saved, had not been able to help, and perhaps even future failures. The whole idea came between her and her sleep on a bad night.

Lydia gave Isabel morphine, but it seemed to have little effect. She and Robert had been studying about how drugs affect everybody differently and Isabel was unfortunate in this way and was soon in great distress, screaming and crying and unable to stay still. Lydia got her up and walked her around the room until she was sufficiently dilated so that Lydia told her it would not be long now, and yet it was.

They were there for five hours and she thought Isabel had been in pain probably for five hours before they got there. It was not that Isabel's pain was unusual, it was just that Isabel's pain threshold would have kicked in hard had she cut her little finger, and Lydia was terrified at one point that she would lose them both, the baby was big and Isabel was tiny.

She wanted to relax Isabel sufficiently so that she was not too bad and sensible enough to push when needed and pant when necessary, but when the child was finally born Isabel was so terrified and worn out that she was exhausted. Even then neither Lydia nor Robert thought she would live for long, she closed her eyes and leaned back and lost consciousness, but just as they were starting to panic she opened her eyes again and even smiled just a little.

When it became obvious that baby and mother would be all right, Robert retreated on to the landing and Lydia went to him just for a moment.

'You thought we were going to lose her?' she said.

He nodded but didn't look at her.

'Well, we didn't and they are both going to be fine.' She tried to be brisk but he shook his head and turned away.

Lydia stayed the night but she sent him home. For the next few days they had agreed that Abigail would go and spend most of the day there so that Isabel had something to eat and was kept warm and clean and the baby latched on to her breasts for feeding. Lydia knew that Abigail liked to help after babies were born.

Before the end of the week Jimmy Slater came in to the front of the shop and was shown by Abigail how to sell and how to take money. He caught on so fast that Abigail was pleased though not surprised, and he seemed to like it. Best of all he said, eagerly, 'Can I see the baby?'

Abigail hesitated. She hadn't expected this and Jay had said that he was to keep to the shop and not see Isabel unless really necessary and that he need not be concerned with anything else, but Jimmy was quick to understand and obviously knew exactly what was happening and his eyes were bright with curiosity and delight. Lads didn't usually react like this, but then so many of them thought it a commonplace occurrence which their mothers went through very often.

'Can I please see the baby? Would Isabel let me?'

Abigail hadn't even known he knew Isabel's first name, and prayed he did not tell his mother, but she took him through into the back where Isabel had finished feeding the baby, and she was neatly covered up with a shawl around her shoulders and the baby was falling asleep.

Isabel stared for a few moments and then seeing that Jimmy was gazing down at the baby with awe she was glad of him there, she warmed to him straight away and then she managed, as she knew she should, 'Thank you Jimmy for coming and helping.'

Jimmy went on staring at the baby.

'He's lovely. What is he called?'

'Allen, like my mam. It was her maiden name.'

'Can I hold him?'

Abigail showed Jimmy how to cradle the baby's head and Jimmy stared at how small the baby was.

'Can he come and help me in the shop when he gets bigger?'

'I'm sure he will want to.'

'That would be just wonderful,' Jimmy said. 'You can rely on me, Isabel, I will make sure that everything is all right.'

When Jimmy went home Abigail stayed, though Isabel said she would manage.

'I do like to be here,' Abigail said, 'and it's such a change for me. I have lots of help in other places and it would be nice to be here for a while.' She didn't say that it would also give Isabel a modicum of respectability.

After a week Abigail left, calling in now and then after she went back to the foundling school, but Jimmy was always in the shop, taking the money and giving people correct change, and as she went in Abigail could hear Jimmy telling people about bargains and special things and how they might not be able to get the same stuff in future and she thought he was a shopkeeper in the making.

# Twenty-six

When Allen was not quite a month old and things had settled somewhat into a routine, Isabel had a visitor. She had been not quite expecting him and yet somehow he was always on the edge of her thinking. It was early evening. Jimmy had just gone and she had locked the shop. She was so grateful to have him there. Without Sister Abigail she might have been lonely because her actions had robbed her of the few people who used to talk to her, some thinking that being a young woman living alone she was a magnet to their husbands or lovers, and she had proved nothing less, she thought ruefully.

Jimmy was now her only friend and she was surprised that she felt like that. How lonely did you have to be before you were grateful for the company of a young lad? Like all the Slater men, she thought, he was clever and useful.

Sister Abigail had said that she would come back whenever she was needed, but with Jimmy in the shop Isabel was starting to think she could manage on her own and to be fair she did like having the place to herself.

She yawned. The baby was sleeping part of the night but he was awake and needed feeding twice and so her sleep was always being interrupted. Jimmy was now eating his meals with her. What his mother thought of this Isabel had not asked, and Jimmy liked being there so much – his only freedom, she thought – that he had grown used to staying until after tea. Now she would sit and doze over the fire until the baby needed feeding again. Then she heard the latch on the back door and was aghast that she had not locked it.

'Who is it?' she called, and a hopeful voice called back, 'It's only me, Matthew.'

It was the miller. She hadn't seen him in months and was not glad to see him now. She wanted nothing more to do with him. She had told him to go and not come back, and now this. She had half suspected it, but was not pleased. She felt angry.

He moved into the light of the kitchen. He looked so middle-aged to her and she had forgotten that he was so much older than she was. He was smiling, it was a happy, gleeful smile that Isabel did not appreciate. She knew exactly why he was here.

'You shouldn't have come,' she greeted him.

He looked surprised, even hurt.

'Don't I have the right to see my boy? My son?'

'I don't know why you should think you have any rights here.'

He looked astonished.

'But I gave you this child. He's ours.' He gazed down at the cot.

'Don't disturb him, he's been awake all day and spent several hours crying. I'm glad of a little peace now.'

'I just want to see him. My son.' He did reach in and picked up the child, despite what she had said, and Isabel didn't like to fuss. The baby cried a little and then went back to sleep. 'He looks just like me,' the miller crooned.

'He doesn't look like anybody yet, he's too little.' Isabel couldn't stand the idea of her child with carrot-coloured hair and eyes like grass. 'Babies always look the same, that's what Sister Abigail says.'

'How on earth would she know?'

Isabel was too tired to argue. He went on rocking the baby for so long that she wanted to ask him to leave, and then he looked at her, a sudden light in his eyes and he said, 'We can go now.'

'Go?' Something cold clutched at Isabel's insides.

'From here,' the miller explained, beaming down at the baby. She stared at him.

'What on earth are you talking about?'

'We are a family now, what I always wanted. A proper family. We can go as soon as you are ready. You can have little to regret behind you with nobody but our child for company. I have waited so long for this time and now it has come. You must let me know whenever you are ready and I will pack my things. I can get a post anywhere you know, millers are always in high demand, there being so few of us.'

'I'm not going anywhere,' Isabel was determined to make her voice heard. She did not want this man to be under any illusions.

He looked at her, taking his gaze reluctantly from the object of his adoration.

'But of course we are. We can't stay here, not like this. We will go somewhere else, somewhere new and have a lovely life together. We would find somewhere easily and then we could make a home and maybe you would even give me another son.'

'I don't think I want to give you anything.'

'Yes, you do. You must care for me, you gave yourself to me so freely and I love you so very much for it.'

The baby, perhaps sensing the atmosphere in the room, began to cry, and when Isabel asked the miller to give back the child he didn't. He turned away from her with the baby in his arms and rocked him, but the baby knew that he was not in his mother's arms and not being used to a man he began to scream.

Jimmy had only just got in the door of his house when he remembered that he had left his book at the front of the shop. His mother was inclined to be cross with him that he 'always had his nose in a book' but it was his escape and this book was very exciting. It was called *The Three Musketeers*. Jimmy loved it better than any book he had read before and badly wanted to be a musketeer when he grew up.

In vain Robert had explained that it was a story and anyway it was in France. Jimmy hated that Robert always reduced everything to boring.

He didn't ask his mam if he could go back because she always said no to everything, he just slipped out of the front door and went to the shop on the front street. When he got there however no lights burned. There was no gleam at all. Isabel had locked up the second he had left, he thought, and retreated into the kitchen, where no doubt she was sitting over the fire. Her face was always white with tiredness and Jimmy didn't like to disturb her again but it would only take five minutes and he was certain she wouldn't mind. She was always telling him what a good help he was, as if she really liked him.

So he ran back up the front street and around the corner and down the unmade back road. She had net curtains up at the windows as everybody did for privacy since people could see over the back gate and back wall, and the neighbours could see in across the yard if they cared to look, so he could see very little, but she was probably just sitting over the fire. She would be hoping that Allen would sleep for a while and she would get some peace, that was what she said.

He went in at the open gate and then paused. He could hear voices as he drew nearer and one of them was a man's voice and it was raised in anger or frustration, Jimmy didn't know which, just that the noise was unhappy, and Isabel, when he allowed her to speak, sounded no happier, with an almost pleading note in her voice.

Jimmy let himself in soundlessly by the unlocked back door and into the little back kitchen where the sink and pantry lay before the step down into the main room.

From the comparative darkness of the pantry he blinked against the light, recognizing the miller, who was quite big and seemed even bigger, Isabel being so short and slight. The miller had his back to Jimmy.

'You can't go anywhere,' she was saying, 'you have a wife and six children.' She sounded as though she was on the verge of desperation and was holding out her hands so that he might give the child back into them.

By now baby Allen was kicking up a fuss and giving it everything he had at the top of his voice so that Jimmy wondered whether the neighbours on both sides might not come to her aid, but since nothing was happening and maybe she being a fallen woman – that what how his mam had talked about Isabel when she had thought he could not hear – was not their concern.

'I would give it all up for you and this boy,' the miller was saying. Isabel couldn't see Jimmy in the darkness of the back kitchen he thought, he was in shadows. 'They would manage. Everybody is looked after here.'

At that moment Jimmy had a brilliant thought. He announced himself by moving back and opening quietly and then slamming very loudly the back door. Then he moved into the lamplight. He said also loudly, 'Hello, Isabel. Hello, Mr Barnfather. My dad said he hopes you don't mind but he needs some stuff for his work.'

There was silence. Both people in the room saw him, the miller frowned as he turned to face the intruder, his face darkening so much that Jimmy turned his gaze on her. Isabel looked almost relieved and Baby Allen gave the room everything he had until Jimmy thought it was a shame that the walls didn't shake, the sound was so very loud and shrill and panicked. Jimmy could hardly bear to see the tiny child in such a state.

'How are you, Mr Barnfather?' Jimmy said, smiling very widely and raising his voice as much as he could, and then he turned and looked solely at Isabel. 'My dad sent me ahead to look for them. I said you'd shut up shop, but he says he needs them first thing in the morning and he'll come when he's had his tea. Is Allen all right? I think he's coming down with summat, he had a really bad rash on his arms and legs this morning. Did you notice? Could it be catching?'

Without seeming to do anything Jimmy moved the short distance between himself and the miller and took the baby from Mr Barnfather before the man had time to realize he was doing it.

The miller stalked out. That was the only word for it, and Jimmy felt like a true musketeer, he had saved the baby and the lass. He was a warrior, a man with a sword and big boots and long leather – what were they called – not gloves, gauntlets. As soon as he was big enough he would set off for France, he swore to himself.

To his horror the man had been gone about three seconds when Isabel started to cry. Jimmy hated tears, he watched as her face sort of crumpled up, like a soggy handkerchief. The lasses in his house had always been on the verge of blubbing, that was what he called it. Thank God the other two had married and left, there was only Hannah and she didn't cry. She prayed a lot and would keep on reading the Bible, the only book he had come across so far that he didn't care for, but Isabel was giving it rock all, oh Lord.

After that she blew her nose on a big hanky, disgusting, Jimmy thought, as she returned the sodden ball to a skirt in her pocket and waffled about as though she had no idea what to do or where to turn, and the baby, who knew Jimmy almost as well as he knew Isabel, settled down to sleep again.

Jimmy didn't like to ask questions but he had already discerned part of what was going on. He had wondered how Isabel had a baby without a man, without a husband. But then the miller couldn't be her husband, he was married to Mrs Barnfather, and as far as Jimmy could work out there were half a dozen of them, so it was as big a family as Jimmy's own. Then what was he doing here?

At last she managed to control her crying and looked at the baby, but hesitated.

'I didn't see a rash.'

Jimmy gave her a pitying look.

'He hasn't got one. I just wanted to get the miller to worry about catching it and give him up.'

Isabel looked puzzled for a few minutes. Jimmy knew that it took lasses ages to catch on, but finally the penny dropped and she looked relieved. Then she was about to start to cry again, for the Lord's sake, he thought, but she didn't, she smiled and he handed Baby Allen to her.

He couldn't stay long, his mam would already have noticed he was gone, so Jimmy went and located his book at the front of the shop on the window ledge as he had left it, and then he went home. He heard Isabel lock the door behind him and he ran up the lane and in at the back door before he heard his mother say, 'Where on earth have you been?' His mam missed nowt.

'I just forgot something.' He wasn't going to tell her, he didn't want her going on and on about books being a waste of time, but luckily she didn't notice.

His dad had finished his tea. He usually went back to the office after tea, Jimmy had the feeling that his dad and Mr Gilbraith talked about what had happened in the village during those evenings. His dad went into the front room and sat down by the fire and began to read his paper which was what he usually did after tea before going back out, and Jimmy followed him in and said softly, 'Dad, can I ask you something?'

They were safe in the front room. His mother complained about the fire. Nobody around here sat in their front rooms, but there had been so many of them in the kitchen that his dad said he couldn't hear himself think and insisted on having the fire lit in there and even lit it himself when he came in if it had not been done before. It was his bit of peace as he called it.

The lasses had rarely ventured in there. In a way it was a man's place. Robert went in to get out of the road of family rows. The lasses would sit around the kitchen table and sew and knit and drink tea, at least they had used to. Now it was only Hannah and his mam, but the idea had not changed.

Robert was not there of course, he never was there, always out with what his mam called in private, 'that hussy', by which she meant Sister Lydia. Jimmy was shocked at what his mother said but it was only ever when they were there by themselves and she somehow assumed he couldn't hear her.

Jimmy waited. His father looked impatiently at the fire as though he really wanted to sit and read just for a few minutes, but with a family he had rarely been able to. Maybe his dad liked that the lasses had gone and thought he might get more peace.

'What is it?' His dad looked kindly at him, because he was the youngest and anyroad his dad liked him. Jimmy knew how lucky he was like that, he had seen plenty of other lads with marks on them from their dads hitting them, with scars such as how they moved back in fear when addressed, how they came to school in rags because their dads couldn't leave the drink alone, and skinny because their dads couldn't leave the cards alone. Some of them, because their dads had gone off and left their mams with seven or eight bairns, their mams were only feeding them because Mr Gilbraith tried to look after everybody, and even then some of the women would buy new stuff for themselves and their bairns did not eat and had no clean clothes or a clean house, while their mam had a new frock to her back and new shoes on her feet.

Jimmy knew that he could trust his mam and dad, for everything they could give him they did. His dad worked hard, his mam put good food on the table, she was always making him change into clean clothes, wash his hands and even clean his teeth, which most lads didn't have to. He knew how much his dad liked him even though he was the last of five children. His dad, once in a good mood, told him that his mam had kept the best for last and although Jimmy, not being daft, knew that his dad was doing what you called soft soaping him, yet he kept it close in his head because his dad meant the whole world and more to Jimmy.

Half invited, he sat in the chair across the fire from his dad, where Robert would have sat had he been at home, and Jimmy explained. His dad's face closed. It looked like a door had come across his expression and Jimmy saw that it was something his dad was not happy talking about.

'She was scared. She cried,' Jimmy said, once he had told his dad about the miller and Isabel.

'I don't see what there is to be done,' his dad said.

'But there must be,' Jimmy said, impatient that his dad was about to dismiss this problem, like it was nowt. 'What if he comes back and won't go? She's just a bit of a lass, she can't put him out. Maybe I could go and stay.'

'Your mam would never agree to it.' That was how his dad got out of stuff, by blaming his mam. Jimmy wasn't having that.

'But what if the miller runs off with Baby Allen?'

'He won't.'

'Or murders her?'

'You read too much,' his dad concluded.

'How come the miller thinks Baby Allen is his?'

His dad looked confused.

'He wants her to run away with him,' Jimmy said.

'He can't do that.'

'Have you seen how big the miller is?'

'She did lock the doors, you said.'

'Dad, have you seen the size of her? She's ever so little and she's frightened.'

'I tell you what,' his dad said, 'I'll do something about it, all right?'

'What?'

'I don't know yet but I will.'

'You promise?'

'I promise. And don't talk to your mam about this.'

'You will sort it and tonight?'

'I will. Don't worry.'

# Twenty-seven

His peace now lost, Jim Slater made his way up towards the fellside house where the boss lived. He liked these evening sessions.
He and Gilbraith sat over whisky and talked in the office. It was
Jim's favourite room, big and full of desks and chairs and papers,
but also it had easy chairs by the fire and the fire in there was
always huge and would have kept an even bigger room warm.

So he told the boss about the problem, and Gilbraith swore.
He only ever did it when they were by themselves and Jim understood his frustration.

'That bastard. He can't let women alone. He left his first wife and
she died and the bairns had to make their own way here, and then
he turned up with a sixteen-year-old – not much more, I think –
with one in her hand and another in her belly. I gave him the job
because of his bairns, and now look. What's with the man? I'll get
somebody to watch the house tonight,' and he went out briefly and
having written a note he asked Miss Proud to get one of the lads
who lived nearby to deliver it. Jim was used to such things.

There were a whole lot of people ready to do Gilbraith's bid-
ding since he paid them handsomely. To watch over a young lass
with a baby even in the cold darkness was nothing to these men,
and if they judged her they had the good sense not to say so
when they were being paid. It was not their business.

'We can't do that every night,' Jim said.

'If he does owt to her then we will have a much bigger problem.'

'I could talk to him.'

Gilbraith shook his head.

'I don't think he's the sort who would listen. What is it with him?'

'There is another way round it. We need somebody to live there.'

'How can we do that?'

'Jimmy could. If my wife would ever agree to it. And maybe Hannah.'

'With a young lad there and a lass like Hannah I doubt he would dare come near. Even so I think for the first few nights somebody should be outside. But look, Jim, it's a lot to ask of you and your wife. Think about it and if it's too much let me know and I'll sort out something else.'

By the time Jim went home he was starting to wish he had not stuck his neck out, but the idea remained a good one and he didn't want to let the boss down. His wife would not agree to Hannah becoming a nun, but this was a compromise and he thought it would do both children good to get away. Even if it was just a few doors down it would present new opportunities and problems.

When he went back everybody but his wife had gone to bed and so he sat her down by the kitchen fire, which was the only fire burning at this time of night, and told her what was proposed. She went very pale.

'So you and Mr Gilbraith have decided?'

Jim felt for her. He was her husband and should have the say, and she would let him if he only laid down the law, but he wouldn't do that to her and now she was being sarcastic. He wished she wouldn't.

'If it hadn't been for Mr Gilbraith we would have had nothing,' Jim said. 'We left Bishop Auckland with nowt beyond the clothes on our backs and five hungry bairns. The lasses have found good lads here to marry and haven't left the village and it looks as though our Robert might become a doctor. Mr Gilbraith has been good to us.'

'He's ruined my family life.'

'There would have been little family life if we hadn't been lucky enough to land here and have him give us this house and pay me as much as he does. And Hannah is restless.'

'Her duty is to me.'

Jim heard the break in his wife's voice and understood that she was losing what she had relied on all those years. Her children didn't need her any more and the loss was huge. And so he said softly, not wanting to hurt her further, 'Her duty is to herself. Surely you didn't bring up your children for them to dance attendance on you. Was that what you wanted?'

He looked carefully at her and then he remembered why he had chosen to marry her, she always looked so honestly into his eyes and did her best every single day, and a lot of them had not been easy.

'Of course it wasn't,' she said now, looking straight back at him. 'But I didn't want her to go to the house of a bad lass like that who got pregnant.'

'The nuns go. And Jimmy.'

'He likes it better than being here.' His wife's voice and look were hard now and Jim cursed himself for not having said the right things.

'Isn't that the point? It's new to him. He's spent his whole life with us and it's only a few doors away. They could have gone much further and possibly will in time.'

'My children only seem happy when they're away from me,' his wife said.

'So you brought them into the world to stay with us and have no lives of their own? We have to learn to let go. We are lucky. They are all still here with us and none of them has been a sick child. That has to be enough. And perhaps with two newly wed daughters there will be grandchildren soon. Have you thought of that?'

'Many a time,' she said.

Jim wasn't sure his two children would want to oblige him, so early the next morning before Jimmy had the chance to dash off to the shop and Hannah had set to work in the house he talked to them. Hannah was so far a disappointed woman. Her mother had set up such a fuss when she wanted to go to Newcastle and become a nun at the convent there that she had relented, but she was frustrated, her father could see.

He explained what he wanted them to do and saw the light arrive in both their faces.

'I can go and stay there with Isabel?' Jimmy said.

'Just for now.'

'And is this because of Mr—'

'Jimmy,' his father warned him and Jimmy shut up. He had worked out by now that for some reason the miller was Baby Allen's dad. Why, when he had a wife and all those bairns Jimmy had no idea, and Isabel was nowhere near as bonny as Mrs Barnfather, not even in the same division.

'I must go and speak to Isabel first,' Jim said, and then he set off for the shop just as Isabel was opening up. She blushed to see him, she was embarrassed, he could see, but he told her that he thought it would be good if Hannah and Jimmy could stay at least for now, and he could see that it provided her with relief.

'Hannah won't mind being in with me and the baby?' she said anxiously.

'I'm sure she won't. She will be a big help with the baby and the house. Hannah is very good and can do all manner of things.'

'She doesn't mind me?'

'She is in no position to judge, none of us is.'

'Thank you, Mr Slater, that's very good of you.'

'And Jimmy can't wait to get here.'

'I have another bedroom so that he can have his own space,' Isabel said.

'Have you beds?'

'I think Hannah might like her own bed, so another single bed would be helpful,' Isabel said. 'I've got plenty of space in that bedroom.'

'Don't worry, I will send you furniture and linen and blankets and pillows and just to make sure – and I know this sounds silly – but I want you to feel comfortable, so we will have some-body watch the house at least to begin with.'

'That's so very kind.'

'Not at all. We only have one hardware shop and we need to look after you,' Jim said.


Jimmy was ecstatic. His life had never been better and though he had the feeling that Hannah might have objected, she didn't. In fact she looked pleased. He had not forgotten when her mother would not let her go to be a nun. Hannah was too good to object and their father had said little, so Jimmy had the feeling that his dad did not want to lose her like that either, but Hannah had been so silent since then that Jimmy had felt sorry for her. He had always liked her best. Maybe it was because she had often looked after him when he was small.

Hannah made and mended his clothes and she had read him stories when he was little. Her mother blamed Hannah for his fondness for books, saying it had made Jimmy want to sit about and be idle. Hannah seemed to get blamed for everything whereas she was much nicer than either of the other two girls.

His mother had taken to making daily excursions down to see the two girls who had married. She said there was nothing to do here so she might as well. She left Hannah to cope with the meals, so Jimmy wondered what would happen when there was nobody to help. He had the feeling she was doing it on purpose because his dad would never let his mam have help of any kind, but his dad would soon think of what generals called a strategy if he came home to cold meat and black grates.

His mam took to leaving a ham sandwich for his dinner in the middle of the day after that. His dad did not look pleased, but then Jimmy was going to Isabel's to live and wouldn't have to listen to the rows between his parents any more. Not that his dad ever said a great deal, it was mostly his mam.

Hannah was much more excited than he had thought she would be at having to move a few doors down. Jimmy was slightly worried about the idea that Hannah would get in the way of his friendship with Baby Allen. Although she did help with the baby if asked, she didn't seem terribly bothered, but seemed to like Isabel straight away. Lasses were like that. Give them a kitchen sink and some dishes to wash and they got on. Jimmy was in the front of the shop so what happened at the back he did not consider to be his business.

Also he had a bedroom to himself. Not that he had minded being in the room with Robert, but it was just that Rob was so very often not there. Jimmy had become lonely without his brother whereas Rob so obviously didn't miss him. That hurt, but he knew that he needed to replace it with something else and thanks to Mr Gilbraith, who Jimmy liked more than anybody except Baby Allen and his dad for what Mr Gilbraith had done for him, he could do this now.

It was the smaller bedroom that overlooked the back lane and there was a bed, a chest of drawers and even a bookcase which was full of books, and Jimmy was more excited about the books than anything else.

Isabel said it had been her dad's and nobody else had been allowed to touch the books, but Jimmy could read them any time he liked when the shop wasn't busy. There was also a table and a chair and she had put on to the table pencils and paper, Jimmy wasn't quite sure why, but he liked the idea that all these things were for him.

Not that he had anybody to write to, but from then on he wrote about his day and he liked the idea of keeping a journal, and both girls thought it a very good idea too and Hannah said she would thread them and make a book of them when he had quite a few so that he might end up with volumes. Jimmy had never been so happy.

The other bedroom was big and now had a single bed in with the double, beside the window.

The meals improved after Hannah got there. He didn't think Isabel knew much about cooking and had always been in the shop and not thought much about anything more when there was Baby Allen to sort out, so it was good that Hannah was there to take charge of the cleaning and mending and cooking.

# Twenty-eight

From as soon as he knew, Mary thought, that Isabel's child was a boy, the miller stopped living at the mill house. He rarely came in, he slept at the mill and his meals were taken there for him. Mary knew this because she was the person who took them. He was no longer good-tempered.

He had only gone once to see the child, as far as Mary could tell. Up to then he was good-tempered, almost sunny, and then he became crafty and leaving no money at all for the housekeeping. Mary knew what that meant, he was saving it for himself so that he and Isabel Norton could run away with the new baby boy.

Mary was frantic and couldn't think what to do. She wished she had somebody to tell. She wondered also whether the nuns understood and if they might do anything. Fran cried a lot, but she also worked because there was so very much to do and between them it took all their time to get through it.

However, since the two newly wed girls had become so friendly and helpful, spending time at the mill house, Fran seemed cheered and she was so used to her husband's odd behaviour that it became the norm.

One Sunday Mrs Slater came to see her daughters and she had with her her other daughter, Hannah, and her son, Jimmy, and where Jimmy went, so he said, Baby Allen went, Jimmy taking the baby out for air in his pram. His mother was pretending the baby was not with them, but since one or the other cuddled the child it didn't seem to matter.

Mrs Slater did not come to the mill house with the rest of the family. She would not have lowered herself to see that man, as he had become known, or his apparent offspring, but Mary liked the little boy and between them both the babies were well cuddled. Jimmy and Mary had gone to school together. She envied him that he could go to school but chose not to, and he envied her that she didn't have to.

'You're clever though, aren't you?' Mary said as they sat outside near the stream, the babies between them on the cold sunny Sunday afternoon.

'Me? How?'

She thought it was nice that he wasn't aware of it. He frowned at her.

'You could always do a lot of stuff that other folk couldn't do,' she said. 'So why don't you go any more?'

'I run the shop and I read to Baby Allen. Do you read to your baby?'

'Haven't got much time,' Mary said, 'there's a lot of us.'

'Your dad seems weird.'

'He does to me too,' Mary agreed.

'And he fathered Baby Allen?'

Mary wasn't happy about this, but nodded. She regarded the baby like she hadn't thought that they were related or possibly could be.

'He's my half-brother,' she finally said, and wrinkled her nose.

'He doesn't look like you.'

She stared at the baby.

'I don't think babies look like anybody, do you?'

'I don't know. Who does Daisy look like?'

'She's bonny like Fran, at least she will be, I hope she doesn't look like us, hair on fire and eyes like goosegogs.'

Jimmy smiled at that.

'Fran says babies only get their looks when they're a few months old and even after that they change a lot.'

'I suppose she would know,' Jimmy agreed. 'Your dad wanted him and Isabel to run away.'

Mary looked at him.

'And won't she?' She held her breath waiting for his reply and when he shook his head half of Mary's worries packed their bags and left. 'Why not?' Mary said.

'I think she doesn't like him, not really. I came in on them and he was getting a bit nasty and she was starting to bubble and Baby Allen screamed.'

'So they aren't going anywhere?' Mary needed more reassurance.

Jimmy shook his head again, looking serious, and Mary thought he was the first boy she had ever really liked apart from Burt and maybe Abe.

'I thought I would marry her when I get older,' he said.

'That would be nice. You could run the shop together.'

'And I would never have to leave Allen, and then Hannah could go and be a full-time nun. She would like that.'

'She's very nice,' Mary agreed. 'Nuns are.'


From the beginning both Jimmy and Isabel encouraged Hannah to go and see the nuns. They could see that she really wanted to, but she said that her parents did not want it for her. Isabel said that she should have a little of what she wanted, so for a couple of hours a day Hannah went to the foundling school to help.

Jimmy was sure it did her the world of good, she always looked so happy and he didn't think anybody could complain because the sisters were often in other people's houses and doing all kinds of things. Also Isabel was managing really well and Hannah had taught her new recipes, and because they were young and energetic everything got done so quickly that Hannah had nothing to do in the afternoons, so she could easily go up the back street to the foundling school.

Jimmy just hoped nobody asked her whether her parents had said it was all right and that she did not encounter her father there.

The two girls sang while they did the washing and since Jimmy took Baby Allen most of the time it was easy. Also because Baby Allen was kept awake all day by Jimmy reading to him and the noise of so many people coming into the shop he began to sleep through the night, which the two girls said was amazing because it made life easier.

The house part of the place was soon immaculate and since the baby was awake, Isabel could help in the shop and Hannah could do the ticketing for the items to sell, and she would scrub the shelves and wash the floor, and between the three of them they were a happy little bunch.

Inevitably, Jimmy thought, Hannah met their dad, but she was at Mr Gilbraith's house at the time and by invitation from Miss Proud, so their dad could hardly complain. Miss Proud and the nuns really liked Hannah, and Jimmy could tell that they did just by the look on Hannah's face when she came back. She would tell him about the cats and dogs and the afternoons with Miss Proud playing the piano, with everybody there on a Wednesday

afternoon. Miss Proud said they must come, and so Isabel actually ventured from the house, and the shop was shut because it
was half day closing.

Jimmy was worried what the other women would say, but at
least because they were in Mr Gilbraith's house they said nothing.
They did look askance at one another, but Miss Proud made a
great fuss of Isabel, Hannah, and Allen. She was so kind, Jimmy
thought, and then their dad turned up, rather white in the face, but
he just smiled and went through into the office and said nothing.

The two girls cried in the kitchen when they got back and Isabel
said she would never do such a thing again and Hannah said that
she must. They didn't bother not talking in front of Jimmy, it
would have been a waste of time and anyway, he and Allen were
the men in the house so they sat down together, and Hannah said
nobody had any right to think they were better than anybody else.

'But Hannah you must know that I'm full of sin,' Isabel said.

'We're all full of sin,' Hannah said.

'Not you,' Isabel said.

'Especially me, tired of my parents telling me what to do and
so desperate to get away.'

Jimmy stared. He hadn't heard this before though it must be
true. Parents, it had to be said, did get in the way of you going
forward and doing new things. He cared very much for them, but
it was lovely being here where they could not get at him, especially
his mam. Here he could wait on customers and read all the rest
of the time, and at night when the girls sat over the kitchen fire
they gave him a candle and he would go upstairs to be by himself.

Those were the best times, his own place and his own time,
and a candle to light his way. Often he took Baby Allen with him
and read aloud, and Baby Allen never fell asleep until the girls
came to bed. Jimmy had no idea why, just that they all agreed he

was a most remarkable child. It was amazing the way that Baby Allen responded to his voice and sat there, gazing at the pages as though he understood them. Jimmy had had no idea that babies could be like this.

The girls dealt with dirty nappies and feeding, and Jimmy thought he had the best of it, because he got Baby Allen to himself so very much and talked, and the baby laughed at him and gurgled and very rarely cried. It was because he had everything he needed to hand, Jimmy thought.

He was looked after and had somebody to see to him and talk to him every waking moment. The girls often sang to him, and they would take him into the back lane and between them sing to him and hold him looking outward so that he could see everything while they hung up the clothes.

Nobody bothered them, nobody dared, and Hannah would make Isabel go to the meetings up at Miss Proud's in Mr Gilbraith's house. Often Mr Gilbraith would come across and say hello and how big the baby was getting and how pleased he was that they had come. He told them all what a grand job they were doing. After that there were no problems, Jimmy thought, and he slept well in his bed at night.

His mam would not lower herself by coming to the shop or the house at the back, and his dad hadn't time, so the three of them plus the baby had a wonderful time together. He hoped it would go on and on because things never did when they were good, in his experience. Enjoy it Jimmy, he told himself, enjoy it now.

Hannah made biscuits and cakes every day so they would have tea as soon as the shop was shut. They were open every day except for Wednesday and Saturday afternoons and all day Sunday, so the meal in the middle of the day was nothing but a sandwich and Jimmy usually had that between customers.

The customers liked him, he thought. He could find anything and he got Isabel to make orders just before they were needed, so that nobody came into the shop and found that what they wanted was out of stock. Isabel congratulated Jimmy on knowing such things and she offered him wages and she offered Hannah wages too, but neither of them would take such a thing. They both liked being there, it was the best things had ever been.

The miller decided that he would leave Isabel alone. It was a tough decision but he came to the conclusion that for now it was the right one. She was tired from having the baby. In time she would understand, and then they would be able to leave. He told himself that he must be patient, he must be happy because finally he had the son he had longed for all his life. When his life seemed impossible he would remember that he had got what he had always wanted and he would have more soon.

She would change her mind. The village would never accept her as she was, and when she understood that she would come to him, and after that they would leave this place together for ever, and it meant that his biggest dream would come true.

In the meanwhile he had to work twice as hard. Fran had been good to him even though she had not given him the son he had so longed for. It was as if now a curse had been lifted. He must not leave Fran destitute. He knew that she would be looked after here, Mr Gilbraith would have nobody hungry or homeless in his village, but it was a matter of pride to Matthew Barnfather to make sure that his family had money to get by on. Abe was big enough to run the mill and could afford to have help.

Mary was always on at her father about money because he admitted to himself that sometimes he had kept them short for

Isabel or the drink. While Mary's moods made him angry, she was just a child and should not speak her mind to him, or have any opinions.

He needed to keep them now. He consoled himself that it was for a short time only. A few months and he would be free.

In the meanwhile he tried to make Abe into a good miller so that he could cope after his father left. Abe was stupid. Matthew was glad in so many ways that Abe was not his son. He did sometimes wish that Burt had been his, but he had been Fran's father's child and, while she had never tried to deceive him, had always said that it was his, he thought that because she could have sons she could have one for him too.

Allen was undoubtedly his as Isabel now was his real love in life. He felt as though he had come home at long last. The knowledge that the child was his made him so happy that he could be cheerful at home and at work. He was civil to everyone and was making more money than ever before.

Because of his good humour and kindness Abe started to pick up things more quickly, more readily, and Matthew saw then that he did have ability, that he could have quickness, he just needed someone with enthusiasm to believe in him, and Matthew wanting to get away so badly, made Abe believe that he could run the mill.

Matthew saw Abe's glowing face at what he could achieve and was glad. Matthew saw that his own teaching was good, the more he praised the lad the better things got, so all he had to do was wait until Isabel made up her mind. And she would, he knew that she would. He would bide his time and make things right before he left so that his family should not suffer. He therefore gave Mary more money than usual right from the beginning. She looked suspiciously at him.

'Is there something the matter?' she said.

He assured her there wasn't.

'It's just that you've never made as much money as this.'

Oh how Matthew enjoyed these small deceptions.

'Abe is being so much more able,' he grinned at the witticism, 'that we are achieving more.'

He smiled that he could be so clever. He had always known that he was clever. Now he was proving it.

Abe was happy at the way that he was praised and worked even harder, and everything was good all round, Matthew thought.

Fran even made room for him in their bed and would have taken him to her had he asked, but he didn't trust her to have a son with him. She had proved she could not, so he feigned tiredness because of work and bided his time.

She was not tactless enough to have the baby in bed with them. He could not bear the sight of it and was pleased that the child slept with Mary most of the time. If Fran looked after it in the night he was never awake to be disgusted.

The house was more comfortable and easier because there was plenty of money. He even managed to give Abe some, secure in the knowledge that Abe, not quite knowing what to do, would hand it to Mary, so it made the miller feel much better.

Mary's face cleared for the first time since he had left home when they lived at Cowshill. He was glad of that. The days became shorter as autumn took hold, and more enjoyable to his mind. He had no need of beer now. He was happy enough to spend his evenings over the fire with his family, thinking that in the future he could leave them having done what he should. He slept and ate well. He didn't even mind that sometimes the nuns came into his house and that Jim Slater's married daughters were often to be found there. Life was sunny.

# Twenty-nine

It was about six months after Baby Allen was born that something occurred to Jimmy. He had seen the Barnfather family and the girls all had red hair and green eyes. The lads didn't, but then neither of the Barnfather lads had a look of the baby. Jimmy was told that all babies had blue eyes, but somehow Allen looked as though his blue eyes would be for always, they were so deep.

Jimmy held the baby up to the little mirror at the back of the shop and he looked at the baby and he looked at himself and he thought the daftest thing. The baby looked like a Slater. He really did. Jimmy then wondered if he had been a magician and had wanted the baby to look like them because he felt like family, but that too was daft.

He dismissed it from his mind and got on with what he was doing. The baby by then could sit up in the old pram at the back of the shop, and it had those things attached to it which meant he couldn't fall out and was quite happy because Jimmy talked to him all the time.

'He does have a name,' Isabel objected. She was a right bugger, some of the lads might have said. She was sinful, that was what the women said and the lads said a lot worse of her, but then they often had to go in the hardware shop so they didn't say it there. If they had, Mr Gilbraith would have known about it – and the more Jimmy looked at Allen and the more he talked to Allen the more sure he was that the baby was one of them.

He got to wondering whether his dad was like Mary's dad and got to doing whatever men did to bonny lasses, but then his dad didn't have time. He found himself looking hard at Mr Barnfather when their paths crossed, which wasn't often. Mr Barnfather didn't come to the shop, Abe did. Abe was slow, he didn't talk, just grunted, but Jimmy somehow worked his way around it. Abe never mentioned the baby but then he never mentioned anything so Jimmy just gave him what he wanted and took his money.

Isabel still got tired and sometimes would fall asleep in the back room, especially in the afternoons, and Hannah would take care of whatever had not been done.

Jimmy gave Baby Allen various stuff off the shelves to handle and play with. You gave the baby a pan to look at or a spoon with the sunshine on it and he was mesmerized.

Also Allen had a lot to say for somebody who hadn't been long in the world but because they did such a lot of talking Jimmy found that he liked Allen a lot more than he liked anybody else.

Therefore it was only on a Sunday evening when Jimmy had gone home to see his dad, and his dad was sitting over the fire reading the newspaper, something he rarely achieved, when Jimmy said, 'Do we have any folk nearby who are family to the Barnfathers?'

His father seemed surprised at the question. Jimmy was also surprised he could put it like that, but he had been thinking it over for some time.

His dad put down the paper and scowled at Jimmy. He was obviously cross to be disturbed in the little time he had away from other things.

'You what?' he said.

'Well, I just wondered if their family coming from up the dale and us coming from here, whether it was something the same.'

'How could it be that? We've just got here.'

This was true, sort of. Jimmy could remember them moving in and it was only a few years ago and he had been little. When the town was started up his dad had been one of the first men to be employed, which was why they had what his mother described as this, 'house right in the way of the winds', but Jimmy's dad said it was one of the best and biggest houses, one of the first to be built, and they had been lucky to get it. It was right on the end, another thing his mam didn't like, but that also meant it was bigger, though if his mam hung sheets out in the back lane she sometimes had to chase after them if the wind got up on a fine day.

'You know very well that we came from Bishop Auckland,' his dad said now. 'My stepfather was a joiner there. Yes, you were little, but it's only a few years ago. Don't you remember?'

Jimmy said nothing to that but he did remember. It was all coming back to him, how could he have forgotten, maybe he had been so unhappy that he had put it from his mind.

How cold it had been, how he had been hungry and cried, and he had the impression that it had taken a long time. He could remember being carried and going to sleep against what he now assumed was his father's shoulder.

Also that there had been rows before they left, a lot worse than what his mam and dad had now, and it was not just them but other people, older people, either his mam's parents or his dad's. He thought there might even have been blows struck. Was that all part of why his mam was never happy, even though they seemed to have so much?

'What then?' his father said.

'I just wondered.'

'Wondered what?'

'Well, Isabel's Allen. He doesn't look like them.'

'Not surprising. I think half the time that man's sons are somebody else's.'

Jimmy frowned. His father said hastily that he was not to say such a thing to anybody, it wasn't true, but it spurred Jimmy on.

'In that case Baby Allen looks like me.'

His father stared at him.

'You what?' he said.

'Like a Bishop Auckland person, blue eyes and sort of dark hair.'

'Half the village looks like that,' his father said. 'It's just a general northern look and also in Fife where I came from. The further north you go in Scotland the darker the men are, so they say.'

'Aunty Winnie doesn't.'

Aunty Winnie lived next door and was his mother's best friend. She had yellow hair and red cheeks and bright blue eyes and apparently had been a Viking. All of which stumped Jimmy. In the first place she was a woman, and in the second place, according to the nuns, the Vikings had left here hundreds of years ago.

His father went back to his newspaper and Jimmy forgot about it but the following day – Mondays were always busy at the hardware shop because of it being shut on Sunday – his dad came to the shop.

Isabel had taken the baby into the back with her. His dad wandered about while Jimmy served various customers, and then his dad left without saying what he wanted, but he came back that afternoon when it was quieter.

It was always quieter after dinner because everybody had a big meal at midday and there was the clearing up to be done by the women and the other jobs they did, so it was mid afternoon by the time it picked up again.

Isabel was lying down probably, though she always said it was book work or summat, and he was reading to the baby. Hannah would be up at the foundling school with the nuns, as she so often was, and in a way he and Isabel felt as if it was something they could give her.

He was reading *Robinson Crusoe*. The baby seemed perfectly happy. Mr Gilbraith liked people to read, and it was one of the things that Jimmy did enjoy and since there were books for the children at school Jimmy tended to bring them home. Sometimes one of the sisters would come down and get them back, but nobody minded because they said a lot of the lads never read at all and Jimmy was happy reading the same book over and over.

Anyroad, there he was reading to the baby in the mid quiet of the afternoon, it was his favourite time, and his dad came into the shop. Jimmy didn't mind that, he was glad that he was in such a responsible position, looking after Allen and the shop, and his dad didn't say much but mooched about for a while. That was fine, sometimes folk forgot what they were doing there, or changed their minds, or found something they hadn't known they wanted – Isabel said that was especially good business. Then his dad came over and looked at Allen and he said, 'He's doing all right, isn't he?'

Jimmy said he was and they both looked at the baby and his dad wandered around the shop for a while and then he left. It was nothing special, people always wandered in and out except for young lads, who weren't allowed in by themselves in case they tried to thieve summat.

Anyroad, he went back to reading to the baby, and then Isabel came in and the shop was busy and when it closed they had their tea.

Jim Slater had no idea what to do. He had tried to brush off the idea that occurred to him and he knew that it was stupid but he couldn't rid his mind of it. He knew their Jimmy was a very clever lad and was proud of him, just as he was proud of their Robert, they were both bright lads. The lasses were his wife's business. There had never been problems since they had come here. He had done well and been able to keep his family and although his wife complained she always complained about everything, that was just the way she was, nowt was ever good enough for her.

Her dad had worked in an office and been upset when she wanted to marry Jim and she had never forgotten it. She was always going on about how she had thought he would rise in the world or she would never have married him.

Jim thought he had done well, he was Mr Gilbraith's right-hand man and proud of it, and they spent a lot of time together these days. It did mean that he couldn't do much joinery work any more, but he had set on two men in their early twenties and they were capable and good. They had to be because otherwise Mr Gilbraith would have had them off the job in no time. Also Robert had gone in with him for a while though never been happy about it and he was glad that Robert had chosen otherwise.

He was proud of Robert though not as proud as his wife was. She would delight anybody who would listen as to how their Robert was as good as the doctor nowadays and so clever and so caring and she had never imagined he would do so well.

He was a moody bugger was Robert, quiet like Jim himself, whereas Jimmy was noisy and forthright, but each in his way was clever and Jim was proud of them. Lasses married and had their own families but the lads would always be there, at least he hoped so. Even if they did marry eventually it just wasn't the same thing.

He had been worried of late that Robert might not stay, since the doctor had taken him up, not just to help Sister Lydia but to learn doctoring in lots of ways, even with women's pregnancies. The whole idea put Jim off, but then again Robert brought home a good wage and that was what counted and though Jim's wife complained about that too, she was ignored.


Jim tried to sleep and succeeded for two nights but the problem kept coming back to the surface and he could think of nothing but that he should ask Robert about it. If he has got that lass into bother he thought, I'll bloody kill him, but he also knew that as the baby grew, if he looked distinctive and was such a Slater as never was, Jim thought regretfully, everybody would work it out.

Half of him wanted to wait and ignore the problem, but also he knew that if you neglected problems the ones that started out as molehills turned into bloody mountains and so he had always thought that the sooner you sorted things out the better it would be.

Still he put it off. Robert was never there. He was at the hospital, he was out with Sister Lydia at all times of the day and night, though his mother had complained bitterly about such goings on and said that she wished they had never come here, she had never thought things would be this bad, and now their Robert – Jim couldn't stand to think of it. If their Robert had gone with Isabel Norton then the babby was most likely his, but then it meant that she had gone with two men at once, which was so disgusting that it sickened Jim to his stomach.

His wife had been right, their Robert should have married Polly Swift when his mam and her mam thought it a good idea. It could be too late now all round, young folk left like that always got themselves into trouble, he thought. He wanted to tell his wife, but she wasn't the kind of woman you could tell anything like that. She would go potty, he didn't know what she would do, and so he had to keep the problem to himself.

He half thought of going to talk to Mr Gilbraith, but then Mr Gilbraith might have a certain opinion about it which Jim did not share, so the first thing was to ask their Robert if he had done it.

It was the first Sunday in January and he knew that if Robert was not busy he might go to the chapel with the nuns because if they had time Sister Lydia would be there, and Robert, rather than going home for whatever reason in his free time, would be there with her.

Jim didn't think there was anything between Robert and Sister Lydia, unlike his wife who was horrified at the casual talk and the circumstances.

Jim was not a churchgoer but he waited outside and when Robert came out with Sister Lydia in tow as ever, Jim asked him if he could have a word. Robert looked surprised, as well he might, Jim thought.

He walked Robert away from the church and out of the village, past the fell house and on to the fell itself. It was for once a dry day but cold and he had got colder through standing around. Robert became impatient, his father could tell by the way that the lad hesitated. He stopped and so Jim stopped, but he had no idea how to broach the subject so he just stood there.

'Summat up?' his son said abruptly. It wasn't that his son did not know how to speak properly but he liked to let go a bit when he was with members of his family because all the rest of the time he was on show – Jim knew that it was a sort of affectation, if that was the word for it. It was a release, a relief, but Jim was slightly surprised and not pleased that his son should use it for him.

If he was wrong about this he would stand his son's anger. If he was right – he couldn't bear the idea that he might be accurate – but then it had to be said. He had thought so much about this it had almost driven him mad.

He stood and didn't say anything. For the first time in thirty years he could feel the tears coming into his eyes. He looked away across the fell, nothing but sheep and sparse grass and the odd windblown tree, further across there were stone walls and gates and the road which went down into Deerness Valley.

'Is me mam poorly?' Robert urged.

'No. No, she's fine.'

'Jimmy? One of the lasses?'

'You'd know first,' his father said and Jim thought yes, he was right, Robert would, but did you ever get used to the fact that your children might know a great deal about a subject you knew nothing about? It took some getting used to. Robert was up on these things, too far up on them, a lot of people said. There had been a scandal when Robert began helping with women's stuff like childbirth, but the doctor had elevated him so high that he was able to help.

Jim turned and looked back at his son. Robert wore what to Jim was an expensive dark suit, you could tell by the cut of it and the material that a good tailor had made it especially for him. The doctor needed to put some distance between Robert and the rest of the village and this was one of the ways in which he did so. Jim had been thinking that the doctor might even ask if Robert could go to Wolsingham and live in his house, and that would make a huge gulf. Jim had not voiced this fear to his wife but he dreaded even more that what he feared might be true.

He took a deep breath.

'I've got something to ask you. I don't want to and I beg your pardon if I'm wrong but it's playing on my mind. I'm just about up the wall with it and I have to know. Did you father Isabel Norton's bairn?'

He waited for Robert to laugh. He waited for Robert to disclaim such a thing, he waited for Robert to deny it, but he saw the look come over Robert's face and after that everything changed.

'Me?'

Jim nodded.

'The miller has such distinctive looks and the baby looks like you.'

There was a long pause and then Robert said, 'The bairn is the miller's, everybody knows that.' Robert did not meet his eyes and Jim willed him to.

'So I understand. Have you seen him?'

'What the miller?'

'No, the bairn.'

'Not since he was born. I was there. Sister Lydia went at first and then she sent other people, including our Jimmy of course.' His voice sounded light and Jim was desperate to believe him, aching to think that his son had not done such a thing. Surely he had not. Surely he could have found a lass he liked, a lass like Polly Swift who was a nice lass, ordinary, just like everybody else, and been content.

'How could you think such a thing?' Robert said.

'Because the bairn looks exactly like our Jimmy.'

Robert frowned. His eyes narrowed.

'Jimmy?'

'Aye. Even Jimmy noticed.'

'Well, he would, wouldn't he? Always ready with a new tale, our Jimmy.'

There was a silence which seemed to Jim to last for ever and the sun was now warming the day because it was noon and he knew that he would be going back to a big dinner and he felt sick to his stomach. He wasn't ready to be assured that this child was nothing to do with his son. And yet he wanted so very much to believe it.

Robert was smiling now.

'I have to get back. We have several cases to see this afternoon,' he said, and then he turned around and walked away to the village.

Jim felt sicker than he thought he had ever felt in his life. He knew his son too well and Robert's eyes had given the game away. How long would it be now before it became obvious to the whole village that Robert was the father of Isabel Norton's child? How could he have been so stupid? Worst of all somehow was that he had not married her. When you did the most stupid thing a man could do you had to ask her to marry you. He was not happy, he had to talk to Robert again and this time he must do something more about it.

He wanted to blame Isabel and in a way it was easier to think that she had used her wiles to seduce his son. He had heard of women who did such things but she was not bonny, not taking, he had never even heard her speak other than in the shop about hammers and nails and such, and when Jimmy and Hannah had gone to live there. She seemed a nice lass to him if he looked at it objectively. It was said that she was shy and polite. Still waters run deep was Jim's conclusion, but he could not get out of his mind that his son who was so clever had done something so stupid.

He had never been like other lads, if he had wanted to marry he could have had Polly Swift ages ago and God knew she was a much bonnier and more outgoing lass than the one from the hardware store who was like a mouse and plain looking. Jim just hoped to God his wife never found out or there would be hell to pay in so many different ways that he shuddered and tried to put it from his mind.

# *Thirty*

Jim was not the only one who panicked and felt sick. All this time Robert had wanted to go to Isabel and say how sorry he was for what he had done, but he was too much of a coward. He had not for a second thought that the baby could be his. He had heard the gossip in the village that the miller was going there and folk didn't like the man, it was rumoured he had done the same thing to his first wife, so it was hardly surprising he had done such a thing again.

Robert thought the miller must be nuts, wanting more children when he already had a clutch of them. What was it with him? But then Robert had tried to clear from his mind the single stupid act that he had gone there and had had the girl, though how or why he was not sure now. It had been very brief, totally unsatisfactory, and was mostly her doing, he told himself. He had not known that lasses were like that. Polly had never done such a thing and he didn't know any other lasses at all well. Three sisters had made him reluctant to go anywhere near them, and now look what had happened.

He thought back to Isabel giving birth and he had been horrified, how long it took, how much pain she was in, but he would not have it that the child was his. It could not and did not have anything to do with him. He had been with her once, whereas according to gossip, the miller had been going there for a while. Even so he felt guilty. He should offer to marry Isabel though it was the last thing he would ever want. He must try to pretend that he wanted to. He must learn to want to. He was so busy that he was able to put this matter from his mind for several days, but in the end the guilt threatened to overcome not just his mind but his work. Even Lydia noticed and asked if there was something the matter.

He decided that he had to talk to Isabel but it was difficult because Hannah and Jimmy were living there. He made an excuse and called in at the shop and when he saw the baby he knew that it was true, the baby was his. The miller had gone to see her so many times and he had been there only once, it was just his luck. He had to talk to her now, his father and Jimmy knew what was going on and presumably Hannah had noticed if she ever noticed anything except what went on in her mind, he thought.

So he had to time things carefully. Hannah left to walk up to the foundling school in the afternoons, he had taken to watching when he could, and it was a routine. So Jimmy would be in the shop and hopefully the door would be closed between shop and house so that he could speak to her without interruption.

He hoped everybody was too busy to notice, but there was no help for it, it was the only time she might be by herself, Jimmy busy in the shop. He was in luck. He lifted the latch on the back door and she was on her own.

Robert didn't say anything to begin with. How did you apologize for something so huge, how did you apologize for not having acknowledged it, for not having helped? He didn't know, just that he was beginning to feel as if he would never be able to concentrate on anything else for the rest of his life.

She didn't say anything, she just looked at him straight into his eyes and then she said, 'It took you long enough.'

He immediately wanted to blame her, call her names, tell her what a slut she was, how she had gone with a married man and then with him. She was a whore, a harlot, a disgusting – no, he couldn't even think of it honestly. She had been young and lost and by herself and scared and she hadn't coped. He hadn't coped either, and God knew about the miller. Did anybody ever manage their lives without making colossal, gigantic and undo-able mistakes? He was beginning to doubt it, and to hate himself for being so weak and stupid.

'I didn't know it was mine. It didn't seem possible,' was all he managed under the harshness of her gaze, and he knew that she was thinking how he had seen her in such pain and perhaps even been glad of it, but he wasn't. He wouldn't ever do that. He hadn't meant to put her through any of that, he had thought from time to time that he had got off lightly, that he had got away with it, and now he understood that it was not so.

'I don't suppose it did,' she said grudgingly.

'I don't know what to say,' was all he could manage.

'Several things might come to mind.'

The baby was lying in a crib by the wall and the only thing Robert could say was, 'Is it all right if I have a look at him?'

'I thought you'd seen him. Jimmy said you came into the shop.'

'Jimmy's too sharp.'

'He works things out.'

Robert managed to get over to the baby. To him it just looked like anybody else's child, dark haired, pale skinned, but it didn't have that bright carrot-coloured hair which would have defined it as a Barnfather, so it could not be the miller's child.

'Blue eyes like yours,' she offered.

Robert felt nothing. He wasn't sure what he was supposed to say or feel, but nothing happened.

'Do you think he looks like me?'

'It's a straight choice between you and the miller,' she said bitterly, 'so I would say yes. Are you frightened people will find out?'

That was when Robert looked at her.

'Frightened? No. I just feel so pathetic, that I could do such a thing and then pretend I hadn't, that I was too stupid to acknowledge what I'd done or try to help, and especially when you went through all that pain.'

'It was awful,' she said, 'I didn't imagine it would be as bad as that.'

'It was the worst I'd ever seen. I couldn't believe it. After that I didn't want to know. I wanted to run away. I pretended it wasn't mine, hoped it wasn't, but I didn't want it to be the miller's either.'

'You just wanted the baby not to exist. You think I'm disgusting?'

He shook his head. He couldn't look at her or at the baby. He couldn't look at anything.

'I think life treated you badly and you were lonely and – he's a piece of shit.'

'I didn't know that. I didn't know anything until it was too late. My excuse for you is that you were the opposite.'

'Was I?'

'Of course. At the time – no, a long time before that – I really thought I liked you. I didn't understand that you were – like you are, all caught up in your own ideas and not caring about anybody.'

'If it's any consolation neither did I.'

There was what felt to him like a long silence and during it he despised himself so much that breathing got difficult.

'If the baby had been his would you ever have acknowledged what you had done?'

'I don't know. Probably not.'

'He asked me to leave with him.'

'It's what he does apparently,' Robert said. 'I think we should get married.'

Isabel stared at him.

'Don't be soft,' she said. 'You don't want to marry me, and though I thought it would be nice to be married to you, I've changed my mind. I don't want to marry you. I've got the sisters and Jimmy and folk have to come to the shop for anything they want. Sister Lydia even asked me to go to the chapel on a Sunday. Can you imagine what folk would think?'

'If I could get us away from here, then I think we might be all right.'

She stared at him.

'Away?'

'Aye, to Edinburgh. I've been told I can go there and study. It would be so different. Nobody would know what happened and we could get married straight away and it would be so much better than this place. We need never come back.'

Isabel stared at him as though her gaze was locked into place.

'What about your family, your mam and dad and – and Jimmy. How do you think that would make them all feel, as though we didn't want them?'

He said nothing.

'Does it seem to you that somehow and miraculously once we get to another place you're going to want me? Robert, that's stupid.'

'It would be better than this.'

'What?' She paused. 'Oh, I see, you feel bad about it and you're trying to shift the feeling by making me feel bad. Do you think I could feel any worse? After all I've been through. If you had cared about me you would have asked me to marry you when we first knew I was having a baby, even if you weren't sure it was yours. But you don't, and to be honest now I'm glad because I think you could possibly be the worst husband any woman ever had.'

He looked at her, surprised, hurt.

'You're selfish, Robert, you don't care about anybody or anything but work. You'd be the kind of man who was always out, like those who spend their evenings in the pub. Not that you'd be at the pub, but you'd have a laboratory or whatever to go to or a study to go to, and you just would never come out of it.

And what do you think I would do in such a place? Sit over the teacups and brag about my husband being a doctor? I don't think so.'

'Edinburgh is beautiful, that's what everybody says. We could buy a fine house and have a family and you could have all sorts of nice things.'

'Do you know it always amazes me when people talk about giving other folk "things". All anybody really wants is to have somebody to come home to who wants to come home to them, to spend time with them, to sit at a table and have a nice meal and kiss goodnight. All the things in the world wouldn't make up for that. I don't think I shall ever have that, but I wouldn't make things worse than they are. Life does that very well and with my assistance I've already got myself into a mess that will haunt me for ever, so if you want to go off to Edinburgh, get yourself away.'

'And what about the baby?' he said.

'I will look after him,' she said.

He had to breathe hard after he left her, he wanted to cry, he was being rejected. He had done his best to help and she didn't want him. He would find somebody better, he would leave here and go away and never come back, and he would make for himself a reputation and be a great doctor.

When he had gone – the way he had come in, Isabel didn't want to give her neighbours anything more to talk about, letting men out of her back door, but she had little choice – she had her tea and sat over the fire and she was glad of having Jimmy and Hannah there, though she let the talk slide over her. She wanted to tell Hannah, she wanted to confide in someone, but she didn't think Hannah would understand and having somebody who didn't understand would be the worst of all it seemed to her.

It was true, she thought, she didn't want to marry him any more, she didn't love him, she didn't want him. He might be clever, but he was weak, and she could never marry anybody weak. She would soon learn to despise him. She was strong enough to go forward now and make a life for herself and Allen.

She thought that Robert would not come back, he had assuaged his guilt, he had done the tiny bit that he felt necessary, and she was sure he would think of her no more and get on with his life in the way that he had chosen. She didn't blame him, she just wished that she didn't blame herself so very much. Why were other people allowed to make mistakes and she was not? Would she be this hard on other people?

For once Allen began to cry. Perhaps he sensed her desolation, her isolation, which she knew was a precursor of the life to come. She would never have anybody but him now, and being a man, one day he too would go and leave her for somebody else.

'I was thinking, Isabel,' Jimmy said, the following day.

'Well, you don't want to be doing too much of that, not at your age,' she said, and he laughed as she had meant him to.

'I'm eleven. How old are you?'

'Nineteen.'

'Right, well, when I'm sixteen we could get wed. That's only another five years and you'll still be sort of young by then, won't you? And Allen will be so bonny.'

Isabel laughed. She hadn't laughed like that in such a long time, maybe before her parents had been taken ill, before her father and then her mother had died.

'Oh Jimmy,' she said, 'you'll want to marry a lass your own age.'

'If I did that I'd have to leave Allen and I don't ever want to and I don't want to leave you. You only have me, and well, and the sisters. Allen is so special, don't you think he is?'

'I think he is of course.'

'So do I. If we got married I wouldn't ever have to go home.'

'Your mam would love that.'

'She doesn't say owt now.'

'She would if we got married.'

'Yes, but if you marry somebody else I won't get to see Allen any more.'

'Nobody's going to marry me.'

'Are you sure?'

'Absolutely.'

'And you won't want to marry anybody?'

'I won't.'

'Will you let me know if you do, and Allen and me, we will run away.'

When she went to bed that night Isabel wondered what it was about these Slater lads. There was something special about them, her heart hurt her and she wondered, as she could not help doing sometimes, what it might have been like had Robert Slater loved her.


Jimmy wished he didn't listen at doors, but nobody told him anything so it had long since become a habit and when Robert had gone he was desperate to tell somebody about it so in the end he told Hannah.

Her eyes grew bigger and bigger much to Jimmy's horror, and then he half wished he hadn't said anything.

'Who else knows?'

'Me dad.'

She stared.

'I talked to him about it. I didn't know what to think, but if you look at Baby Allen he does look like us. And so me dad worked it out and told Robert, and then he came here. She says she won't marry him.'

'But they have to get married now.'

'She won't.'

'But everybody will find out. Then what will happen?'

'I think I should tell Mary.'

Hannah stared at him even more.

'Whatever for?'

'Because just think when her dad finds out that it isn't his. You know what he's like.'

'I can't say I do.'

'Well, he— you know. You know he did.'

'And our Robert too?' Hannah looked as though she felt sick, Jimmy thought.

Robert went to talk to Mr Gray at the hospital when they had a few minutes to spare. He didn't know what to say, he couldn't say what he thought he should, he just said that he thought he was ready to go to Edinburgh to study. The doctor sighed.

'I know. I should have mentioned it to you before now, you are ready to learn much more than I can ever teach you and I think now that the hospital is set up and we have sufficient capable people, Sister Lydia can probably manage without you.'

Robert felt slightly injured that the doctor dismissed him so easily. He had thought that the doctor could at least regret his going. He felt as if he must get out of there before the baby became so obviously his.

Lydia didn't react as he had thought or hoped she would either. She just sighed and said, 'I knew the day would come. I wish I could go.'

It had not occurred to Robert that she would want any such thing, though in his heart he felt that she would make a much better doctor than he, but he had the need to get away. Lydia couldn't go from here unless she gave up being a nun, and he couldn't see that happening.

Mr Gray wrote to Edinburgh University and the response was favourable. Robert could go there and start at the medical school in the term that began after Easter, which was no more than three months away. That was when Robert decided that he must tell his father. The trouble was he didn't seem to be able to get his dad by himself, his mother always popped up as she had never seemed to do before.

The front room became general territory like a railway station, and since she wasn't used to having him home for any length of time and since he was the only one who lived at home, even part of the time, she tended to cling to him, to make food for him, ask whether he was hungry, what he had been doing and how long he could stay, until he wanted to get away more and more. He became impatient.

The doctor's second response was that he must try and replace Robert, and that didn't please Robert either. He would write to the people he could think of who might be able to find someone to help, preferably an already qualified doctor. Robert couldn't believe how petty he felt, he didn't want to be replaced and yet he knew that somebody would be needed to help, and he wanted to be gone so much that he could barely sleep.

Neither Mr Gray nor Lydia mentioned the matter again. Nobody said that they would regret his going, nobody wished he might find he couldn't let go, and yet he must.

The days went forward and and he began to wish that the time wasn't ticking by. He put off telling his parents until the acceptance became reality and plans were put in place, so in the end he had to go to the house on a Sunday and tell them that it was only a matter of weeks before he left. He had not realized how difficult it would be, he had not known that his father would be so displeased. His mother burst into tears. Robert couldn't look at either of them.

'I thought you weren't thinking of going any more,' his mother sobbed. 'You are needed here, Mr Gray is getting old and that nun couldn't possibly do all that work by herself, even if she was half as clever as folk think she is.'

His father sat there like somebody had stuffed him.

'Mr Gray and Mr Gilbraith think it is the right time,' Robert offered. His father got up and wandered around as though he couldn't think of what to do or say.

'You can't think that now is the right time,' his father said softly, perhaps hoping that his wife had suddenly lost her acute hearing.

'It's exactly the right time,' Robert said.

'Who will look after you?'

'There are lodgings apparently, a place to sleep and eat, and the university will provide everything, Mr Gray says.' He didn't like to add that he had a great deal of money. He had offered it to his parents but they had refused. Now it would come in more useful than he had expected. He could go whenever he chose. Also he couldn't bear that he should still be here when his replacement arrived, and he felt sure that somebody much more experienced and perhaps older would come here and take his place and people would talk about it and how much better he was than Robert could ever have been.

'I wish we had never come here,' his mother said for perhaps the four-hundredth time. 'I wish I was well away from here and none of this had happened.'

She ran out of the room. Robert could hear her footsteps, which were usually light on the stairs, but now she was making enough noise for three people in her despair. When she slammed the bedroom door so hard that the house shook his father looked at him. Robert looked at the floor.

'You're going to get married?' his father guessed.

Robert had known but tried not to think about the fact that he hadn't told his father directly that Isabel's child was his. Now he had to face it.

'She won't have me.'

His father had never heard that one before, Robert surmised with tight lips.

'What is she going to do?'

'I don't know.'

'You didn't ask her?'

'She won't have me, all right?'

'It isn't all right Robert, it's anything but. You are running away from the situation which you caused. No man does that.'

'Lots of them do, I feel sure,' Robert said.

'Any man calling himself respectable marries a lass who has his bairn.'

'Well, maybe I don't call myself anything of the sort,' Robert said, becoming as angry as his dad.

'She cannot bring up a bairn here on her own.' Robert was surprised at the way that his father's voice rose. His dad never shouted.

His father said nothing more and didn't look at him.

'What do you want me to do?' he demanded, becoming more angry in his turn.

'I want you to persuade her to marry you. You can't just leave her.'

'I'm not leaving her, I'm going away to become a doctor.'

'No son of mine would run away and leave a lass with a bairn, it's not right, and no talking about it will make it right.'

Robert tried to get out of the house at that point, but when he moved his dad got hold of him and swung him around. He had never done such a thing before.

'You have to talk to her.'

Robert, without using force, tried to shrug his dad off.

'Let go of me,' he said. 'I've done everything I could and she won't listen.'

'She likely knows that having done such a thing you don't care about her.'

'Well, maybe I don't.' Robert was too angry now to pretend. 'I didn't ever care about her and she doesn't care about me. And besides—'

'And besides what?'

'She let the miller have her first so—'

He got no further. His father hit him. His father had never hit him before and it wasn't just something small, it knocked Robert into the side of the wooden dresser so that the furniture tottered.

Half of it was surprise because he was so much younger and fitter than his dad that in usual circumstances his dad wouldn't have been able to do such a thing. And his dad hit him, not like he would hit another man with his fist, he slapped Robert hard around the face as you would slap somebody who wasn't worth the respect of your fist. Robert was too aghast to do anything but get himself upright, and after that his dad hit him on the other side of his face so that it matched and sent him against the table and chairs, and after that his mam came crashing down the stairs and into the room, face pale and eyes darting from one to the other.

'Isabel Norton's bairn is our Robert's,' his dad said, and his teeth were clenched with fury so that the words came out in an audible hiss.

Robert couldn't move. He couldn't have got across the room and out of the door had the building been falling around him. He couldn't look at his dad, but he knew that his dad had never looked at him in such a way before, like he was the lowest most vile thing on the planet.

His mother didn't seem to grasp it, but she was a quick learner,

Robert knew, and within seconds she worked it out as well and she put her thin hands up to cover her face and began to wail in despair.

'Oh, the shame of it,' she managed, 'the shame.'

'Go upstairs and get what's left of your things,' his dad said, pointing as though Robert didn't know the way.

Robert didn't move.

'Go on, and then get out of my house. I don't want you here ever again.'

Somehow Robert climbed the stairs, stuffed his clothes and the few books he had left here into a bag, and within less than five minutes he was out of the house and into the street.

Jim took his wife into his arms and she sobbed and sobbed against his shoulder. He put up one hand and stroked her hair while she sobbed away the disappointment, the betrayal, what the village would think of her son, and how things would never ever be any good again.

# Thirty-one

Mary had known that something would go wrong. Her experience of life had taught her that. When she had been younger, before her dad had left her mam, things had been good. She had thought they always would be. Now that things kept on going wrong again and again she felt as though some rhythm had left her life, that having turned itself into horror it would not settle.

She told herself that it was time for them to be happy, why shouldn't it be, after everything they had gone through? Fran carried Baby Daisy around with her now and sang to her, and Daisy was an easy baby, Mary thought, much easier than the two little girls before her had been. Maybe that was something to do with the fact that Fran was happy. Mary could not remember her mother happy somehow.

Abe had become almost as good a miller as her dad, so her dad said, and though Abe was never going to be the sort of person who talked a lot, he had given to smiling under his dad's flattery, and spending as much time as he could with Burt, and Burt adored him.

They had sufficient money to eat well and live well. Maybe the future was coming together. Mary had almost stopped worrying. Her dad spoke civilly to her, and he was almost as nice as she had believed him to be before he walked out and left her and the others and her mam. She was ready to forgive him, to think well of him, to be grateful that he was her dad.

He even encouraged her to go to school, and when Fran said she couldn't manage by herself he said he would ask Mr Gilbraith if there was a woman who could come and help in the house now that Sister Abigail was too busy to come more than a couple of times a month. Mary suggested that she would contact Sister Abigail and ask her, and he seemed to be in favour of this.

She decided to stop by and tell Jimmy. She quite liked the hardware shop and could live with the memories of what it used to be like. Isabel was never in the shop, presumably she had enough to do at the back, what with the baby and everything.

Mary thought that if she talked to Jimmy about the fact that her dad had said she could go to school, Jimmy might want to go too. Then she thought, no, Jimmy would never leave Baby Allen, he loved the little boy so much, almost as much as she loved Baby Daisy, although she was feeling rather left out now that Fran had taken the baby to her. There was a space in Mary's arms and in her heart, which the baby had inhabited. She would fill that place with school.

Jimmy was dealing with a customer and Baby Allen was nowhere to be seen, something of a disappointment, Mary thought, though she did not want to talk to Isabel. She didn't think they could ever be nice to one another, too much had gone on. The customer left.

'Where's the baby?'

'The lasses have got him in the back. He was crying, summat to do with his gums,' Jimmy said, lifting his surprisingly long-lashed eyes to the ceiling. He would be nice-looking when he got older, Mary thought, and she quite liked him as a friend. He was nothing like the men in her family, and he seemed to like her too, it was good to talk to somebody else.

And since nobody came in after the customer left Mary proceeded to tell him what her dad had said about her going to school.

'I'm glad it's not me,' Jimmy said, 'I'm never going back there. Besides, Isabel needs me here to see to the shop.'

'If your Hannah took the baby she could manage the shop by herself,' Mary said.

'I don't want her to. I like Allen.'

'I know you do.'

Jimmy looked as if he was going to say something, and then stopped.

'If you came to school we could read more books and talk about them,' Mary said.

'I can just go and collect them, or Sister Abigail brings me new ones. There's nowt at school for me. I like having a job, I like being in charge, and I do the ordering and sort out the shelves.

Hannah cleans them, I don't like that bit, but I help her to take everything off the shelves and I put them where they are meant to be, and I can find everything in the place. And me mam might think I should go back and live at home, and that's not going to happen,' Jimmy said. 'The shop makes money and Isabel would pay Hannah and me if we would let her, she's really nice.'

'I've never liked her.'

'Well, that's because of your dad,' Jimmy said.

'She should have left him alone,' Mary said, for once annoyed because somebody was talking her dad down.

Jimmy frowned and Mary wished she hadn't said it.

'It isn't his anyroad,' Jimmy said.

'It isn't his what?' Mary said, going very cool considering

what a sunny day it was outside. It was never a nice day in here, she had never liked the shop, it was gloomy and had a mouldy smell. The big window at the front offered the only light, the shelves and corners and walls were laden with big boxes of hooks and nails, the walls were lined with yard brushes, sweeping brushes, and tools like axes and hammers, so that it gave off an atmosphere in the dark shadows which wasn't quite pleasing to her.

'Nowt,' Jimmy said. 'I've got to get on. Other folk will be in.'

And then she understood and although Jimmy tried to walk away, she went with him.

'Baby Allen? Baby Allen isn't my dad's?'

'I didn't mean that.'

'Yes, you did. What did you mean? What did you mean, Jimmy?' She was squaring up to him, glaring at him, and she meant to.

Jimmy stopped then and seemed to consider. Then he said haltingly, 'Well, we talked about it, hair on fire and goosegog eyes. Baby Allen doesn't look like that.'

'He could look like Isabel.'

Jimmy gave her the look that he gave when he knew he was right and everybody else was wrong.

'Isabel has brown eyes and brown hair. He wouldn't look owt like her in a month of Sundays,' he said.

'So what does he look like?'

Jimmy considered, his brow went into lines, she could see.

'Well, he looks like a lad from Bishop.'

'Like you?'

'Aye, sort of.'

'How come?'

'Well, because,' Jimmy said. 'Some folk do. And some folk

look like other folk from way back when, I read about it. He doesn't have to look like anybody.'

This wouldn't do, Mary thought. Jimmy wasn't glancing even in her direction never mind straight at her.

'So,' she plunged, 'your dad is just like my dad.'

Jimmy was looking in her direction now, blue eyes lit.

'My dad is nowt of the sort, Mary Barnfather, don't you say such stuff.'

'That's right, isn't it?' Mary said.

'My dad would never do owt like that, he only cares about me mam and his own bairns. My dad's not like that.'

'Well, he must be, mustn't he? I know that much anyroad, I know as much as you.'

'You don't then,' Jimmy said, 'Baby Allen is our Robert's bairn, there now.'

Mary knew disaster when she saw it straight in front of her. She had learned to see it just as it came over the hill towards her, she recognized it in silent agony, her world was going wrong again and she had thought it could not, they had been through so much.

Jimmy looked as though he wished himself far away. She didn't think that she could be made more miserable than knowing Isabel's baby was her dad's. She had thought it couldn't get any worse, she had been wrong. She had known even though she had tried not to think about it that her dad's world was complete now that he had his own son.

He was a different person, like all his Christmases had come together. Her dad was happy, he was like the dad she had known when she was little and she had been his favourite and her mam had still been alive.

She was back at the little house in Cowshill and her dad was at work and she was playing in the stream. Her mam was making her a new dress and was embroidering butterflies all around the bottom of the skirt. It was a yellow dress because her mam said that yellow suited her, and the butterflies were red admirals and painted ladies, orange, white and black, and little tortoiseshells, brown and orange.

Then the images left her and there was a horrible hard feeling inside her stomach which grew and grew until it filled all of her and she wanted to go outside and be sick. Yet she could still hope. It was amazing that even after your life shattered in front of you, you were in some ways so far behind that you were like a man jumping off a cliff who still saw firm land beneath him until it was too late. And then she understood and was afraid.

# Thirty-two

Lydia was in her room when Robert arrived at the hospital with his belongings. She knew him so well by now that she could see he was distressed, and then she saw his face, the marks and the way that he didn't look at her. For once she had been congratulating herself that the world was not falling apart.

Nobody was seriously ill, the doctor had not called for her to go to some emergency, and this was her life, so with little to do other than read books about yet another form of medicine she was rather lost. She was therefore almost pleased to see him. He had just gone in and dumped his bag on the bed and she was about to say something ordinary when she could see everything was wrong.

'You've been in a fight?' she said, ready to be horrified.

'Not exactly, no,' he said.

She went in and was about to touch his face when he drew back hard. She didn't usually go into his room and he didn't go into hers, it was an unspoken rule, so she wasn't quite sure why she had forgotten it but she was concerned about him, her instincts were shrieking.

They both liked the little privacy they could manage, so it was a case of polite knocking on doors and hesitating even when the door was half open, so in some ways she just wished she had not seen him come in and then she thought he had not come in like he usually did.

'Are you hurt?'

'I'm fine, Lydia.'

He spoke impatiently and there was something just that little bit disrespectful about the way that he used her name unpunctuated by 'sister', and that was unusual too.

'Maybe you could leave me alone.' And then, as she stood in the doorway, not quite beyond it, he said, 'Mr Gray has agreed that I should go to Edinburgh to study medicine and Mr Gilbraith thinks it's a good idea and it is going to be sorted out, so I can leave at any time and start up after Easter, the new term.'

'Well, I know, but that gives us time to get used to it and Mr Gray thinks he will find somebody new,' she said, looking hard at the bag which he had dropped on to the bed.

'I can go to Edinburgh now.'

'Right now?'

Robert said nothing to that, so Lydia tried again.

'Have you told Mr Gray you're going straight away?'

'I don't need to, it's all been settled by the doctor and Mr Gilbraith, so why should I stay here any longer when I can afford to get away?'

'Were you going to leave without telling me?'

'Why should I tell you?'

Lydia smelled a rat or perhaps even several rats.

'Have you told your parents?'

He looked at her then. She thought he had never looked so pale or haggard and so very unhappy that his eyes betrayed it.

'My dad didn't want me to go. We had a row and my mam cried. I've had enough, Lydia. I know it means more work for you, but the system at the hospital and the clinics is so good now that you should manage, and I have to get out of here. There will be another doctor here to replace me in next to no time, you'll see.'

'It's perfectly understandable that your mam cried. You were all she had left, it's been like Exodus from your house.' Lydia was striving for humour to try and mix the recipe a little. 'She'll learn to cope. Your Kitty looks to me like she's expecting. I was down there yesterday and I think it's a bit early to say, but she has all the right symptoms. Your mother will be so pleased. I think she's been fretting when nothing happened. Bless Kitty, she thinks she has some horrible disease, she's so tired and aching and low.'

Robert didn't react. He finished stuffing his clothes into the second bag, and then he just walked out.

Lydia didn't understand. She knew that his parents would not want him to leave, but even Robert's mother wouldn't expect him to stay here when he had a golden opportunity like this. She didn't know what to do, she wanted to run around telling everybody what had happened, but that seemed childish and gossipy and after all what Robert did was his own business.

Yes, she thought he was selfish, going like that, but she knew also that if she had been given such an opportunity in such circumstances she would have left too. But she liked being right here, she liked being a nun, she liked belonging to this place as she had never belonged anywhere before. Her life prior to this was just a working up towards it. And he had wanted to go for so long, talked about it for as far back as she could remember, so maybe he just couldn't stand any more waiting, she wouldn't blame him for that.

As she worked on she became more optimistic. Life without Robert would certainly be different, but he was right, they could manage quite well without him. Mr Gilbraith would need to find somebody else to ride with her. She did know many of the farms and cottages and could go to most places by herself now, but it was a stupid idea as Robert had always told her. If she turned an ankle or had an accident with the horse she could be lost for a very long time. She must always leave word where she was, but in the dark she would need help.

At the hospital all went on as usual, and she got a note from the doctor saying that he had found a chemist who would be able to help them, a lad who had come from Stanhope originally and had now come back here from wherever he had been studying. He and his sister, who was an excellent nurse and knew almost as much as he did, would be happy to move here. That cheered her. Things would go forward and the doctor must know that Robert was leaving, or was planning ahead as they had to.

That afternoon the doctor came to the village as he usually did to help at the hospital and in the clinics. Lydia tried to take as much of the work from him because she could see how tired he was. It was obvious from the first that he did not know Robert had gone.

'Where's the laddie?' The doctor was fond of them both, but Lydia could see that he wanted Robert to succeed him. There was nobody else in the clinic at that point so Lydia was able to tell him what had happened. He said nothing at first and then he sighed.

'Robert has demons to fight and I think just at the moment they are bettering him. Yes, I wanted him to go away, but not yet, not until the new chemist and his sister will be here. I thought ahead there, thank goodness. He is a local man, went away to train and now wants to set up home with his sister and come here to us. Very enthusiastic. Also I am trying to get somebody to help you, otherwise the burden may become too great, but

I've heard nothing positive. I wish Robert had waited, but I think he has since lost patience, grown tired of this place and the responsibilities which he has chosen not to shoulder.'

Lydia stared. They had not talked about this, but then the doctor, like Mr Gilbraith, knew everything that happened.

'If he must go then it is best he should go now and we will have to move forward without him. Try not to worry about it so much my dear.' When the doctor 'my deared' her, Lydia felt better. He didn't do it often, but she knew that when it came to love the doctor loved her very much. She loved him too, he was the kind of man quite the opposite from her own father, who was a gentleman and did not work, but they were also alike in some ways for her own father had the same manners, the same ideas, and had let her become a nun against his own wishes.

Lydia therefore got on with her day and tried to take heart. There would be more people to help and even though Robert had left abruptly like that it would have been only weeks until he went away, and she could see that the doctor and Mr Gilbraith were thinking well ahead and that everything would be all right.

# Thirty-three

It occurred to the miller that Isabel would need some time to get her things together before they could leave the village. He didn't really doubt her willingness to go with him, why wouldn't she, and now the baby was a little older they could travel easily. So that Friday evening after the shops closed he made his way to the back of the shop and banged on the door.

To his surprise a young woman he didn't recognize opened it. She didn't seem to know him either and that was unusual. This was a small village, everybody knew everybody. Whatever was she doing here? What a nuisance that there was somebody else living at the shop.

'I've come to see Miss Norton,' he said, like a casual visitor.

'Yes, of course, do come in,' she offered, and then he was in the kitchen and he remembered being here with Isabel, holding and kissing her. She came to him and then he remembered all the love he had for her and for their child.

The other girl melted into the background, she went off into the shop, and then he had Isabel to himself.

'Matthew, what are you doing here?' she said.

'The time is right for us to go,' he said.

She stared at him.

'Go where?' she said.

'Away from here, you, me, and the baby.'

She stared at him as if she had never heard of such a thing.

'What?' she said.

He said nothing and then she shook her head and half smiled, and then she said, 'I'm sorry Matthew but I can't do something like that.'

'How could you not?'

'Well, because the people here have accepted me.'

'But you have my son.'

She seemed to linger over the next reply, and then she looked at him and said, 'He isn't yours.'

'He isn't what?'

'He's not yours. I'm sorry, I should have said something, but he isn't, and he doesn't look like you, and there is no point in pretending.'

He stared at her, he didn't understand what she was talking about. There couldn't be anybody else, the whole idea was ridiculous. He stared at the crib where the child was apparently sleeping. Isabel saw him looking and she went over and took the little boy into her arms.

To the miller the baby looked just like every baby he had ever seen.

'What's different about him?'

'He has dark hair.'

'You have dark hair.'

'And blue eyes.'

The miller said nothing, and then he just looked at her.

'His eyes are closed.'

'Believe me, Matthew, he isn't yours.'

'He couldn't have been anyone else's. Of course he's mine. You couldn't have done such a thing. No woman would do such a thing.'

'Men do it.'

He stared at her, thought of how crudely she spoke, and then he thought of her doing what she had done with him with another man, and he was horrified. And it was worse than that. It was awful. And she had deceived him. She had pretended to him.

'He isn't mine? And all this time I made plans for us and money for us and I – I sorted everything out so that I could take you away.'

'I can't do that, I'm sure you understand.'

'Understand? That I don't have a son? You told me I had a son.'

'I told you nothing.'

'You didn't tell me I was in competition, you didn't tell me there was somebody else. Who is he? I will kill him, taking what is mine.'

Isabel drew the baby closer, and then she shouted, 'Hannah!' and the other girl appeared in the doorway.

'You led me to understand that that baby was mine,' the miller said.

'I didn't know whose he was,' she admitted.

'My God,' the miller said, horrified, 'you didn't know?'

He took a step towards her as if to take the baby, which wasn't necessarily his intention, he just wanted to appeal to her, and Hannah got between them.

'I think you should leave now, Mr Barnfather,' she said.

'I will do nothing of the sort.'

'Yes, you will, because if you don't Jimmy will go for my father who is only a few doors up and he will go for Mr Gilbraith and the other men, and they will stop you.'

The miller stared. He stared and stared while he tried to make sense of what was happening. It could not be true, this baby was his, but even as he thought that, the baby opened his eyes and it seemed to Matthew that the baby was looking straight at him as if it knew that it was not his child, and then he knew that he had been deceived, that he had laboured under some delusion.

This child was nothing to do with him. She had played him, she had taken him for an idiot, she had let him comfort and be there for her in the most basic way possible while she was playing the same game with another man. He had never met a woman who had done such a thing. It was not possible, and yet it had happened. Why was she not apologetic? Why did she not ask him to forgive her? Why had he gone down this road? He did not have a son. He did not have the only thing he had ever wanted in his life.

The other girl stood there and she was between them still, and he did not doubt the fire in her eyes and that she would make sure that the boy went for their father. The sound of her voice had brought Jimmy in from the shop, and he could see by the look on the boy's face that he would run out from either the front door or the back, and he could return with his father at any time.

Matthew knew that Jim Slater was a man to be reckoned with, as the girl threatened him, and then he saw it all so clearly. Jim Slater had fathered this child, but he had the village behind him, he had the kind of influence here which the miller could only dream of, whereas the miller had no real friends. He had people who would drink with him, but that was all, and only when he was paying. There was no friend for him here, nobody to help him, nobody to speak or plead for him, but this child was not his so there was nothing to be gained by staying.

He somehow got himself out and through the yard and into the unmade back street. There he stumbled as he never had before. There his last hopes of having a son left him and he thought of how his mother had given him up, how the woman who had taken him had never wanted him, how the people in the home had starved and beaten and abused him, and he felt worthless. He had got what he deserved. He would never have the boy he could love, the boy who would get the affection he had never had, the boy who would make up for all those years when nobody had cared, when he did not belong.

It was only when the miller and his wife took him in that he had any life at all, and it was never enough, it did not make up for all that time when he had felt so worthless. He had hungered for a boy, he had wanted so much for somebody to better the life that he had had, he had wanted to give away the love that had never been there for him because only by giving it away could he earn it, only by passing on that love could he gain it for himself. Nothing would do that now, he had tried and tried. He had tried so very hard, and it had cost him the love of two women and of his daughters and of the sons who could never be his. It had cost him everything.

He staggered down the road and all the way to the bottom of the hill. He could see Mary as he drew near to the mill, she had the baby girl in her arms. She was standing beside the stream. It had begun to rain and she was showing Baby Daisy what rain looked like when it fell into the water, so she did not see her father running very quickly towards her. She did not see or hear him as by then he could make no noise, it was as though his very voice had died within him. He could do nothing other than as he reached her he put his arms out to her for comfort, for she had always been his favourite child and he needed her now as never before. The impetus of his grasp carried her and the baby forward with him and into the river.

Jimmy had run after him and was yelling, but nobody heard him yell, as he was completely out of breath by that time, and he could not stop as he reached the water and so the four of them plunged into the depths of the mill stream.

# Thirty-four

Robert got as far as Berwick before he changed his mind. He hadn't even changed his mind, he told himself, he was just angry. He tried to make himself stay on the train, he went through all the reasons he had for leaving and it made him tired, because even though he was sure he was right to go, even though he had a dozen good reasons for leaving, in the end it was not enough and, cursing himself and everybody under creation, he got off and stood there as the train for Edinburgh left without him.

There was a good-looking hotel in the middle of the town, The King's Arms, so he went there and got a room and sat looking out of the window trying to decide whether to go back or go on.

He wanted to cry from frustration but he could not put from him the image of his father hitting him. His father had never lifted a hand to him before. His father, he dared say, had never hit anybody in his life, and it made him want to cry that he had so upset his parents and most especially his lovely dad, that he had caused Jim such distress.

His father had always done his very best for them even though to Robert many a time he had felt like scoffing at his father's limited mind. It was a limited mind compared to his own, but his father was of a different generation and had other skills that

Robert did not care for, but he acknowledged for the first time now that he could not do as well as his father did.

His father had not run away from his responsibilities, he had got on with what the good Lord had sent him, and Robert did imagine sometimes that although his wife had given him five children it must have been hard for him to live with. If she had been an easier woman he had the idea that his father would have spent more time at home, but she was always complaining and carping, and she was an easy woman to dislike. She was not very bright, she didn't seem to move forward, and he knew that in her heart she wished she had not felt obliged to leave her family. But he loved her, she had been so good to him, so good and so wonderful and so intensely irritating.

It was a great sorrow to her that she had had to make choices that seemed almost impossible and that to some degree she blamed his father just for being who he was and not what her parents would have chosen for her. She was the kind of person who wanted things to stay as they had been, possibly even after they had reached the little hilltop town.

He thought that she did not have a very clear memory of the journey from Bishop Auckland, whereas he could remember the girls crying and his father silenced and carrying Jimmy in his arms, and how they had to sleep outside and it had rained and they had trudged on and on. They had no money.

He didn't know how but his mother did not remember the hunger or the trudge or the way that they had had to sleep where they could. In her mind somehow they were still in Bishop Auckland, she had her family around her, and Jim had found a respectable office job such as she always wished he would. She felt that everything had gone wrong here in the village and her children had left her in some ways, and she could not get her thinking around the fact that things did move forward and that if you did not go with them you got left behind.

And now Robert acknowledged that the son Isabel had was his own, and how he would be left because Robert had not the guts to go forward in the right way and take responsibility for what he had done. Also his mind presented him with images of Isabel in pain having his child.

How could he leave her? He wanted to howl. He didn't of course, but his throat ached with unshed tears and his mind whirled with frustration and regret. His imagination gave him his future without Isabel, alone in Edinburgh without his family and without the little town he loved so much and the people who had helped him, the nuns and Mr Gilbraith, and the doctor, and most of all Lydia. My God, how ashamed of him she must be that he had run away and left her to manage.

They were a partnership such as men and women never were. It was not like marriage, it was quite different and yet just as vital. He needed to be there with Lydia as much as with Isabel. He doubted that Isabel would have him back now, but he felt as though he must try.

Having made the decision, everything worked against him so that had he been less determined he would have gone on to Edinburgh and tried to forget about it all, but he couldn't. At some time in the future he might be able to go, but it was not now.

He stayed at the hotel and tried to eat his dinner but couldn't, and then to sleep, but he couldn't do that either, so he just lay down on the bed and waited for morning to arrive and then he paid his bill and went back to the station.

First of all there was no train for hours, so he sat there with his bags and tried not to think that he should have been near

Edinburgh by now. It would have been easier in so many ways. He wouldn't have had to face his parents or the village or Lydia or most particularly Isabel.

He would go now, if there had been a train he would have been on it. Luckily perhaps there was no train in either direction for so long that he thought he would grow old in Berwick, which despite its castle and pretty streets was fast losing the little attraction he had thought at first that it had. He told himself that if he could go back to the hotel and stay another night to think more, then he would have worked this out, headed north, and everything would be different, but he could not leave the station, his mind would not let go of his legs.

He waited and waited until there was a train south and then got on it, furious with himself that he was doing such a thing, and then he began the journey back which stretched out endlessly before him until he wanted to shout aloud.

# Thirty-five

It took Isabel several hours to work out that it wasn't true, she didn't want to stay here, she didn't want Robert to go off to Edinburgh without her. At first she felt a triumph in the things she had said to him, that she didn't need him, that she would prefer a single life with a bastard child rather than being with him. The trouble was that now she could see that life before her.

Hannah was spending more and more time at the found-ling school and Isabel encouraged her. She wanted Hannah to have the life that she longed for. There was no reason why she shouldn't. Jimmy ran the shop so efficiently, and there was little to do except see to the baby and the meals and do a bit of cleaning in the back. In fact life was going to become boring and it was all she could see before her.

No friends, no companionship, because although Jimmy was lovely he was just a half grown child. Her lot became harder every day and it had been doing that for so long now, she just wouldn't admit it. It took no more than a day before she broke down in tears. Jimmy would grow up and leave her, Hannah would become a nun, and she would be left there friendless, the loneliness eating away at her minute by minute.

Without Hannah she would not go to the meeting at Mr Gilbraith's house because often the miller's wife was there and

Isabel dared not speak to or look at her, and Fran ignored her. She could not go, she had nothing but that little back room and her bedroom, and she was not sleeping well.

From her room she could hear Jimmy's softly taken breaths, not quite snoring, and she thought what it would be like when something else was found for him to do and there would be nothing but silence in the night until she began hoping that Baby Allen would awaken.

Sister Maddy had gone to see Mrs Slater about Hannah. Mrs Slater was in no mood to be crossed. Her husband and elder son had had a fight and Robert had not come back. She had longed to go to the hospital to see him, but her husband was so angry that she did not go. Her first loyalty must be to Jim, and to be fair they were closer than they had been in years, but it made neither of them happy.

She felt as though she was on the brink of losing everything, with the two girls married and so much in love with the idea of being wives that she knew they were not thinking of her, Jimmy living with that awful girl and her baby, and now Sister Maddy came to her begging that she give Hannah leave to go to Newcastle and become a nun.

Mrs Slater was so angry that she couldn't speak. She had never thought she would lose all her children and so quickly. Nobody ever came to see her, she always had to do the running, and she would not go to the shop to see Jimmy or Hannah. She was feeling very lost and left out and by the time Jim came home, had his tea and went back out, she was beside herself and sat over her kitchen fire, remembering how good it had been when her children were small.

So Sister Maddy could not have timed it less well, and Mrs Slater was inclined to give the woman a piece of her mind except that somehow Sister Maddy carried with her an air of authority which slightly scared Mrs Slater.

Sister Maddy, Mrs Slater thought uncharitably, knew exactly what to say and when to say it, she had had such a lot of practice at manipulation. Mrs Slater knew that she ought to have asked Sister Maddy into the front room and it was always warm, either because the day was seasonal, or if it was cool if she would put on the fire there and Jim might not go out after tea. She was becoming desperate in some ways.

'I was hoping that we might talk about Hannah,' Sister Maddy said after Mrs Slater frigidly asked her to be seated. Sitting over the kitchen fire was far too homely and she regretted that she had not asked the nun into the other room, she would have felt more in command of herself with her pretty furniture around her.

Mrs Slater did not look at her unwelcome visitor.

'I know that she spends a great deal of time with you and the other nuns, though her father and I expressly forbade it,' Mrs Slater said.

'I'm sorry.'

'I didn't even want her to go to the shop. That was done without my will. Jim will go on and on about what the children want. Does anybody ever think about what I want, what my needs are? My house is empty.'

'I don't completely understand,' Sister Maddy said, being more frank than Mrs Slater had thought she would. 'I had no mother and will never be one. My love for people I'm afraid remains general.'

'I thought you came from well-to-do people,' Mrs Slater said, surprised at this confidence.

'My father was a brilliant architect but a very selfish man, my mother died before I knew her.'

'Families,' Mrs Slater said, thinking of how her parents had begged her not to marry Jim and had not been in touch ever since. She missed them.

Mrs Slater sighed.

'I was going to say that I don't want to lose Hannah, whereas in fact she was the first child of mine to be lost to me. I didn't understand right from her being little. She always did everything I asked of her, but she was never there somehow. I so wanted her to marry a nice man. My other two daughters, their husbands are all very well, but neither of them will ever rise to be anything much, and although I know it sounds shallow it is nice for a woman to boast that one of her children has satisfied her silly ideas.' She managed to smile at this, she didn't know how. She was amazed at the effect the nun was having on her and yet Sister Maddy said nothing very much at all. She was powerful, Mrs Slater thought and Hannah would be something like her. Perhaps she too would found a new village and make space for families like the Slaters.

Mrs Slater attempted not to cry when she gave her permission for Hannah to go on and become a nun, and afterwards to her own surprise she was rather pleased at what she had done.

She did cry into the dirty dishes later though, reflecting bitterly that there was little more to go wrong.

# Thirty-six

It was mid evening, cold rain falling softly down, and both the young Smith men were about to go off to the nearest pub for a few jars. The two sisters were at Kitty's back door as they were about to get together over the teacups by her kitchen fire. So all saw the miller running down the hill at a great pace and plunging into the water with his two daughters with Jimmy in pursuit, and Jimmy going in after them as being so close that he couldn't help it.

Both lads saw the situation and ran towards the river, and as Jimmy reached the bank Alf tried to catch him mid leap, but Jimmy's body was thrust too far forward and so they both went in, Alf struggling with the slippery stones and the force of the water against his chest as Jimmy went under for the second time. Alf floundered against the stream that caught him, and then stepped back as slowly as he could, Jimmy's wet self heavy against him. When they reached the bank the two young women were there. Alf handed Jimmy to his sisters and, Jimmy safe, Alf also went back into the water and Harold handed the baby to him. Harold was holding Mary by her clothes, but pulled her up further against him, then Alf took her, but the miller had been carried away by the force of the stream, being bigger. They ran along the bank and between them they reached him where the stream was running shallow in one place, where he was now thrashing and floundering. He went under. The two young men went in together and between them they pulled him, so very heavy now, being a big man, exhausted and barely breathing. They pulled and pushed him on to the grass where he lay back, finally losing consciousness.

He was alive. They turned him on to his front and then he came to and he coughed and coughed, so they sat him up and as he did so the water ran from his mouth and down his body. Both lads were panting and Fran had reached them by then and she screamed and cried and took both Mary and Daisy into her arms and sobbed over them as though her heart would break.

Neither did she turn her back on the miller, for once the children were safe and could go to the two girls, she got down beside the miller and wept.

'Oh Matthew, you stupid fool, what in the name of God and all the saints were you thinking of?'

And this was progress because she had only learned these words through spending so much time with the nuns.

The miller did not reply because he could not hear her. He was breathing however, and they got Abe to come out and help the two men to carry his father home.

Mary was crying and the baby was screaming, but with help from the two sisters Fran managed to get them both back to the house where they were wrapped in warm blankets and given hot tea.

Harold carried Jimmy back up the road, not to the shop though. Hannah and Isabel were standing outside so that they knew Jimmy was back with them. After passing the women Harold went on to the Slater house and when Mrs Slater saw her youngest child she cried out in horror while Harold said, 'He's all right, Mrs Slater, honest, he just took a tumble.'

Jimmy was by then blinking, but he lay still in his brother-in-law's arms.

'Why is he so wet?'

'He – he fell in the river.'

'And you got him out?'

'Me and Alf and the others.'

She stared at her son-in-law as Hannah came in.

'Get your father,' Mavis said.

Hannah ran off the short distance towards the fell house where the offices were, and Harold stayed there with Mrs Slater until her husband should come. She didn't say much but her lips were trembling.

'We should get his things off, he's cold,' Harold prompted her, and she nodded and then she said, 'What happened?'

'Let's just get him down,' Harold said, and so they put him in blankets and Harold sat by the fire with the little boy in his arms and they stayed like that until Jim Slater appeared, his face dark with concern. 'He's all right, Mr Slater, he just fell in.'

'And you just happened to be there?'

Harold nodded.

'Me and Alf were standing outside with the lasses, about to set off for the pub.'

'Thank God you were.'

'What were you doing letting Jimmy run down to the river like that?' Mrs Slater accused her daughter.

Hannah stood as though rooted.

'I ran after him but when I got there – when I got there it was all right, the lads had dealt with it. I went back to tell Isabel. It was just that . . .' Here Hannah fell silent and said nothing more.

'And to think that I wasn't sure you were worth your salt,

Harold,' Mrs Slater said as her child came round now safely in his father's arms.

'You all right, son?' Mr Slater said.

'The miller,' was all Jimmy said.

Harold left, but Jimmy's parents sat over the fire and the tears rolled down Mrs Slater's face and slid into her collar. 'It has something to do with that lass, doesn't it?' she said.

Jim looked blankly at her.

'We'll talk about it later. Let's get this lad into bed first.'

They did, and Jimmy, who usually didn't shut up, didn't speak another word, and they sat over him until he fell asleep, white with shock, and then they ventured downstairs.

'I'm going to the mill,' Jim said, 'I won't be long.'

So his wife sat over her fire, rocking herself for comfort, and the time that he was away seemed to go on for ever but finally he came back and by then she had partly worked out what had happened. When he came in at the back door she looked straight at him and said, 'Tell me then, I think I have the right to know who tried to drown my bairn?'

Jim sat down with her.

'Nobody did.'

'So what happened?'

'He put himself in the river trying to rescue Mary and Daisy.'

Mrs Slater stared.

'He can't swim,' she said, ridiculously. 'Jimmy doesn't swim. Nobody here swims.'

'No.' Jim frowned. 'No, it was Mary. It was Mary and Daisy. The miller had gone to the shop to try and persuade Isabel to leave with him, and when she said that her baby wasn't his he lost his reason. He ran out crying, and Jimmy could tell that no good would come of it so he ran after him, and then the miller pulled Mary and the baby into the stream.'

'That dreadful girl, Isabel. She causes all the problems in this place. She's like the devil,' Mrs Slater said.

'That's not true, Mavis, you mustn't blame her.'

'Who else can I blame?'

'Nobody. There is nobody to blame. The miller is a very sick man.'

Mary was most worried about Daisy, and although it was reassuring to hear her cry straight away so that all she had had was a ducking Fran kept saying, Mary was shaking, and it was not the cold water, it was not what had happened, it was what her dad had done. Her father had finally reached that stage where he could not be relied upon ever again, she thought.

Abe and the other men had carried the miller into the house and upstairs to the bedroom, and Fran had taken Mary and the baby. The other children just stood about, not understanding what was happening. Hester and Kitty were looking after them, and when Harold came back it was to the mill house, and his wife greeted him by throwing herself into his arms, which people hereabouts did not do.

'Nay, nay, lass, it's all right now,' he said, holding her at arms' length with embarrassment, and Alf just made a joke of it.

The miller said nothing. He opened his eyes, he was awake and conscious, but he didn't speak.

It was left to Jim Slater to see how Isabel was. Hannah, being the best lass in the world, had stayed there with Isabel and she now went with him. The evening was well advanced and the darkness was falling as Jim walked near to her, and he wished it was a lot further so that he could contain himself better. The thought of his child being drowned was not something he imagined he would ever recover from, but he made himself go.

They went in by the backyard to find Isabel putty-faced and the baby half awake.

They went inside and Jim explained as briefly as possible so that Isabel should not be more upset than she already was. Isabel had the baby clutched so tightly to her that Jim was surprised the child wasn't howling. She was so white she was grey.

'It's all right, lass, it's all right now,' he said.

'Are you sure?'

'The miller has been taken home, and Jimmy is in bed.' Jim thought it was pointless to tell her anything he didn't have to.

'Can I hold him?'

The look on her face made Jim ashamed of himself. This girl had been left to manage without help of any kind after her parents had died, and had turned to the miller, thinking he was her friend, and he had betrayed her because he couldn't help himself. As for Robert, Jim couldn't think about his son without wanting to knock his block off again. He too had taken advantage of Isabel's loneliness and vulnerability, but Jim could also see that the look in her eyes was not just for the child. He had the feeling that she loved his son, and Jim felt scalded that Robert had chosen to run away rather than face up to what he had done, and because of it three children had almost died.

Isabel gave him the baby. The years fell back and Mavis was lying in bed and she was putting Robert into his arms. He was the spit of his dad, and Jim had to fight back the words so that he would not say anything so tactless.

'Mr Slater, I'm so very sorry for what I did,' Isabel managed, and Jim found that he could look at her with sadness and joy, and that in fact he liked this lass and might even have loved to have her in his family. She had been badly treated by the whole village and then cast out when she knew no better than to give herself in love to two men who had both betrayed her.

'You didn't know any better,' he said, trying to control the harshness of his voice, which didn't quite hide his emotion. 'How could you, you're just a bit of a lass of no age and you were left all alone as folk should never be. He's a grand little lad and I'm glad he's ours.'

When Jim went home, his wife was just coming down the stairs and reported that Jimmy was sleeping and that the colour was starting to come back into his face. When he and Mavis were sitting over the fire he said to her, 'That lass is one of us now even if our Robert is no better than he should be, and she must come to us. It isn't right otherwise.'

'I don't want her in my house.'

'None of it can be undone, Mavis, you know that, she's just a lass like any other, and if she was wrong by God she's got her just desserts, and it's enough. We have to look after her now. You know we do. Wait until you see the bairn, he looks like you. You and Robert.' He didn't say 'and me', but he wanted to, he wanted his first grandchild to look like him, whatever the circumstances.

Lydia was called to the mill house. The evening was late by then, so all she could do was be reassuring, and she was certain that Mary and the baby would be fine after they slept. The miller she was a lot more worried about. He said nothing and turned his face to the wall when he could move, so she said she would come back in the morning.

She still wanted to go and see how Jimmy was. She did not like Mrs Slater, but there was nothing else to be done. The doctor was so tired and Lydia had assured him that she could manage this by herself, so she walked up the hill towards the top and banged on the back door. It was opened by Mrs Slater. Lydia could see the woman stiffen, but she said, 'I would like to take a look at Jimmy if I may.'

'There's nothing wrong with him.'

'Perhaps you would let me be the judge of that.' Lydia was not having this kind of thing from anybody in the village and all Mrs Slater did now was stand aside, so Lydia trudged up the stairs. Mr Slater was sitting in a chair by the bed and Jimmy was asleep. Mr Slater smiled at her.

'He's all right, Sister, but thank you for coming, it was good of you. How is the miller?'

She shook her head.

'Alive. I am going back to see him in the morning, but Mary and Daisy are fine and none the worse for it. If Jimmy ails anything please bring him straight to the hospital.'

'Thank you Sister, I will.'

She left and went back to the hospital, she didn't bother with Mrs Slater any more. The doctor had done the rounds of the wards and gone home. Lydia couldn't wait for her bed, she didn't think she had ever been so tired.

Fran sat over her husband all night until finally in the depths of it he went to sleep, and then she could not help remembering how kind he had been to her when they had first met, how he had rescued her, and he knew by then that she was having her father's child so there was no deception from the start.

Her father made her miserable every day of her life. He was always shouting at her mother and throwing things at her. He stormed out most days, but the nights were what she dreaded. He had been going to her bed for a long time by then and hurting her, and her mother dared not stop him. She had long since tried to reason with him over anything. They were not allowed out and nobody was allowed to come to the house other than for necessities, and he doled out the money so that they never had a penny extra for anything.

She had never forgotten the first time she saw Matthew Barnfather, and how tall and good-looking he was. She knew that he was married and lived in Cowshill, and that he had been adopted a long time back by the family, and when his father had died he ran the mill by himself with one young lad.

He was not afraid of her father and when he saw that she was pregnant and bruised and cowed he had taken her from there and installed her in a little cottage so that her father could reach her no more. Her father was too much of a coward to face a man as big and young as the miller, and she had loved that cottage as she had never loved anything in her life.

It was her haven, a tiny place with two rooms and a garden, which was nothing more than a small piece of grass, and here she sat because most of the time she was alone. It was heaven. After her father, she had thought she would never give herself to another man, but she had learned to love the miller and when it was obvious that after giving birth to Burt she was pregnant again they decided to leave. She could not let her conscience interfere. Everybody knew, but she must take Matthew, he was all the opportunity she had ever had.

Now, looking at him, he seemed so old and defeated. When he awoke in the morning he didn't seem to know where he was or who she was, until she worried that life had defeated him and his mind had gone.

Sister Lydia arrived very early so perhaps she had worried about him overnight. Concern came into her face because by then the miller wasn't even turned to the wall and he wasn't asleep. He looked straight up at the ceiling and did nothing other than blinking from time to time.

He would sip water but take nothing more, and even then the water ran down his chin. Abe went to the mill, and Burt and the little girls kept near to home.

Mary was downstairs with them. Fran kept the baby close to her even though Daisy seemed not to have suffered at all, but then the Smith lads had been so fast at pulling everybody out. She would never cease to be grateful to them. Even now Kitty and Hester came to help, and they would take the two little girls and Burt if Mary found it became too much for her, which it soon did.

Mary was the one who suffered most Fran thought, but between her husband and her beloved stepdaughter Fran was torn, and she was only grateful that in the afternoon when the two little girls and Burt were gone to Hester's house Mary took herself wearily to bed.

Fran checked on her after a few minutes. The day had cleared and since the curtains were open the afternoon light was pouring into the room and Mary was tucked up, fast asleep. Fran breathed a few sighs of relief and went next door. Matthew was also sleeping.

That afternoon Mr Gray came. Fran was surprised to see him, but he had said that Lydia wanted him to take a look at the miller and so she tried not to be concerned.

Lydia hadn't known what to do or how to go on. She had feared that the miller would die if he would take no sustenance at all, and the doctor saw as he always did that she needed an older hand at the wheel so to speak. He even reassured her. He knew that Robert's leaving was affecting her badly. He was her partner in the medical sense, they had been through a great deal together, and now her confidence was shaken. In vain had the doctor told her that everything would be all right.

Yes, the new chemist and his wife would soon be there, but Lydia would still be fulfilling a double role and the doctor did not think it was the right time to find another doctor to help. Lydia needed her place here and she was very bright, and so she must learn to manage as best she could. They must also however find another man to go outside the village with her, somebody who understood, somebody who was not dangerous in any sense of the word, and Mr Gray could see the difficulties of this.

Mr Gray was not inclined to take the miller into hospital because the man was already looking so much better. Sometimes a huge shock like that could change a person's life, he thought.

Fran ached to cry when he had gone but she trooped back upstairs and saw for the first time that her husband recognized her.

'Are Mary and Daisy all right?' he said, his voice barely a whisper.

She nodded dumbly.

'Oh Matthew,' she said, 'what were you doing?'

He didn't answer for a long time, but his eyes did not look vague any more and in the end he said, 'All I could see was that nobody wanted me.'

'What do you mean?'

'I wanted somebody to myself.'

'Nobody ever has anybody all to themselves.'

'My boy.'

'He wasn't your boy, Matthew.'

'I used to wake up in the night and I didn't know where I was. It happened again and again.'

'You aren't alone.'

'Why don't I feel that?'

'Maybe you will. Maybe you will in time.'

She gathered him into her arms and for the first time in his life he sobbed into her shoulder, clinging on as he had not been able to as a small child.

'I love you Matthew, I think you are worth loving, but you must change your ways and understand that the world goes on and we have to try our hardest to get by each day. You may never have a son. You have to face up to that, but you have children who love you and if you give them a chance there is no reason why we shouldn't strive for a little happiness.'

'I will,' he said from his safe place in her arms. 'I will do better and learn to love what I have.'

'You have so very much.'

She held him away from her and smiled into his eyes and she thought that his face was clearer now than she had seen him in years. Maybe he had needed to come to a crisis, to the idea that he could lose everything in the attempt to gain something which was not his right.

# *Thirty-seven*

Robert wished there had been another way out of the mess he had made. He wanted to go on to Edinburgh, he tried to talk himself into leaving and never going back, but his feet wouldn't let him do it. When the Newcastle train came in he jumped on it before he could think any more. He sat on the left side of the train which looked out over the world's most beautiful beaches. He saw the tiny stone houses and the high green sand dunes and the flash of pale cream sand as the train made its way south.

He felt sick. How could he be so stupid as to go back, but he couldn't do anything else. He changed trains in Newcastle and then in Durham and so his journey took him all day, and when the train didn't go any further he trudged the few miles home, and it was home, a place he loved and hated all at the same time. The bloody place had eaten its way into his soul, he thought ridiculously. He wanted to laugh at his stupid self but somehow he couldn't. It was very late indeed when he made his way with his heavy luggage all the way up the back lane to Isabel Norton's shop.

He doubted she would be in bed yet and he was right, the lights were on in the little back room and he thought he could make out her figure beyond the net curtains. He put down his bags and knocked on the door. Nothing happened at first. He didn't want to bang too loudly since it was late, he didn't want to frighten her or alert the neighbours, but the door opened after the second knocking and there stood Hannah.

'Why, Robert,' she said, and then for the first time in her life she threw herself into her brother's arms and he hid his face against her neck. He couldn't manage a single word. She smelled so sweetly of baking that it made him think of his mother. She took him into the house and pushed his bags against the pantry wall and then she led him into the little back room which he had promised himself he would never see again, never wanted to see again. He had thought he didn't want to be there and it was true, but he was changed, he was different, he had to be there now.

He looked into the little plain face of the girl he had treated so badly, and then he said, 'Isabel, I'm so sorry, I'm so very sorry for what I did.'

She didn't say anything, she turned away toward the fire, but he could see how her lips quivered. Robert took two steps towards her and then stopped. Her back was thin, she was so skinny and worn, and if he had never loved her before this he certainly did now and then he was glad he had come back, he could not leave her like that. She was not like other girls, she was not brassy and pushing forward like some, or coy and daft like others. He knew that he couldn't leave her again, he couldn't go anywhere if she wouldn't go. If he had to stop in this wretched little village which had taught him so much he would stay.

'Will you forgive me?' he said.

'I thought you'd gone,' was all Isabel said in a very small voice.

'I got as far as Berwick.'

Hannah very softly at this point tiptoed up the stairs.

'I can never remember whether Berwick is in England or in Scotland.'

'I stayed in a hotel,' he said.

'Nice hotel?'

'Aye, the best.'

'Well, as long as it was,' she said, and then he couldn't say any more, because his throat closed, and she didn't say anything either. He didn't know how long they stood there, all he could see was the baby lying asleep in a cot to one side of the fireplace.

'I'm not going,' he said finally. 'I can't.'

'Is Berwick pretty?'

'Every place is bonny compared to this dump,' he said, and then she turned around and smiled at him and he tried to smile back. 'I tried not to care about you. The trouble was that I thought I could get by without you, without anybody, but from the very first time I ever saw you behind the counter in your dad's flaming shop you mattered to me. I spent years pretending it wasn't true while the feelings got worse and worse. I tried telling myself that you were little and skinny and had nowt about you, but none of it worked, and I just got to the point where I couldn't keep my hands to myself any more even though I know that bloody old man had – had pushed himself on you when you knew no better. I wished I had been first, isn't that stupid? I wished I had been there before him like the stupid person I am, but most of all I wished I hadn't been so bloody selfish and then I ran away.'

Robert started to cry. He couldn't believe he was doing so and in front of a lass, in front of the very lass he cared about. 'Clown that I am, I thought I wanted – I don't know what I thought I wanted, but it wasn't in Berwick and it sure as hell won't be in Edinburgh.'

He despaired of her ever speaking to him again. And just when he was about to run out of the house and up to where his parents didn't want his presence, she put her arms around him and her face was the face he had always loved and she was sort of shining up at him like some daft little kid.

'Yes, it will. You should go. You can do a lot better than this place, and if you wanted to come back in time and help here you could, but you might want to go on and do something else, something more important.'

'I'm not sure there is anything more important.'

'You must go. You know I'll be all right here.'

'I don't think you will. I think you are lying through your teeth and pretending that it would be all right, when you know damned well that it wouldn't.'

'I thought I might manage. It wasn't until you went that I knew I couldn't. Folk aren't meant to be left on their own, it's not natural, and it's empty and lonely and just awful. Did you know that silence has a sound of its own? It's the most horrible sound in the world.'

Robert pulled her further into his arms and held her there against his shoulder.

'I'm not going anywhere without you and our Allen.'

'Our Allen,' she said.

The following day Jim didn't go to work. His wife, having thought she wanted to see more of him, wished that he would, he was in the road right from getting up and being useless. He would sit over the front room fire all day if she would let him, and she didn't like it. Men shouldn't be at home, she would remind herself of that the very next time he set foot in this house other than for a meal.

Jimmy slept long into the morning and then he got up by himself and dressed and went downstairs to be greeted so affably by
his parents that he stood back.

His mam made him poached eggs on toast and then he was
very hungry and had two cups of tea while they stood about
like pigs at a fair, he thought, so that he felt he had to say, 'I'm
all right, you know.'

'What were you doing, going after the miller like that?' his
dad said.

Jimmy sat back and considered.

'He was in this funny mood and I didn't trust him. He's a bit
odd, a bit, you know, and I thought he might hurt somebody cos
he had no idea where he was or what he was doing, and then he
got right down to the bottom and I could see Mary and Baby
Daisy, and he pulled them into the water with him. I don't think
he did it on purpose, it was just that he sort of needed somebody
there and he wasn't thinking clearly and he didn't want to go
there by himself.'

Nobody spoke and Jimmy could hear the fire crackle. Both
his parents were staring at him now.

'You went into the water to get them out?' his father said.

'I didn't,' Jimmy protested for once truthfully and against himself, 'I just couldn't stop meself, that's all.'

'But you could have drowned,' his mother said.

Jimmy shook his head.

'I don't think so,' he said. 'At that point the mill stream isn't
very deep. I don't think he knew what he was doing, it wasn't
deliberate, it was just like the only thing left. He wanted Allen, he
wanted Isabel and Allen to run away with him and when Isabel
told him about our Robert he lost his mind right at that second.
So he couldn't be trusted, could he? And he never liked Daisy,

he wanted Allen to be his. Daisy is a lovely baby, nearly as nice as Allen.'

Robert stayed at Isabel's house that night but he slept in the back room. He didn't want to make any more mistakes, and besides Hannah was there. They told him what had happened and he couldn't sleep. He just lay there and wondered whether his mam and dad would ever forgive him, and wished he was anybody but who he was.

The following morning Isabel persuaded him to go up to see them. He was still the coward, he thought. He didn't want to go, he didn't know what he wanted any more, just that he couldn't leave Isabel and Allen ever again.

He opened the door of his own home, went in the back way, as everybody but visitors always did, and Jimmy was sitting at the kitchen table and his mam and dad were hovering over him like he might disappear. As they all turned at the noise, he ushered Isabel inside and everybody stared at everybody, and then he found his voice.

'I didn't know whether to come in or not,' he said hoarsely, and then he was even more scared that he might start to cry for the second time within a few hours, 'but I thought you might like to know that I was back and that we are going to get married. We thought you might like to come to the wedding.'

Hannah had declined the invitation to join in the family reunion, she went on up towards the foundling school. She had the feeling that she would soon be in Newcastle doing what she had hoped and prayed for, that she would have her own life and her own ideas and learn things that she had always wanted to know. She went up to see Sister Maddy to tell her what had happened. She was sure the sisters would love to know.

Mary turned over in the almost darkness which was falling on her bed and knew that something was troubling her. She tried to go back to sleep but she turned over twice and then remembered what had happened. She crept out of her bed. The door of her parents' bedroom was open. Her father hadn't left that room yet and she had not dared to venture inside until now, but as she did so he heard her and he turned his head towards her and he even smiled.

'Mary,' he said, and he held out his hand to her.

Mary wanted to burst into tears. It was like he was again the man he had been before he had walked out and left them. His look, his gaze, it had all changed. She hung back a little, unsure.

Fran came in with Daisy in her arms and asked him hesitantly how he was feeling and he said that he was better and that he was hungry, and she told Mary after they left him that he had slept and was better now than he had been in so very long.

She could hear the sound of voices down below. Fran sounded worried as she would be, but the children were happy. Abe was taking on a lad to help him in the mill as they had no idea when the miller would be back to help. Abe was doing well, Mary just had to see how grateful Fran was. He still didn't ever say much, but he was just like that. He was becoming a very good miller though, everybody said so, and the money was coming in.

Ben Walton was starting that morning, a bright lad so Mr Gilbraith said. He had advised them on the matter, so that would make life easier. Mary ventured downstairs and she thought that it was an awful thing to think, but things were so much easier now that her father was not taking part in the day-to-day doings. The little girls could run around and make as much noise as they wanted. Burt could go to the mill, and they trusted Abe to make sure he came to no harm, and Daisy was Fran's biggest joy so she had taken to saying.

Fran was also thin and pale and Mary knew that in spite of everything that had happened Fran did love her father. He had been the man to solve her problems and later to start some more, but Fran was grateful to have her family around and smiled just a little at her as Mary came downstairs.

'Your dad ate all his dinner earlier,' she said. That was a first, that was good, Mary decided.

Later that day she took the little girls outside to play. Sister Lydia came to the house daily to see how the miller was and she had also stopped by Kitty Smith's house. It was the biggest secret in the village that Kitty was expecting, and it was such a relief to them all that Mrs Slater now had something to look forward to.

The small children treated Hester and Kitty's house much as they treated their own, and Alf and Harold, having been so good when things went wrong, were like family, that Mary felt in some ways since the ducking in the river it had all got somewhat better.

Jimmy was down there that afternoon, and he and Mary sat on the riverbank and talked about books.

'Our Robert came back,' Jimmy said, lifting his gaze heavenward.

'So we heard.'

'They're getting married and going to Edinburgh,' Jimmy said. After that he was quiet.

'Me mam isn't overly keen on them going,' Jimmy said, and after that he was quiet again.

'You'll miss Baby Allen.'

'Aye.'

That was all.

Jimmy went home for his tea and Isabel and Robert were there because it was late Saturday afternoon. They were practically haunting the place, so Mrs Slater said, but in a good way because she could hardly keep her hands off Baby Allen.

Jimmy felt unused, unwanted. They were going off to Edinburgh that autumn so that Robert could study, and apparently there was a new chemist coming to Wolsingham.

Jimmy thought sadly that he was the only one who had been left out. Nobody seemed to care. He was still going and helping at the shop, but Isabel would be leaving it and somebody else taking over, though it wasn't known who yet, and he wouldn't see Baby Allen. Maybe he would never see him again.

When he got home he reflected now that after his short-term of glory, Baby Allen was the star in the house. Everything would alter and he had the feeling that whoever took over the shop would not want him there any more. He would have nowhere to go and no place to be.

At tea Jimmy could hardly swallow knowing that in a few months he would be left here by himself, and he couldn't stand being in the house a moment longer. The shop was formally closed since it was Sunday night, and he mooched about outside away from the baby talk. His dad was up seeing Mr Gilbraith, so presumably he was tired of all the cooing and doing baby talk. Baby Allen understood real talk perfectly well, Jimmy knew, because Jimmy had had him long before Robert knew anything about him. More than anything in the world he would miss Baby Allen.

Robert followed him outside.

'Boring, aren't they?' he offered about his mother and wife-to-be.

'Lasses always are,' Jimmy said.

'Look Jimmy, I wanted to say summat to you.'

'You already thanked me, though for what I don't know. It was nowt to do with you.'

That wasn't true, they both knew it had everything to do with Robert, in a way, Jimmy thought privately and rudely, it was their bloody Robert's fault, all of it.

'No, it's not that. I talked to me mam and dad, and although me mam says she will miss us, especially the baby, she'll have Kitty's baby shortly, and I think maybe since everything is changing so much that you might like to come with us.'

Jimmy didn't take this in for a few minutes and then looked so hard into Robert's face that Robert shrugged.

'Well?' he said.

'Go with you?'

'Yes.'

'What, to Edinburgh?'

'No, to bloody Siberia, yer daft sod. Me mam doesn't want you to go, but Isabel and me, we think it would be a good idea. You care about Allen and you were the first person he really knew other than Isabel, so I thought you might not like to be parted from him. You have to come, Isabel says she won't go without you, and you'll stop me getting bloody big-headed the way I have sort of got lately. That's what she says. You might have to go to school, but I think the schools in Edinburgh would be a lot more up your street than the one here. You're way past anything the nuns could teach you.'

Jimmy was stunned.

'Edinburgh is supposed to be a lovely big city so there'll be lots you can do. There'll be libraries and museums, and big parks so we can walk Allen there on Sunday afternoons. I think you need like me and Isabel to go somewhere different, to something new.'

Jimmy still said nothing.

'Well?' Robert said again.

'That would be grand,' Jimmy said, trying to say no more than polite, and then he couldn't help smiling and the smile became wide. 'I'll be able to teach Allen to read. He really likes the *Three Musketeers* you know. I was going to go to Paris to become a musketeer, but I suppose I could always put it off for a few years.'

'You can do Paris later,' Robert said.


It was, Maddy thought, the biggest wedding the village had ever seen, and she knew that Jay had deliberately done this because he would have nobody able to go on and on about Isabel's wickedness, so the whole place was invited. Also he was doing his best to be tactful, and since Isabel's mam and dad had had their funerals at the Methodist church he sorted it out, and the wedding was held there. It was just as well it was a fine day because the chapel was not very big and most people had to wait outside.

Maddy was worried about Lydia. She thought that Lydia was possibly the only person who was not happy that Robert should leave. Mr Gray had not said that another doctor was coming to the area, but they really needed help, and she was worried that Lydia would feel discarded and left out.

Lydia was very quiet even though Abigail did her best at cheering her.

Isabel was very skinny still in the pale cream dress that Miss Pretty the local dressmaker had made, but she looked happy, and Robert looked happy, and Jimmy looked even happier and he carried Allen everywhere. All the Barnfather family was there

Elizabeth Gill • 326

except for the miller, who was being looked after by a nurse Mr Gray had provided.

The Slaters were all there, including both the Smith husbands and, despite it having been a Methodist affair, Jay had provided plenty of beer and whisky and sherry as well as a huge spread in and outside of his fellside house.

Abigail was already saying that she would get a horse and ride around the district helping Lydia with her patients. Maddy had made it clear that she could not manage everything by herself. Also she had the horrible idea that if Mother were to find out, she would be sending new nuns any minute to take the places of the two who had gone off to do different things.

Mr Gray was also at the wedding but briefly, he still had patients to see to.


Lydia didn't enjoy the wedding. She felt left out. She felt rather jealous that Isabel and Allen came first with Robert now, even though they ought to. And even though she didn't love Robert as Isabel so obviously did, she would miss so much having him around, just being there for her and having him to discuss all her work with. There would be a great raging gap and in it would be new people whom she didn't want to know.

'You aren't spending enough time in the chapel,' she told herself, 'You've got so big for your boots that you are putting yourself first, you wretched stupid nun.'


Abigail drank two glasses of whisky and told Maddy that she would not change her mind. She was definitely going to accompany Lydia on her outings on horseback.

'Have you ever ridden a horse?' Maddy said, enjoying sitting next to Jay, and how everybody had turned out for the wedding. It wasn't often that all the denominations spent time together, and she was not kidding herself that it was a popular move, but since everybody in the area owed Jay their very existence in this place they were not about to object when he told them they were invited to this very special wedding.

'If Lydia can ride then so can I,' Abigail said.

'And what am I supposed to do, run the school by myself? And what do you think the Reverent Mother will say?'

'She'll say, "Sister Madeline I will send you another nun and this time you must try to keep better control of her",' Abigail said, and smiled gleefully.

'Did you hear that?' Maddy said to Jay.

'I should think they could hear it in Durham City,' Jay said, Abigail being the tiniest adult there, but with the biggest voice. 'I can't wait to see two nuns riding about healing the sick around my doors.'

'Very funny,' Maddy said.

'No, Seriously, Sister Madeline—'

'Seriously your backside,' Maddy said very softly, being glad nobody could hear her but him.

'Has it never occurred to you that Mother knows what is going on here and perhaps even approves and is proud of the abilities and strength and stamina of the women she sends here, and that she has not only her own will in mind but perhaps God's too?'

'I shall tell her you said so, Mr Gilbraith. I'm sure she'll be delighted to hear it.'

\*

As soon as she could get away Lydia made her escape back to the hospital. She was eager to go. She preferred things to be as normal as it ever got around there. Mr Gray however had a long face and a letter in his hand.

'I thought I had found a replacement for Robert, but I have had a letter from Mr Temple and he has changed his mind about coming here to help,' he said. 'He thinks that somewhere so far out of the way would not suit him.'

'What a shame,' Lydia said, inwardly rejoicing.

'We do have the chemist and his sister to look forward to of course.'

'But they will be living in Wolsingham,' Lydia said.

Mr Gray eyed her.

'And why do you sound so pleased? It couldn't be that you think Mr Partridge would get in your way here?'

'Certainly not,' Lydia said.

'He would be a brave man to do it,' Mr Gray said almost to himself.


The newly married couple were seen off to the railway station when the time came that summer, complete with Jimmy and Allen and Mrs Slater, who insisted on waving them away and who had cried for various reasons at least once a week since the wedding and obviously had no intention of stopping any time soon, so her husband thought.

Hannah would be going to Newcastle any day now, both their sons were gone, so it was only Kitty and her new baby that held his wife's interest. He hoped that his daughters had many many children, it would keep Mavis out of his hair and out of his way, and perhaps he would get down to read his

# Acknowledgements

Thanks to everybody at Quercus and, most of all, my wonderful Editors, Emma, Celine and Ajebowale.

newspaper of an evening occasionally and have a bit of peace in his own parlour.

When Robert, Isabel and Jimmy got settled his mam and dad would be going to Edinburgh, and there Mavis would be able to brag afresh about her family. Just that morning she had talked of how Hannah would be able to come back, if she changed her mind because Ralph McFadden still wasn't married and he needed a nice wife to take care of him.